THE ROSE OF WINTER

K WHITE

Published by Blushing Books
An Imprint of
ABCD Graphics and Design, Inc.
A Virginia Corporation
977 Seminole Trail #233
Charlottesville, VA 22901

K White
The Rose of Winter

Print ISBN: 978-1-63954-266-6
v1

Chapter 1

Greenwell was Paradise.

This was a well-known fact. The jewel of its system, it was a large planet, swathed in shades of green. Broken only by the jagged grey-and-white slashes of mountains, the serpentine winding of rivers, and the occasional blue jewel of a large lake, it was renowned for its temperate climate and lush vegetation. Coveted by the rich for the vacation homes they knew they would never be able to have, as Greenwell was completely off-limits. Which, of course, made it all the more desirable. And as a result, the various agricultural goods it exported were always in high demand. Everyone wanted a piece of the veritable Eden.

Alexia hated it.

Of course, it had its perks. The open, endless plains and the lush, verdant gardens. The profusion of flora and the peaceful fauna that roamed its wilderness. But when even Paradise is a prison, one can grow to hate it. For that was what Greenwell was to the only child of its empress, no more than a gilded cage for her to be kept in. Her mother, Empress Yvonne, was a tyrant, running her empire and her business with a titanium fist, and along with them, the life of her daughter. Alexia wanted nothing more than to explore the galaxy, venture to distant systems and see the wonders their planets held.

She was lucky if she got to set foot outside the family estate. And never alone. No, not for the precious pearl that was the empire's sovereign heir. There was no freedom, no exploration, no blasted *peace* at all. It was enough to drive even the most mild-mannered of women mad, and Alexia of Greenwell was far from mild-mannered.

"Your Highness?"

Alexia groaned as the voice of her handmaiden reached her ears. Vienne was a good girl, sweet and devoted to her mistress, and surprisingly capable of putting up with Alexia's temperamental nature. But at the moment, she was the last person Alexia wanted to see. Undoubtedly because she was one leg out of the window of her bedroom, and was now dreading the flutter her favorite attendant would go into at the sight. Thinking quickly, the heiress drew her leg back in and tried to settle lazily on the padded cushion of the window seat. To add to the illusion, she plucked up the nearest book and opened it, staring unseeing at the pages.

Vienne rounded the corner and came to a stop, peering suspiciously at her mistress. It was an expression Alexia could see even in her peripheral vision, and she glanced up from her book, piercing green eyes setting upon the other woman while pale-skinned, aristocratic features adopted a purely innocent expression.

"Yes, Vienne? What is it?" Her tone was cool, composed, a direct contrast to the unsettled twisting of her stomach. She watched Vienne's warm, earthy gaze drift from her face to the book in her hands, and glanced at it.

It was upside-down.

"Forgive me for interrupting your reading, Your Highness." Alexia's eyes snapped back to her handmaiden, narrowing at the blatant note of sarcasm in the older girl's voice, before she closed the book forcefully and dropped it to the floor. "Your lady mother has just boarded a shuttle and asked me to send her apologies that your afternoon outing must be canceled."

"Mother is *gone*? Where did she go?" The princess practically leaped from her seat, silver-blonde hair swaying about her shoulders and brushing the tops of her thighs. Hurrying to the far window, she pushed open the glass and leaned forward, craning her neck in an attempt to see the landing pad on the far side of the estate. It was fruitless, although she did catch a glimpse of a speck ascending through the atmosphere's thick layer of clouds.

"Ah, to the Golden Cloud system. It would seem she has a meeting with Lord Chancellor Mallen, and...Your Highness!"

There was no disguising her excitement as the princess pushed past her handmaiden, bursting from the warm, wood-paneled suite of rooms that she called her own and into the gleaming white stone halls of the keep. Servants were bustling everywhere, chatting over data slates, carrying linens, and hurrying to their next duty. Guards could be seen standing at the junction of hallways, stark and resplendent in crisp uniforms of sage green and gunmetal grey, hands at their sides and able to grab energy pistols or plasma shields at a moment's notice.

None paid much attention to the wild streak of pale hair and lilac robe that was their princess, even when she hiked the long skirt up to her knees and took off running through the honeycomb of passages toward the eastern exit. She positively flew out of the portal as it slid open at her approach, skipping lightly across the grassy incline that led down to a lofty building of greenish stone, and finally skidded to a stop within the cool, shady confines of the royal stable. The scent of honeysweet seeds filled the air, an odd, musky-floral aroma that she associated with freedom, entirely because they were the seeds from which Green-well's plains grasses grew. It was the main food source of the moss-deer, a native species of the planet, and treasured as the royal family's favored mounts.

The moss-deer were quadrupeds and, on average, stood roughly two meters tall at the crest of their vaguely vulpine heads, with sturdy seven-toed paws at the end of each long, slender leg. But it was there that their appear-ance to mammalian creatures ended, for in every other aspect, they appeared more like living plants. Their bodies were covered in fur and feathers that resembled grass more than anything, with vine-like follicles sprouting from the back of their necks and their rumps. The royal stables housed eighteen of the creatures, sixteen of which were particularly muscular beasts, with their neck-follicles bred and styled specifically to look as though they had wings. Those sixteen pulled the lev-carriages that the empress, her daughter, and their servants would occupy on the occasions when they left the main royal residence to visit other portions of Greenwell. The remaining two were the personal mounts of the empress and her heir.

Normally, Alexia would stop in to visit her mother's moss-deer, a robust and lazy specimen who preferred to spend his days dozing in his stall. But Garth was in the far corner of his box at the moment, and she wasn't going to venture in there. Not when she had a brief taste of liberty within her grasp. The rapid tread of her feet led her down to the far end of the stables, past the stalls housing the burly brutes that hauled the lev-carriages and several empty cubicles. She was still more than three meters away when a white-eared head poked over the stall door, and an eerie trill emanated from the moss-deer's throat. At that, Alexia couldn't help but grin.

"Did you sense me coming, Lella?" She reached out to pet the moss-deer as the creature lowered her head, happily nuzzling her snout into the crook of her rider's neck and snuffling at her skin, crystal blue eyes peering at the princess from behind a thick fringe of jade green lashes. Lella was slightly shorter than most moss-deer, but she was lithe and long-limbed, with speed no other could match. She loved to run free across the plains of Greenwell —just as Alexia did. "Mother is gone. We can finally go for that long ride we've been wanting."

"Your Highness!"

Again? Alexia spun around, her jaw dropping as she saw Vienne come hurrying up, her chestnut curls in disarray and her sun-browned cheeks flushed from running. She also looked quite annoyed, a fact that had Alexia clamping her mouth shut to suppress a snigger. Vienne wasn't exactly in the best of shape, with rounded curves and a bit of extra weight, something that she had thought certain would keep the handmaiden from following her. Apparently, she'd been wrong.

"Your Highness." Wheezing the address, the handmaiden came to a stop a few paces from her princess, pressing her hands firmly into the curve of her waist as though that would support her lungs and force her breathing back to normal. When Alexia arched a brow at her, she scowled and huffed a sound that was pure annoyance. "You know your lady mother has decreed you aren't to leave the grounds unattended!"

Ah, of course. Her mother knew she was prone to bolting off into the wilderness at a moment's notice. Alexia pondered this, her lips pursing into a thoughtful frown, before an idea occurred to her.

"Certainly, Vienne. If you'll please assemble a handful of ladies, we'll leave immediately."

"Leave? Where are you intending on going, Your Highness?" Vienne was looking at her warily, as though this reasonable response were too good to be true.

"For a ride in the plains." It took everything she had not to burst out laughing as Vienne's expression only darkened at her calmly-stated answer.

"A ride? Do you mean for the ladies to ride in the lev-carriage, then?"

"Mother would never allow that. I think a lev-pod will do. Ethan will drive." As expected, the blood drained from Vienne's face, and Alexia was forced to bite the inside of her cheek to keep a victorious grin from spreading across her face. Her master of the hunt was even more wild than she was, and his depth perception was nonexistent, thanks to an eye he'd lost when she was just a girl. Vienne would sooner throw herself from the top of the keep than ride in a lev-pod driven by Ethan.

"If you're certain, Your Highness, I'll notify Ethan and assemble the ladies. Pardon me." She'd discombobulated Vienne enough that the woman didn't even curtsy before she hurried away, and once she was out of earshot, Alexia allowed herself a giggle. Only then, did she turn back to Lella, opening the stall door and leading the moss-deer out.

"That will give us at least a fifteen minute head start, I think. Are you ready to run?"

The moss-deer trilled her excitement, prancing lightly on her paws, before kneeling down to allow her rider onto her back. Alexia carefully gripped the violet follicles growing out of the moss-deer's neck and hauled herself up onto the blue-tinged back. With her hands wound through the follicles, she pressed her heels gently against the creature's sides and bent low over her neck as they sped out into the wide-open plains.

Greenwell was miserable.

It was too bright, too warm, and the blasted plants were making his nose itch.

"My lord, are you unwell?"

His pale grey eyes lifted from the data slate in his hand and darted to the steward at his elbow, who was doing his best not to look amused. Zavier, Iron King of Ironhold, scowled and, with a grumble, turned back to the data slate.

"This is why I never leave Ironhold." Even from the corner of his eye, he saw Benji's lips twitch with the urge to smile, and growled. The steward had been with him since he was barely a man, which was the only reason he didn't reach out and throttle him at that moment. Aside from the fact that Zavier wasn't actually as foul-tempered and violent as people made him out to be, of course.

"If it's any consolation, my lord, your business is nearly concluded. You have but to verify the agreement, and we can return to your ship." Accustomed to his employer's mercurial moods, Benji pointed this out casually, but there was no mistaking the iron king's reaction. He perked up a bit in his seat, skimming the data slate more swiftly, before finally reaching the bottom. It would've been perfectly acceptable for him to send an emissary to attend to this matter, but Zavier had always preferred to see exactly what he was buying firsthand and settle all business arrangements himself. Which was precisely why he pressed his thumb to the data slate's screen, allowing it to register the whorls and ridges of his fingerprint, and effectively applying his recorded signature and seal to the contract.

"There. Consider it done."

The plantation owner looked up in shock, seemingly surprised that the iron king had so readily accepted the terms, and scrambled to his feet as the iron king did, reaching out to take the offered data slate.

"Oh, I… Thank you, Your Majesty."

"Your thanks are unnecessary. Your product is superior and precisely what I require. I expect the first shipment to arrive within an Ironhold month, understood?" Zavier pinned the glorified farmer with a firm look, made all the more striking by the contrast of his nearly translucent eyes, pale skin, angular features, and the shoulder-length black hair that hung around his face. Naturally, the plantation owner nodded and scurried back into his home. Archaic thing of wood and glass that it was, he thought with a disdainful sneer.

Spinning away, he cast a baleful glare toward the sun, which was beating down mercilessly upon the fields, and the king that stalked past them. He should've known better than to wear dark colors on such a disturbingly warm planet, but he absolutely despised brighter hues and refused to bow to the foolish whims of galactic fashion. High-necked coats with long sleeves, trousers, and sturdy boots. He would wear nothing else. Even on agricultural cesspools like Greenwell.

He barely noticed when Benji hurried up to his side, struggling to keep pace with the king's long-legged strides, and tapping fitfully at the data slate in his hand. He only glanced over when the steward began to speak, his demeanor already thunderous.

"My lord, you really should visit the empress before—"

"No."

"But, my lord—"

"I said *no*, Benji. Bad enough I have to put up with Yvonne at my brother's court once a year, I refuse to visit the harpy in her own territory." Under any other circumstances, Benji's open mouth and horrified expression would've been thoroughly amusing. As it was, Zavier just felt more disgruntled. This planet was making him absolutely boorish. But he was mere meters from his shuttle, and if he could just get aboard...

Something caught his eye. A flash of pale color streaming beneath the sun. For all his faults, admitted and otherwise, his greatest one was perhaps his curiosity. Unable to help himself, the king stopped, turning to look for the source of the visual disruption. The last thing he expected to see was a figure with streaming silvery hair galloping by on the back of one of those bizarre creatures that only lived on Greenwell. What were they called again? Moss-deer?

As he watched, the beast and its rider veered toward the forest of ancient growth trees that bordered the plantation. Possessed by some strange compulsion he didn't quite understand, Zavier began walking again, his pace soon quickening to a trot, and finally into a full-on sprint. He ignored Benji's calls as he veered around his waiting shuttle, easily vaulted a low stone wall, and crossed the grassy span between the plantation and the forest. Within moments, he was in the cool shade of the looming trees, shade-loving ferns slapping at his arms and legs as he ran, trying to find the creature and its rider.

He didn't know why, but he *had* to find them.

There was nothing better than the wind in her hair and Lella's muscles rippling beneath her. Freedom was such a precious rarity in her world, and Alexia knew it couldn't last. She had to savor it, stretch it out for as long as she possibly could. She knew there would be guards and daintily distressed handmaids behind her before long, but if she could evade them... There was no choice in the matter. She had to get out of sight.

Farms and plantations passed on either side, but her attention was firmly fixed on the forest that rose tall and untouched ahead of her. She could hide in there for a time, at least, she felt certain. They wouldn't think to look in the woods, and she could only hope none of the agriculturalists had seen her go by. Within moments, the mount and rider were beneath the shady branches, pace dropping from full tilt to a lazy canter as they made their way between the ancient trunks.

"We did it, Lella. We might be able to... Woah girl, what..."

Her praise and patting of the moss-deer's neck became anxiety when the creature began to toss her head and trill in alarm. The last thing she expected was for her only true friend to suddenly come to a stop, rearing up on her hind legs and screaming in fear. Surprised by the uncharacteristic motion, Alexia was unable to keep her hold on the animal's follicles and went soaring through the air.

Time itself seemed to slow as she tumbled toward the ground that was too far away. For a moment, she thought she saw someone step out from behind a massive trunk. Then pain filled her world, and everything went dark.

Finding the rider had been easier than even he had anticipated. The forest was eerily quiet, save for the sounds of his own feet and those of the running quadruped. He could hear that the rapid four-beat tread of its paws had slowed to a more sedate three-beat canter, crunching through the fallen leaves and undergrowth. He was close. Close enough to hear someone speaking. The rider. She was talking to her mount, praising it, in a voice that was warm and husky. If her voice was that lovely, how would her face look?

Slowing from his mad dash, Zavier suddenly stepped around a tree, confronted by the sight of the girl on her moss-deer. He still couldn't see her face, not with the beast's head in the way, but any moment now...

He watched with a dawning sense of dismay as the animal suddenly threw itself up onto its hind legs and screamed, dislodging its rider in the process. He was already moving forward even as the girl tumbled from the creature's back, and for one glorious moment, he saw her face, shrouded by a wild tumble of silver-blonde hair. Then she impacted the ground with a sickening thud and rolled to a stop.

Zavier rushed to where she'd fallen, bypassing the moss-deer that was trilling and kicking with fear, and knelt beside the unconscious girl. His fingers pressed to her throat, and he was beyond relieved to feel her pulse, a glance downward showing him that she was still breathing, if shallowly. She didn't appear to have broken anything, no twisted limbs or jutting bone. With the utmost caution, he rolled her onto her back and gently pushed her hair away from her face.

He stopped breathing. She was beautiful. No, beautiful was too mild a word for such utter graceful loveliness. Her skin was fair like the most exotic Ureltz marble, with a bone structure that only the finest sculptors could hope to achieve. High cheekbones, a delicate, pert nose, a chin that was perfectly suited to her full, lush mouth, and wide eyes with thick lashes set beneath gracefully arched brows.

What color were her eyes? Would they be blue like the sky? Perhaps some fantastic shade of gold or amber? Maybe a hypnotizing and enigmatic violet? Regardless of their color, he knew they would be utterly captivating. Just like her voice. Just like her face.

He had to have her. He didn't know who she was, or where she'd come from, but this girl would be *his*.

Ignoring the panicked flight of the moss-deer, he carefully scooped the unconscious woman into his arms, cradling her shoulders in one and her knees with the other. Her head lolled over against his chest, and Zavier felt a wholly unfamiliar and powerful surge of possession. He moved as swiftly as he dared, a brisk walk so as not to jostle her too badly, and retraced his steps out of the woods. As he emerged into the daylight, he could see Benji standing beside the shuttle, his face filled with a questioning light.

Zavier ignored him and boarded the shuttle, laying the girl gently on the cushioned bench in the passenger bay. The nano-gel within immediately conformed to the shape of her body, cradling her securely in its grasp as the shuttle's engines activated beneath the king's touch on the console. Within moments, both Zavier and Benji were strapped into their seats, the loading bay ramp slid into place, and the shuttle rose from the ground. As it streaked through the sky, heading for the flagship hovering in orbit, the iron king silently marveled at his prize. Soon, he would know her name, and she would know that she belonged to him.

Chapter 2

The darkness faded slowly. It almost felt like emerging from the depths of a pool, pushing through the water until the world was no longer distant. Even when she surfaced, she kept her eyes closed, reaching out with her other senses first. It was quiet. Not the quiet of a keep at rest, or even an infirmary. The lack of noise was complete and almost unnatural, and it reminded her of the time she'd fallen out of a tree and awakened in a healing pod. She'd broken both legs, and they'd feared she would hinder her recovery, so she'd spent three months in a comatose state while her body healed.

But even as she compared that instance to this one, Alexia knew she wasn't quite right. With her eyes closed, she could hear the faintest of hums, as though of some great machine toiling away at a distance. She shifted ever so slightly and became aware of immeasurably soft fabric, both underneath and on top of her body. She was also lying on a thoroughly plush surface, one that automatically adjusted to her movements, cradling her perfectly. Just like the nano-gel that filled her bed.

"You're awake."

Her eyes snapped open at the sound of that voice. A masculine one. Which was an oddity in and of itself, because her mother absolutely never allowed men into her wing of the keep unless she was anywhere else. Pushing herself upright, she looked around. There was faint light visible beyond swathes of fabric that hung from a point above her, gauzy lengths of blood red and black. She slid off the bed, sweeping the semi-transparent hangings out of the way, and edged forward, her bare feet moving cautiously across the plush rug below. Finally, she emerged from the canopy and saw him.

At first, she wasn't sure if he was a statue, he was so still. What person could stand with such lack of motion? Not to mention, he looked like a statue, there was that little color to him. Even his eyes seemed colorless, the irises a shade of grey so light that they nearly blended into the whites, with inky black hair that reminded her of the obsidian beads her mother had gifted her once. And surely, no living person could have a face that sharp and angular. His cheekbones seemed on the verge of pushing through his skin, his nose vaguely aquiline, with a strong, square jaw. It was only when he blinked that she realized this man wasn't a statue. He was very much alive, and he was staring at her with an intensity that was as thrilling as it was terrifying.

"Who are you?" She was barely aware of the fact that she'd spoken. The words didn't sound like herself, said in a voice rendered breathless and almost meek. Alexia of Greenwell was many things, but meek was not one of them. The thick, dark brow that he arched in response had her squaring her shoulders and attempting to look down her nose at him, which was quite impossible, given he was a good head taller than she was, if not more.

"Iron King Zavier, of Ironhold."

Her brow crinkled slightly at that, a ponderous frown appearing on her lips. She had no idea what he was talking about. Her mother was the Empress of Greenwell, of course, but she knew nothing of worlds beyond her home, or who ruled them. The connective 'ni' between his name and his planet indicated he was the ruler of Ironhold, of course, but beyond that... He was staring at her like he expected a reaction, or at least one different from what he got.

"What are you doing on Greenwell?" Her voice grew accusatory. Why had this foreign king come to her home world? And more importantly, why had he brought her to some bizarre keep that was so unlike her own? She had so many questions, but she would parse them out carefully, to disguise her rising concern.

"I *was* on Greenwell to secure a business arrangement with one of the planet's agriculturalists. We are no longer on Greenwell."

No longer on Greenwell? Alexia felt her throat close up as her heart began hammering in her chest. What did he mean, they were no longer on Greenwell? As though sensing her unspoken questions, the man who had named himself Zavier stepped forward, peering at her with an almost predatory focus.

"We are on my flagship, the *Nightfall*, approximately three hours from arriving at Ironhold."

There was no longer any use denying it: Alexia was panicking. It was true, she'd always wanted to see the entirety of her home world, and if possible, the worlds beyond it. But not like this. Not being captured by some unknown king and carted off to his domain like... like *chattel*. Her gaze darted from him to her surroundings, looking for something she could use to defend herself.

Luckily, there was a table full of sparkling stones only a few steps away.

Her eyes were green.

That was the only thing he could seem to think when the unnamed girl vacated his bed and came within view. Of all the possibilities he had contemplated when wondering about her eye color, somehow, green hadn't been among them. And yet, the moment he saw them, he knew it could be nothing else. It suited her. They were a vivid and striking emerald, more brilliant than even the purest of gems which bore that name, as vibrant as the grasses of the world he'd taken her from.

Her questions hadn't been unanticipated. He suspected anyone who awoke in a strange location would have such questions. But she didn't offer any indication of her identity, and it became obvious within moments that she didn't know they were no longer planet-side.

The last thing he could've predicted was that she'd go completely mad.

She was bloody *fast*. One moment, she was standing there, pale and wide-eyed like a frightened *malit*. The next, she'd sprinted across the short distance between herself and his mineral collection. What did she mean to do with those? He had barely a heartbeat to step forward and hold his hand up in warning, before she picked up a fist-sized sample of uncut pink moonstone and lobbed it directly at his head.

"Kidnapper!"

Zavier barely managed to duck in time, both hands now raised, this time to protect his head. He peered between his fingers at her, mouth agape in disbelief, and jumped to the side as she hurled another stone at him.

"Scoundrel!"

"Now hold on—" His words were cut off by a thoroughly undignified grunt when she finally managed to nail him, right in the gut, forcing his arms down to cover the aching spot. And more importantly, his groin, because that seemed to be her next target if trends were going to continue in this manner. He narrowed his eyes at her, thin lips claimed by a furious scowl, and growled in his most threatening tone. "Woman, stop throwing those damned rocks at me!"

That seemed to do the trick, as she froze with her arm cocked back, clearly ready to throw another stone at him. Whether it was the authority in his voice, or the fact that he'd cursed at her, Zavier had no idea, but he certainly wasn't going to let this opportunity pass him by. Taking advantage of his long legs, he lunged toward her, and though she tried to scramble backwards with an ear-splitting shriek, his equally long arms were capable of an extensive reach. Within moments, he had thin, strong fingers wrapped around her wrists, and forced them down to her sides.

"Let go of me, you—"

He nearly choked on his tongue when she cursed at him. He'd never heard any female use such a word, and he wondered if she even knew what it meant. But his concerns almost immediately shifted when she began squirming and thrashing, doing her best to knee him in a very sensitive spot. Thinking fast, he lifted her arms and spun her around, then crossed them over her body as he pulled her back against his chest. That made it much harder for her to kick him, let alone hit him, and the height difference was great enough that her attempts to ram her skull into his face resulted only in her bashing the back of her head against his sternum. Which, while unpleasant, was far less painful than what she intended to do.

"You're absolutely mad, do you know that? Now stop flailing about like an angry spike bear and let's talk like rational adults." His voice was firm, his grip even more so, making it clear he had no intention of letting her go until she could behave herself. When she gradually stopped fighting, he lowered his head, allowing himself to inhale her scent. It was sweet, floral, but with a unique tang that he couldn't quite place. Some kind of melon?

"You're hurting me."

Her voice was sharp, but it was the words that snapped him out of his reverie. He immediately released her and felt a touch of remorse when he saw her rubbing her wrists. Perhaps he'd been gripping her a bit too tightly, but in his defense, she'd tried to both knock him unconscious and render him infertile with rocks. Still, he took a few steps back, giving her space while she turned and eyed him with obvious wariness. Taking a deep breath, he tried to regain his composure and his regal bearing and spoke in as even a tone as he could muster.

"Now. You know who I am, so I only think it's fair you reciprocate. What is your name?"

She let her hands fall and squared her shoulders, and in an instant, Zavier felt his universe tilt on its axis.

"Princess Alexia of Greenwell, daughter of Empress Yvonne, and heir to the Flora Crown."

It was, she mused, entirely too gratifying to see this high and mighty king look like he was about to choke on something. She'd suspected he hadn't known who she was, but being struck with the knowledge seemed to be an unpleasant surprise. Of course, now that he knew her identity, he would turn his ship around and take her back home.

"What kind of princess goes out riding on one of those strange creatures completely alone?"

Blast. He'd seen that? She'd hoped that her little venture had gone without witness, but apparently, she wasn't that lucky. Confidence was key if she was going to get him to take her home, so she planted her hands on her hips and raised her chin defiantly. "I hardly see how it's any of your business what I do on my own planet. Clearly, this has been some sort of grave misunderstanding, so you will take me home immediately."

Rather than respond, he stared at her, his cool gaze assessing. What was there to assess? He'd taken a princess captive—unknowingly, she admitted, but that didn't exactly excuse his actions—and the only way to avoid an intersystem war was to take her home. Surely, he didn't want to cause a galactic incident?

Her eyes widened when he suddenly moved toward her, and her hands fell from her hips as she scurried backwards, trying to escape him. She misjudged how much space there was, however, and gasped when her back abruptly met with the cold metal of the bulkhead. Then she was rising up on her toes, trying to keep as much distance between them as he could. Which seemed to be entirely in vain, as he pressed his hands to the wall on either side of her head and leaned in until his face was mere inches from hers.

"No. I saw you. I wanted you. I took you. Now, you're mine." His voice was cool, but his eyes burned with a fire that she'd never seen in anyone before. It seemed ready to sear right to her soul, making her shudder and sputter her response.

"Wh-what? You can't... you can't just *take* a member of the royal family!" She tried to muster up righteous indignation, to fill her voice with it and force him to obey her. It worked with the servants. But it appeared he was made of sterner stuff, as his lips curved into a smile that she could only call cruel.

"I can if I mean to make her my queen."

"*Queen?*"

She positively screeched the word, causing him to wince. Did the woman have to be so damned loud? His smile became a grim smirk as all the color drained from her face. He probably shouldn't have found it so satisfying, but she'd been nothing less than a giant pain in his arse since shortly after she woke up. As far as he was concerned, she deserved to be shaken up a bit for attempting to knee him, if for nothing else. He halfway expected her to swoon, which meant that when her eyes suddenly sharpened to a venomous shade of jade, he tensed.

And none too soon, as she tried to emasculate him *again*. It was only quick reflexes that allowed him to turn his pelvis to the side at the last moment, though he grunted when her bony knee collided with his hipbone. The glare he shot her was positively icy, and he was thoroughly pleased by her wide-eyed look of panic. Intent on staving off any further attempts at assault on his person, Zavier did the only thing he could think of: He pressed himself against her.

The moment his body aligned with hers, sandwiching the princess between his lithe form and the smooth wall, he realized this was not one of his better ideas. She was so soft, so warm, and so very distracting. A low, growling moan rumbled in his chest as his hands slid down from the wall, gliding over the bare skin of her shoulders before settling on her hips, his fingers curling to grip her firmly. Her sharp intake of breath drew his attention squarely to her bosom, and he couldn't help but notice how the lilac fabric of her robes draped over those full mounds in a most fetching fashion.

He should stop this. But when he saw her tongue sweep across her lips from the corner of his eye, and he looked at her deliciously full mouth, he knew he couldn't. Not just yet. He needed something of her, just a little taste, to sustain him until he could make her his wife. Drawn inexorably forward, his head lowered, seeking to take her mouth with his own. As he neared, however, she turned her head away, clenching her eyes tightly shut. When presented with the graceful curve of her neck, he realized he had a wonderful opportunity. One far too good to pass up.

The tip of his nose brushed against her pulse point, and he noticed with some pleasure that her blood was rushing swiftly through her veins. Was it terror, or excitement? Either way, he was affecting her, and that was all he truly wanted. His focus moved to the shadow of her jaw, nuzzling just below the lobe of her ear. That maddeningly luscious scent was stronger here, so close to her hair, and unable to resist the temptation, he buried his face in that pale, gleaming mass, inhaling deeply. He didn't know what she used to make her hair smell so good, but once they were wed, he'd buy her a lifetime supply of it. The thought of not immersing himself in this aroma every day was simply unacceptable.

She was trembling, her curvaceous body quaking in his

grasp, as his hands moved up over the curve of her waist. Was there anything more arousing than the feel of a woman rendered speechless in his presence? Not that she was just any woman. She lit a fire in him like no other had before, and he was unable to resist the urge to thrust his hips against her, his confined desire rubbing against the soft flesh of her belly. Gods, he'd never wanted anyone like this before. If he didn't have her soon, he was going to go stark raving mad.

Just as his hands began to skim downward again, his unsteady fingers starting to gather up the skirt of her robes, intent on feeling her bare skin beneath his touch, a chime rang out in his quarters. The sound made him freeze, his head snapping up to level a purely murderous glower on the speaker so high above. When Benji's voice came across it, he unconsciously bared his teeth in a snarl.

"Your Majesty, there's an incoming communication from Ironhold, labeled urgent. Should I patch it through to your holo-comm?"

Dammit all. If it was urgent, he really should take it. Besides, his steward had definitely killed the mood. Forcing himself to step back, he barely noticed the way Alexia slumped in relief, sliding down the wall until she was sitting on the floor, looking up at him with too-wide eyes and a dazed expression.

"No. Send it to the bridge. I'll take it there." He knew his tone was clipped, strained, but it couldn't be helped. Not when he was so wound up with need and unable to do away with it. As Benji acknowledged his order and cut off the communication, his gaze dropped to her. She looked flushed and uncertain, and much as he wanted to haul her into his bed, he couldn't. It would've been a grave mistake, anyway, to do so before they were married.

Crouching down in front of her, he gripped her chin none too gently between his thumb and forefinger, making her gaze focus on him. He smirked, seeing the ire rising in her eyes. It made him want to kiss her, but he held back, knowing that if he did, neither of them would be leaving this room unscathed.

"You can't leave my quarters, but you can enter the lounge. Surely, you'll find something there to entertain you. And don't break anything. I'll be quite angry if you do, and I'm not afraid to punish a princess."

The way her jaw dropped was far too rewarding. Zavier didn't bother to silence his chuckle as he let go of her, rising to his full imposing height. Without a backwards glance, he turned on his heel and strode briskly out of the bedchamber, tugging his coat down in a futile attempt to disguise his lingering discomfort. Still, he was smiling to himself as he left.

He was going to have such fun bending her to his will.

It was several minutes after he left before Alexia felt steady enough to stand. By then, she was fuming. How dare he accost her in such a manner! No one had ever even tried to touch her like that before, and she was quite frankly very confused about her reaction. She hadn't wanted him to kiss her, of course, which was clearly what he'd been trying to do. Mother would be aghast if she knew her precious sheltered daughter had seen servants kissing, but how else was she supposed to learn about the ways of men and women? But it had felt strangely appealing when he'd run his hands over her sides…

"Clearly, you've lost your mind. Stop dawdling and find a way out of here."

Her conviction seemed hollow in the vast space of this empty room. She needed to formulate an escape. Surely, he wouldn't actually lock her in these quarters? Walking briskly to the door he'd gone through, she was somewhat surprised when it slid open before her, but when she stepped through, she realized why. A room full of dark, sturdy-looking furniture lay before her, complete with a desk, chair, and a bar adorned with decanters full of variously colored libations. There was another door on the far side, and it was to this that she scurried, hope giving her speed.

To her dismay, the door remained stubbornly closed at her approach. So he really had locked her in. Stepping back, she began to stroke her thumb across her lower lip as she considered her options. The voice over the intercom had mentioned a holo-comm... perhaps she could find it and send a message to her mother? As she turned to face the room at large again, her attention landed on the desk. That seemed like a logical place to start.

Within moments, she was rifling through the drawers, searching for... well, she honestly wasn't sure what. She wasn't permitted communications from off-planet, so she'd never even seen a holo-comm, though she knew her mother kept one in her chambers. There were lots of pieces of paper, a few data slates, some pens, but nothing that she remotely thought could be what she was looking for. Frustrated, she flopped into the desk chair and grimaced at the desk.

"Where is that blasted holo-comm?"

As soon as the words left her mouth, two small panels lifted on either side of the desk. She yelped, jumping back in surprise as they lit up, casting a holographic display into the air above the smooth wooden surface. A pleasant but entirely average male face greeted her, smiling widely, and she heard a voice coming from somewhere within the desk as the lips moved.

"Hello, Your Majesty! I thought… Oh. You're not… the iron king."

So it was voice-activated? Interesting. Leaning forward, she examined the technology as best she could, then glanced up at the hologram. Very advanced AI for a comm system, to so easily mimic human facial expressions and speech patterns.

"No. I am Alexia of Greenwell, and I insist that you connect me to my mother, the Empress Yvonne."

"Ah, um, I'm… I'm sorry, Your Highness. I'm afraid I can't do that."

Drat. Of course, it couldn't be that easy. No doubt he'd activated some kind of security protocol with the ship's AI when he left the room. That didn't make it any less annoying, but an AI was basically just a highly advanced computer system. Maybe she could short it out. To that end, she crouched down, searching the underside of the desk for a hidden panel. There had to be wires in here, if she could just get to them… She was unaware of the hologram attempting to crane forward and see her. Fruitlessly, of course, as she'd gone out of range of the camera.

"Um, Your Highness? What are you doing?"

"Trying to find a way to short circuit you so I can bypass your security protocols and contact my mother." She grunted the words as she pressed and pried at every seam and panel she felt. Blast it all, where was the bloody access panel?

"Oh. Wait, I'm not an AI!"

The statement startled her, and she jumped, smacking her head on the bottom of the desk. Muttering curses, she crawled out from under the item to fix a vaguely sheepish look on the hologram. Which was, apparently, a visual of a real person. That was embarrassing, to say the least. Especially since the pleasant-faced young man now looked mildly disgruntled by her assumption.

"Forgive me. I didn't think your iron king would be inclined to employ a real person where a program would serve just as well."

"I think you don't know the iron king well enough to be making judgements about his personality, Your Highness."

She blinked. Whoever this person was, no doubt some lowly communications officer aboard the ship, they sounded unexpectedly loyal to their liege. She found it hard to believe anyone would be inspired to loyalty by such a man. But didn't that assumption simply reinforce what the male had said to begin with? She pondered this, worrying her lower lip between her teeth, until the officer glanced off to one side, drawing her attention back to him.

"I'm sorry, Your Highness, but we've all been given strict orders not to allow you to contact anyone. The best I can do is dispatch a guard with any items you might want. Do you require anything?"

Well, that answered her questions, didn't it? Murmuring a negative response, she sighed as the holo-comm deactivated, and the little panels sank back into the desk. It seemed she truly was trapped aboard this ship, and soon, she would be equally captive on a strange planet. Slumping in the chair, she looked up toward the distant ceiling and grumbled to herself.

"Well, I have always wanted to see other planets. Although I didn't quite mean for it to happen like this…"

The Iron King of Ironhold was in a foul mood. Nearly two hours of conversing with the head of his guard and the situation that had just been quelled on his planet had left him with a headache and far too much tension in his shoulders. The sparse crew that occupied his flagship scurried out of his way as he stalked through the passageways, intent on returning to his quarters and having a very strong drink. More importantly, he wanted to be around Alexia again. Even as she stirred his blood, something about her was undeniably soothing.

He was expecting her to attempt another assault, which was why he kept his distance, standing back a few paces from the door to his personal lounge as it slid open. Much to his amazement, she didn't launch herself at him. His brow wrinkling in puzzlement, he stepped into the room and looked around as the door once more slid shut behind him. It took him a few moments of searching to find her, and then, he bit back a burst of laughter.

He'd give her points for creativity and determination. The last thing he'd anticipated she would do was turn one of his own collection of crystals into a weapon. He wondered where she'd even gotten the length of wood from, then realized she'd destroyed one of his chairs and bound the broken, jagged bit of crystal to it with a strip of bedsheet, to form a rudimentary—but very effective— spear. Although, apparently, at some point after finishing her crude weapon, she'd managed to activate one of his data slates. It wasn't connected to the ship's comm array, but held a vast wealth of knowledge about the galaxy, and she was huddled on the floor in front of his sofa, deeply immersed in information about the Golden Cloud system.

Now *that* was puzzling. Why was she researching the heart of galactic society and politics?

"I'll count myself lucky you got distracted. A crystal spearhead sounds like a very unpleasant thing to be stabbed with." His wry drawl was tinged with amusement, a feeling that only grew when she jumped and whirled around to glare up at him. His lips twitched with the threat of a smile, arms crossing as he leaned against the side of the sofa.

"I suppose you're going to take it from me."

Her tone was accusatory, vaguely petulant, and a perfect match to her defiant expression. She was adorable when she was mad, he thought, but realized sharing said thought would almost certainly incite her to stab him. Instead, he cocked a brow, looking from her face, to the spear, to the data slate, and back again.

"Your crude weapon, or the data slate?"

"Both."

He couldn't help himself. He chuckled. She had such a timorous personality, how could he not find her funny? The way her eyes spat fire, was both attractive and comical, but he'd managed to avoid getting attacked thus far, and he wanted to keep it that way. So, Zavier silenced his mirth and cleared his throat.

"Actually, no. I hope to persuade you the former won't be necessary, and I see no reason not to let you keep the latter, for now. You can't send a message to your mother from it, after all." The abrupt surge of pink across her face made it obvious that had been the first thing she'd tried. Not surprising. Benji had immediately alerted him to her virtual encounter with Communications Officer Mathias. Now his steward was hastily reassuring the crew and sending messages ahead to the staff of the keep, informing them of the iron king's guest. There would be quarters prepared for her and the royal seamstress ready and waiting to get her measurements. Soon, she would be dressed like a queen, and once rings and a diadem were made...

"Why are you being so lenient? I thought I was your prisoner."

Zavier blinked out of his thoughts, reining in the mental vision of her in nothing but a crown of Ironhold iron and opals, and frowned at her question. Rounding the sofa, he moved toward one of the wingback chairs nearby and sank onto the plush cushion. She watched him warily, but he was distant enough not to reach her easily, not to mention his lounging position made it clear he had no intention of grabbing her. Propping his elbow on the arm of the chair, he leaned his cheek against his fist and sighed.

"I know it seems that way, but I'm just trying to prevent you from contacting your mother. I didn't know who you were when I took you, and now that I know your identity, things have changed. Before, I would've simply made you my mistress." Her sudden sharp inhalation made him pause, and he smirked at her flushed cheeks and indignant expression. He saw no reason not to be honest, but her reaction was certainly worth it. "But that's hardly possible now. I intend to convince you that marriage is the best option, and it's my hope we can become... friends."

"*Friends?* Marriage isn't about being friends! It's... it's about..."

The way she sputtered and faltered, made it clear what she was trying to say. Zavier couldn't stop his lip from curling in disdain as he spat his reply.

"It's about what? *Love?* Love is a luxury that royalty can't afford. I need a queen and an heir. You will inherit the rule of Greenwell, thus bringing it under my control when Yvonne dies. Our firstborn will sit on the Obsidian Throne of Ironhold, and our second will wear the Flora Crown. It's politics. There is no room for emotion." The words were coldly spoken, bitter, and he knew he'd been more than cruel. She had jerked back, withdrawn from him like he'd struck her, and he felt a momentary ripple of remorse. But she was so naive. Surely, it was best for her that he did away with her silly delusions of love and romance?

The silence that fell in the wake of his words was weighty, nearly oppressive. He fully expected her to begin protesting once more. Which meant that the abrupt sparkle of something undefinable in her gaze was all the more startling. Rather than begin whining about her situation, she squared her shoulders and gestured toward the data slate resting on her lap.

"I haven't been able to find any information about Ironhold on here, except for its size and estimated population, and that you're the ruler, of course. Why is that?"

That was... unanticipated. She'd been trying to find information about his world? Was she perhaps not as averse to the idea as it appeared? Or did she simply want to know about the next battlefield she'd be facing him on? More importantly, what should he tell her about his planet? After several moments of consideration, he began to answer her, weighing his every word carefully.

"Ironhold is seen as both unimportant and yet vital. It's the galaxy's prison planet. It allows other planets to maximize the use of their own territory for more profitable ventures to support the law-abiding population by not having to build incarceration facilities. So, the scum of the universe are sent to Ironhold... even if those scum are simple petty thieves."

He could tell the information shocked her, but oddly, she didn't seem concerned. If she believed he would keep her safe from the aforementioned criminals, she was, of course, correct. But there was much information about his world that he had no intention of imparting to her. Not for quite some time. Instead, he elected to sit there and observe her.

Watching Alexia think was fascinating. Her face was so

open and expressive that he could see every little thought reflected in her features. The widening and narrowing of her eyes, the crinkling and smoothing of her brow and nose, the pursing of her mouth, and occasionally, how she would take that plump lower lip between her teeth and worry it in the most charming manner. Did she realize how utterly delectable she was?

Before he could do something foolish, like attempt to seduce her, he heard the low hum of the ship's light speed drive cease, and he perked up. Had they already entered the Ironhold system? He glanced toward Alexia, who had also noticed the cessation of that almost subliminal tone, and stood, offering a hand to her.

"Come. You can have your first look at Ironhold."

"Your Majesty, there's an urgent message waiting on the holo-comm. It's from Greenwell."

Yvonne groaned. She'd only just stepped into her guest quarters in the Golden Citadel, and already, she was being pestered. Probably her steward, insisting there was a matter that only the Verdant Empress could handle. Carefully disentangling her circlet from her tawny curls, she handed the weighty item of gold and emeralds to her handmaiden and approached the small table that bore the holo-comm. Just as she'd expected, her steward was waiting for her, but the woman's face was drawn with worry. Even more concerning, she saw the stern, scarred visage of Harald, her Guard Captain, hovering beside the steward's.

"What is it, Portia? I've only just returned from listening to that insufferable oaf blather on about his most recent conquest, and I'm in dire need of a bath to wash the ego off me." Her sharp green eyes narrowed as her steward and captain shared a look. Something was wrong. The sense of it invaded her very bones, making the tall, elegant woman shiver.

"Your Majesty… The princess is missing."

Everything seemed to stop. Even her heart ceased to beat. A frigid numbness spread throughout her body, and Yvonne fumbled for the nearest item of furniture, leaving her to clutch the back of a chair in a white-knuckled grip. Alexia was gone? Surely, there must be a mistake.

"Explain," she snapped at the pair, uncaring when Portia cringed, which led Harald to step forward and do as his empress commanded.

"The princess slipped away from her handmaiden, took her moss-deer, and fled the estate. We were just about to go out and retrieve her when the creature returned, without the princess. As of yet, there's been no way to determine which direction she went, but we've begun questioning the inhabitants of all plantations and farms within a five kilo radius. If nothing is turned up by tomorrow, we'll begin a planet-wide search."

Yvonne couldn't believe what she was hearing. Most alarming was the knowledge that Lella had returned to the royal estate without Alexia. Her daughter and the moss-deer had a strong bond, and the creatures were bred to be loyal. The animal never would've left Alexia unless it was absolutely necessary… which meant that either her daughter was gravely injured and unable to return on her mount, or they had been forced to separate.

Either option was terrifying. But the worst possibility was that Alexia had been taken captive. She'd kept knowledge of her daughter and only heir's identity as ambiguous as possible. Most of the galaxy knew that she existed, but little more than that.

And for very good reason. If anyone found out about her deepest, darkest secret…

The numbness in her body seemed to have spread to her ears, filling them with a muted buzzing, moments before the edges of her vision darkened. The last thing she saw was the holo-comm tilting bizarrely onto the wall as she swooned, collapsing onto the floor.

Chapter 3

At first, Alexia had been skeptical of his offer. In the end, she'd eschewed taking his hand, not trusting him to refrain from accosting her again. But she did follow him as he moved to one wall of the lounge, clutching her makeshift spear in one hand and the data slate in the other. When he touched his hand to the wall, it almost seemed like the metal went opaque, and it took her a moment to realize she was looking at a large video screen of some sort. What she saw made her gasp.

It was obviously some sort of exterior camera feed, because she saw the blackness of space speckled with stars and a pale circle growing steadily larger in the center. That circle solidified into a planet, its surface a pale blue-grey, studded here and there with mountains and dark spots that she couldn't identify. Rising almost violently from the center of the planet, from her perspective, was a massive and forbidding fortress city of black stone and metal.

"This is Ironhold, and that is the Ebon Citadel. My home... soon to be your home."

She glanced at Zavier as he spoke, her lips pressing into

a thin line. She refused to accept that this cold and unfeeling place would be her home. She'd find a way to get word to her mother, and the empress would retrieve her. Admittedly, the princess had no idea exactly how she'd manage this, but she was determined.

"Why is it that color? And why does it look... fuzzy?" She tilted her head, stepping nearer to the screen, as though that would help her determine her own answers, but it seemed the ship had stopped as the view grew no closer. Maybe they were in orbit. She was so fixated on the image of the planet that when the screen suddenly darkened, she jumped, only to squeak in surprise as his hand gently grasped her upper arm.

"I'll give you answers while we walk to the shuttle. I'd prefer not to force you, but I will if you don't come peacefully."

She could tell by the warning in his tone that he was absolutely serious, and she briefly considered attacking him. But her curiosity was winning out over her desire to do him bodily harm, much to her chagrin. So she set aside the data slate and followed him as he moved toward the door to the passageway.

When the door opened, she pulled up short and clutched the spear to her chest. She hadn't exactly anticipated a whole unit of guards and what appeared to be a servant of some sort. It seemed everything happened all at once, as the guards noticed her weapon, and suddenly, there were nearly a dozen energy lances pointed at her. She gasped in alarm and dove behind Zavier, who made a sound suspiciously akin to a laugh, before clearing his throat.

"Stand down. The princess is our honored guest, and she's not going to hurt anyone. Isn't that right?"

She glared up at him when he looked over his shoulder

at her but begrudgingly nodded as she stepped out to stand beside him once more. The guards immediately raised their lances and moved into position, assuming a square formation for the royals and the steward to occupy. She stepped into the formation beside Zavier and his steward and glanced anxiously at the guards as they moved to surround the trio. Though she didn't much like it, she was forced to stick close to both the iron king and his servant as they moved through the passageways toward the shuttle bay, their pace swift enough that she was barely able to look around.

"Allow me to introduce you to my steward. Princess, this is Benji, who has been serving me most of my life. Benji, Princess Alexia of Greenwell, heir of the Verdant Empress."

She looked at Zavier as he introduced her to the man with the warm eyes and bald head, who bowed to her as much as he was able, given they were in motion. When he lifted his head, he smiled at her, and despite her anxiety about this situation, Alexia found herself smiling back.

"It's my great honor to meet you, Your Highness. I hope you'll enjoy Ironhold. It's not as lush as Greenwell, but it has its own beauty. If there's anything you need, you can, of course, summon me directly, but I'll see to it we find you an appropriate handmaiden as soon as possible after we arrive at the Citadel."

She couldn't stop her eyes from widening at the steward's words. So it seemed this man, at least, was aware of his king's plans and didn't seem to object to them. Was he indoctrinated, or simply loyal? Or did he somehow think that this was a good plan? Alexia was too caught off guard to respond, so she simply nodded her understanding and continued walking. She very nearly reminded him about his promise, but as soon as she opened her mouth, Zavier began speaking again.

"Ironhold is covered in thick mist, almost like a very low and constant cloud-cover, likely because of our distance from this system's sun. The vegetation is all the sort that survives without much light in very damp situations, as a result, and you can easily put together how that affects the cycle of prey and predator lifeforms. It looks fuzzy, as you put it, because of the mist, and the fact that the majority of the terrain is rocky gives it that coloration you noticed."

Well, that explained a lot. It also made her heart sink. Greenwell might have been a veritable prison for her, but it was still a vibrant and living prison. She couldn't imagine living on a world where it was mostly rocks and cold, damp mist, with little flora to speak of. And what sort of creatures must be native to such a planet? It gave her a lot to think about, and she remained silent as they entered the shuttle bay, boarded the waiting shuttle, and descended to the Citadel.

Alexia was being far too quiet.

Zavier supposed she might simply be struggling with information overload and having a hard time processing everything she'd just learned. But considering she was holding a weapon, it made him quite nervous. Not that he didn't think he could disarm her. He easily could. He was larger and heavier, with a longer reach. But she'd probably be able to get in at least one strike, and that would undoubtedly hurt quite a lot, which was something he wanted to avoid.

Even though he knew, logically, that she was still

dangerous, his heart went out to her as the shuttle traveled through Ironhold's atmosphere. She looked so small and young, huddled in her seat, watching the Citadel grow larger through the shuttle's viewports. It made him want to take her in his arms and comfort her... which would *definitely* result in him getting stabbed. She didn't like him, let alone trust him, and touching her uninvited wouldn't help the issue.

This meant the shuttle was uncomfortably quiet as it finally landed on the open square in front of the Ebon Citadel, until the hatch opened and the low rumble of the assembled staff entered the vessel. Climbing out of the shuttle, he straightened and turned to offer his hand to Alexia. She hesitated visibly, but apparently whatever she saw in his face convinced her that she could at least trust him not to do anything to her where others could see, because she placed her delicate hand in his and exited with his assistance. Tugging her gently up to his side, he stepped forward and addressed the gathering of staff and guards with a loud, strong voice.

"I know you've all heard rumors of the situation, but let me confirm it right now. I have brought Princess Alexia of Greenwell here to be my queen. You should treat her with all the respect she is due from this moment forward." He was ready for some sort of hubbub, but instead, silence met his ears. It was pleasing to see them all bow or curtsy to the princess, and he even caught a few half-hidden smiles. Good. They would hopefully adjust quickly to having a mistress.

When he stepped forward, however, she yanked her hand out of his. Zavier froze, seeing the shocked expressions and hearing the whispers rippling through his staff, then slowly turned to face her. She stood there, grim-faced and defiant, gripping her crude spear and glaring at him.

"I am *not* going to be your queen."

The moment she pulled free of him, Alexia knew she was about to do something potentially foolish. But Zavier's reaction to her proclamation made her seriously reconsider the past few minutes of her life. His grey eyes seemed to darken threateningly, and he clenched his jaw as a vein began to pulse in his brow. While she somehow felt certain he'd never strike her, and certainly not in front of witnesses, she nonetheless tensed when she saw his hand clench into a fist.

"Benji."

She blinked as he summoned the steward, who hurried wordlessly to his liege's side. He wasn't going to yell at her? Maybe he just didn't want to make even more of a scene in front of his people. Even when he addressed the shorter man in cool, clipped tones, his frigid gaze never left hers. "The princess is clearly overtired. Select a handmaiden and a few individuals for her personal guard, and see she's escorted to her chambers."

"Of course, Your Majesty. Right away." Benji barely got the words out before the iron king was stalking off, anger vibrating in every line of his body. As he disappeared into the towering Citadel, she felt some of the tension leave her body and exhaled a breath she hadn't realized she'd been holding while the steward sent the crowd scurrying back to their duties. Alexia watched him carefully as he spoke with a young woman, her hair hidden beneath a pale blue scarf, and a few uniformed women with energy lances. After several long moments, he led the group of six over to where the princess was standing and gestured to them.

"Your Highness, allow me to introduce Elea. She'll be

your handmaiden. The others are your personal guards, and they can tell you their names as they like. Now if you'll pardon me, I must attend to the iron king."

Before she could protest, the steward hurried away, and she turned back to the women who were all looking at her. Elea had the most brilliant blue eyes she'd ever seen, and she suspected a streak of mischief, judging by the way the girl smiled as she dipped a not-quite-perfect curtsy.

"If you'll come with me, Your Highness, I'll lead you to your chambers."

"Um… yes, that would be greatly appreciated, thank you." She tried to muster a smile but failed miserably as the quintet of women fell in behind and to either side of her, clearly intending to prevent any attempted escape. She could feel eyes on her back, which made her unconsciously straighten and hurry her pace to keep up with the brisk strides of Elea. Their pace didn't slow even as they entered the Citadel, but that didn't stop her from looking around with great interest.

The place was nowhere near as stark as she'd expected it to be. The light within was warm and vaguely yellow, softening the hard lines of the corridors they passed through, and many of the walls were covered with rich hangings and detailed tapestries, which helped to stave off the chill inherent to such dark stone surfaces. She lost count of how many twists and turns they took before Elea finally stopped in front of a door. She pressed her palm to the surface, and the door slid to one side, revealing the room within.

Despite her better judgement, Alexia couldn't stop herself from almost running into the sitting room. The walls had been covered with diaphanous layers of green fabric and paintings of landscapes that were so realistic, she half expected to be able to reach right into them and touch the greenery they contained. The furniture all appeared to be made of some sleek black metal but had been covered with green and white fabric and cushions to make it softer. She imagined the bedroom furniture would be much the same, but that was hardly her concern at the moment. Because what really thrilled her were the planters and vases, full to bursting with flowers and exotic plants she'd never seen before.

She reached out to touch a brilliant orange blossom nestled in a bed of vines with four-lobed leaves, and then leaned in to inhale its intoxicating scent. But almost as soon as she'd done this, something occurred to her, and she straightened, turning a confused look upon Elea. The handmaiden was lurking by a panel that she assumed was a video screen, trying not to appear amused by her new lady's distraction.

"These chambers were prepared for me? Where did the plants come from?"

"From the Citadel's garden, Your Highness."

The Citadel had a garden? She'd never have imagined such a dark place would have a location like that in its halls, but now that she knew it existed, she positively itched to see it. Nodding firmly, she started toward the door.

"You will take me there."

It had taken quite a bit of cajoling, wheedling, and demanding, but Elea finally conceded that there was no harm in taking her to the garden. When they arrived at a large set of double doors constructed from that same black metal and shining crystal panels, she could see the smudged green shades of flora just beyond. She wanted to proceed through the doors and immerse herself in something familiar, but the pair of guards standing to either side of the doorway, energy lances slanted in an X across the portal, gave her pause.

"I wish to enter the garden." She made her tone firm, certain they would give way and do what she wanted. But when they simply exchanged a troubled look, she felt a ripple of worry. Surely, Zavier wouldn't be so cruel as to bar her entrance to the one place in this grim fortress that would be familiar to her?

"Has the iron king expressly forbidden the princess to enter the garden?"

She was surprised to hear one of the guards speak up from her right, and Alexia glanced at the woman. She could see a hint of vivid orange curls beneath the imposing female's helmet, sharply contrasted against the mahogany coloration of her skin, with a scattering of scars and red eyes. Alexia had never seen anyone like her before. Where did she come from? Why was she here? She didn't voice these questions, only watched as the two guards before the door shuffled their feet, one of them shaking his head in response to the question posed.

"Then I suggest you step aside and let your future queen do as she wants."

Although she bristled at the suggestion that she'd actually marry their brute of a king, Alexia was nonetheless grateful when the female's steely tone and reminder caused the guards to lift their energy lances out of the way. Wasting no time, she hurried forward and pushed the doors open.

It was beautiful. Towering trees rose to a trio of massive crystal domes so perfectly clear that she could almost swear they weren't even there. Ferns as tall as she was were scattered among squat shrubs and flowering plants. So many different kinds of plants in a rainbow of colors, enough to almost hurt her eyes. And yet she couldn't look away. There were no paved pathways, only thick grass with round grey stones just large enough to step upon, wending their way through the untamed flora. She could hear water trickling and knew there must be a pond or an artificial stream in here somewhere.

A few minutes of walking, reaching out to touch every leaf, petal, and branch that came within range, led her to what she was looking for. But when she rounded a bend and found herself confronted with not just a pond and a stream, but a man-made waterfall, she froze. For sitting on a bench in front of the water festooned with flowered lily pads, was the very source of her current predicament. Although in that moment, she couldn't reconcile the sight before her with the man who'd accosted and bullied her since the moment she awoke.

The iron king was hunched over, his elbows on his knees and hands turned upward, his brow resting against his palms with his fingers immersed in his hair. He looked so weary, utterly broken down, that she felt a pang of sympathy. Was it because of her? Or was there something else troubling him? She stepped forward, the skirt of her robes rustling against the leaves of a fern, and the noise was enough to alert him to her presence. She froze as Zavier's head snapped up and turned toward her, not because she feared his wrath, but because his expression was one of anguish.

"What are you doing here?"

Even though the question was devoid of reproach, she felt herself taking half a step backwards as everything about him changed. Gone, was the moment of vulnerability, replaced by the distant and haughty demeanor of a king as he stood and turned to face her. But she had seen it, and there was no forgetting the way he'd seemed completely alone and adrift in the universe in that split-second of naked emotion.

"I saw the flowers in my chambers, and I wanted to see the garden they came from." Her response was almost absently murmured, her mind barely on her words, because she was far more curious about what had brought him here. Did he seek solace in the garden, too?

"Well, now you've seen them. I'll leave you to it." He grumbled the words, tugging his jacket down in a gesture of obvious discomfort, then stalked past her, giving the princess a wide berth. Almost like he was afraid to touch her. Perhaps it was contrary of her, but Alexia reached out and grasped his sleeve as he passed. Even that light contact was enough to stop him, his back rigid as he shot a silently questioning look over his shoulder at her.

"Why did you take me?" It wasn't what she'd meant to ask, but as soon as the softly spoken question left her lips, she knew it was the right one. She needed to understand. He'd said he wanted her as his mistress at first, until he found out her royal status, but why?

She watched as his lips thinned, his gaze turning away from her and settling on a nearby plant. Her heart was tripping over itself while she waited, and waited... then it sank into her stomach when he turned away and spoke gruffly.

"Return to your chambers. The seamstress should be waiting to fit you for new gowns."

Her hand fell from his sleeve as he stepped away, hurrying back in the direction from where she'd entered. Was she doomed to spend her days a prisoner in this keep, with no one for company except some servants and a man who didn't want to speak to her? It was a grim thought, and one she didn't particularly relish as she retraced her steps to the doorway, where a white-haired old man bowed to her before stepping into the garden.

She didn't hear his gasp of surprise, as she was following Elea back to her chambers, but the guards at the door did. One of them turned to the bent elder, his face claimed by a frown.

"What is it, Warren?"

"The garden, sir. I've never seen it so alive."

The seamstress was indeed waiting for her upon her return, but Alexia barely did more than greet the woman and her assistants as she stripped out of her robes and stood upon the waiting stool. They'd apparently had enough forewarning of her arrival to put together the basic shapes of some gowns, and she found herself in a familiar position, with arms out to her sides as they measured, pinned, and marked the sleeve-less, unfinished garments. By the time they were done and had bustled off to make her new wardrobe, she became aware that she was famished. How long had it been since she fell from Lella's back? As she donned her robe once more, she turned to Elea, who was examining a data slate in her hand.

"Where are the kitchens?"

"Your Highness?" Elea looked at her questioningly, and Alexia realized that things would be different here. She wouldn't be allowed to simply go to the kitchens and take whatever she liked. Even her mother frowned on it, but with no one around to see other than the staff, the empress hadn't stopped her. Ignoring her flush of embarrassment, Alexia squared her shoulders and spoke.

"I haven't eaten since well before your iron king took me from Greenwell. I'm in need of sustenance." That was clear enough, though she wondered at the uncomfortable look on Elea's face as the girl fidgeted.

"Ahh, well, His Majesty has issued a command that you're to dine with him tonight."

Oh. That explained her discomfort. And although Alexia knew it wasn't the servant's fault, she felt a surge of anger. Making decisions when she was angry never ended well.

But that didn't stop her from doing it.

"No."

"What do you mean, she said *no?*" Zavier snapped as he whirled on Benji, his pale eyes alight with fury. First, the chit invaded his garden while he was trying to think, asked him a question he really didn't want to answer, and now she refused to eat with him? To his credit, Benji didn't quail under his king's rage, but then again, he was used to these displays, after more than twenty years of service.

"Exactly what I said, Your Majesty. Elea informed the princess that you had commanded her to dine with you tonight, and her response was—and I quote," the steward cleared his throat, looked down at the data slate in his hand, and continued, "'no.' Just that."

"Just..." His hands curling into fists, Zavier took a deep breath to stifle the urge to begin cursing. That girl was going to drive him completely mad, he felt sure of it. It took several long moments of pacing and measured breathing to rein his temper back in, but there was still a thread of anger when he spoke again. "Unacceptable. I'll handle this myself."

"As you wish, Your Majesty." There was a note of amusement in Benji's voice, which had the iron king shooting him a sharp glance, but the steward's expression was carefully blank. Of course. He was familiar enough with his king's temperament to know better.

Ignoring the robed man, Zavier left his chambers at a swift pace, heading down a flight of stairs and into the portion of the royal wing where Alexia's current chambers were. It wasn't a permanent arrangement, after all. Once they were married and she was crowned, the queen's chambers, connected to his own, would be fitted for her occupation. But for now, it was best that he keep her away from him. *Far* away. His temper had risen again by the time he reached her chambers, ignoring the salutes of the guards and the curtsy from Elea as the door opened.

"What do you mean by refusing to dine with me?" He snapped the words as soon as he spotted her, sitting calmly on a chaise lounge with a data slate in her hands. He didn't want to admit that the princess was utterly fetching, or that his abdomen tensed with desire when she looked up through her lashes at him.

"I'd think it's obvious. You kidnapped me, you're proclaiming your intent to marry me against my wishes, and you were rude to me in the garden. I don't want to be around you, let alone be forced to share a meal with you."

His jaw clenched. Her tone was perfectly calm, but there was a spitting fire in her gaze. He knew she had a temper. It had been turned on him a few times since she awoke on the *Nightfall*. Was she holding back in front of her handmaiden? Without even looking at the servant, though he could sense her hovering anxiously behind him somewhere, he growled a command, "Out."

He heard Elea squeak in surprise and hurry out the door, which slid shut behind her. Suddenly alone, he could see the flash of wariness in Alexia's face. *Good.* He wanted her to think very carefully about what her next move was.

Pressing one hand to the sloped back of the chaise, and the other to the padded arm beside her, Zavier leaned down, down, down. And with every inch closer that he came, the princess tried to withdraw, until it became obvious there was nowhere for her to go. He had her penned in, his large body effectively preventing her from rising, and the positioning of his arms keeping her from moving to either side.

"Listen to me, you little harpy. This is *my* domain. Everyone here answers to me. And from the moment you set foot on my planet, that included you. So you can either come with me and act like the lady you are, or I'll throw you over my shoulder and cart you out of here like a misbehaving child."

Her eyes widened at the threat, and then narrowed. He could see her trying to weigh whether he was bluffing or not. Then she raised her chin defiantly, and he had to suppress a purely malicious grin. He knew what she was going to say even before the words left her pretty mouth.

"You wouldn't dare."

"Put me *down!*" She kicked, rather ineffectually, and pummeled her fists against his back as Zavier strolled calmly out of her room and down the hallway. It felt like she was striking a stone wall, for all the good it did her, not to mention his back was apparently nothing but hard muscle. The chuckle that rumbled in his chest did nothing but infuriate her, and she growled her frustration as she kicked again.

"No. I warned you. You didn't believe me, so this is your fault."

Her jaw dropped at his nonchalant tone. She couldn't believe he was treating her this way! She was an imperial princess, and he was carrying her around over his shoulder like a sack of grain! It seemed fighting would achieve nothing except humiliation, though, so she elected to simply deal with it for now, and enact revenge once she was on her feet again. She heard when a door opened before their approach and looked around the room they entered, a gasp falling from her lips.

It was full of books. *Real* books, with embossed bindings and paper pages, she could tell even from this distance by the scent of book dust and leather. Alexia was so taken aback by this unexpected delight that she barely noticed when he stopped beside a square table set for two, though she came back to her senses as he set her down. She looked up at him warily, taking a step back as her hands clutched against her chest.

"What is the meaning of this?" She knew she sounded wary, and that the question was probably absurd, but she didn't trust him. It seemed she'd only served to amuse him again, however, as he arched a brow and smirked. That expression was infuriating, and she wanted to slap it right off his face, but she had the strong sense that wouldn't go over well.

"This room is comfortable, and I saw no point to dining in formality when it's just the two of us. Sit. Eat."

She turned to watch him suspiciously as he rounded the table, but to her mild shock, he simply pulled out one of the chairs for her. Anticipating deceit at any moment, she cautiously sank onto the plushily padded item and allowed him to scoot her closer to the table. Amazing, that this brutish king could act like a gentleman when he chose. It took her a few moments to realize that, rather than calling servants to tend to them, he had deactivated the energy dome on a hovering serving cart and was dishing out food onto their plates himself.

Alexia couldn't help it. She sniffed delightedly at the fragrant, vaguely spicy aroma of the unfamiliar meat and vegetables as they were placed before her and felt her stomach grumble. Which only made sense, given she hadn't eaten in… at least a full day, she realized. But also it just smelled spectacular. Without waiting for an invitation, she lifted her fork and speared a bite of a pale pink root and the aromatic red meat, plucking it daintily yet hungrily off the tines while Zavier poured them both measures of a rich, violet wine.

"I'll have to give my regards to your cook. This is wonderful." She had to fight back the urge to moan as the mélange of intricate flavors washed across her tongue, though when he hid a smile in his wine glass, she gestured angrily at him with her utensil. "This doesn't mean I'm going to forgive you for treating me so terribly."

"Of course not." She could practically see the sarcasm dripping off his words, and she glared at him again, before pointedly shoving another bite of the dish into her mouth. He seemed to find that funny, too, as he chuckled quietly.

The man was infuriating. But he had a beautiful garden and a library full of actual books, so she could at least admit that he had good taste. But she didn't like him and vowed she never would. Not after he'd abducted her from her own planet and tried to… She didn't even want to think about what he'd tried to do and felt her face warming as she recalled that embarrassing scene in his bedchamber aboard the flagship. Trying to dispel her blush, she sipped at her wine and did her best to ignore him. Until she noticed one of the books on the nearest shelf.

"Oh, is that a copy of Tirone's *Essays on Love*?" Her fingers twitched with the urge to reach out and grab the tome, which looked old enough that it might very well have been an original printing, but she restrained herself. Barely.

"It is. I'm surprised you know it. It doesn't seem like the sort of thing Yvonne would let you read."

Her gaze darted from the book to Zavier, who was chewing on a bite of his dinner while looking at her with obvious curiosity. She couldn't help but grin, her eyes flashing with mischief.

"Mother has no idea. I stole a copy from one of the scholars."

The way his eyebrows shot upward in shock was thoroughly satisfying, and she giggled almost wickedly to herself as she brought her wine glass to her lips to sample the vintage it held. An intense flavor of *idriv* fruit washed across her tongue, paired with the burn of alcohol, and she coughed slightly. Her mother had only let her have wine on rare occasions, and she still wasn't terribly fond of it.

"Imagine, stealing from your servants. I didn't think you had it in you."

"There's a lot you don't know about me." She fired back the words without thinking and immediately felt her skin heating again when he leveled a look on her that was far too intense. Why did he look at her like that?

"I'd like to learn. It's only fitting if you're going to be my queen." His voice was deep and smooth and sent a shiver down her spine. Squaring her shoulders, she gave him her haughtiest look.

"I'm not going to be your queen. How many times do I have to say it?"

"You can say it as much as you want, but I *will* have you." Her eyes widened at the promise in his words. Swallowing thickly, she decided it was safest just to bury her focus in her dinner, which she ate with gusto, ignoring his considering looks and the awkward, heavy silence between them.

When her plate was empty and her wine glass drained, she tried to think of a way to get out of there without his help. Which was hard to do, considering everything felt just a little... fuzzy. Perhaps she shouldn't have had that entire glass of wine, she mused. Just as she was about to push her chair back and stand, she realized he had already done so and was rounding the table. She found her eyes widening as he leaned over her, her head craning back to keep eye contact.

"Tell me, Princess... have you ever been kissed?"

She was so alluring. The way she looked up at him, with those full lips slightly parted, pupils dilated, and cheeks flushed... She had no idea how beautiful she was, did she? Zavier wanted nothing more than to claim her lips, haul her body against his, and take her on the very floor beneath them. But the way she stammered and stumbled over her response gave him a better idea.

"I... What? No, of... of course not."

His face was claimed by a wide and purely devilish smile, and while he let one hand fall to rest on the back of her chair, the other rose to capture a silky tendril of that silvery hair. Twirling it around his index finger, he reveled in her sharp intake of breath. He affected her. Even if she didn't want to admit it, he knew he did.

"No, I would think not. No one even knows what you look like, so who would be bold enough to kiss you? Such a shame... You have a mouth for kissing. I wonder if you taste as good as you look?"

She began sputtering as the color in her cheeks rose,

and Zavier uttered a husky chuckle. His hand slid around the side of her head to cup the back of her neck, while his head dipped lower. Just when she seemed ready to fall out of the chair simply to get away from him, he paused, the tip of his nose barely brushing against hers.

"I'll have you begging me to kiss you by the time you wear my ring... Alexia."

He felt the way her body trembled beneath that promise, or perhaps it was how he said her name. He burned with desire for her and had no doubt it carried through into his voice. But he was a man with an iron will, perfectly in control of himself, so he let go of her and straightened, then turned away and moved to the nearby bookcase. Retrieving the copy of *Essays*, he flashed a heated look at her, before venturing out the nearest door. He'd send Benji to escort her back to her rooms, and leave her wondering. It would be far easier to catch her unawares that way.

Chapter 4

I t was a restless night for Alexia. The stone walls of her room left her feeling too separate from the outdoors, not to mention the landscape outside was so different from what she was used to. The world she could see through her bedchamber's window was too flat, too lifeless, nothing at all like Greenwell. She'd wanted so badly to see the universe beyond her planet, but now that she was gone from her home, she missed it terribly.

This left her in a thoroughly disgruntled mood when she awoke the next morning to the sounds of rattling porcelain from the sitting room. Sliding out of the bed, she shrugged on a robe of rose pink and shuffled into the other room with a yawn. Not expecting the sight of a full breakfast and tea service sitting on the low table, she stared at it, uncomprehending, before turning to Elea.

"Your king hasn't demanded my presence for breakfast?"

"No, Your Highness. His Majesty had to leave the Citadel on urgent business, but he asked me to assure you he'll be back in time to share dinner with you."

Oddly, she felt displeased by this. For someone who claimed to want her as his queen, Zavier didn't seem all that determined to spend time with her. Then again, he'd said this would just be a political union. But after his behavior last night... that somehow rang untrue. Irritated with herself over her own conflicting thoughts and feelings, she dropped unceremoniously into a chair and began to eat, consoling herself with the knowledge that the food, at least, was delicious enough to be worth all this trouble.

An opinion she thoroughly rejected not even two hours later, when she was inundated with servants. The seamstress had returned to get more precise measurements, this time for what would be her bridal gown. On her heels, were the jewel smith, to fit her for her crown, and the shoemaker, to size her for 'proper footwear'. Alexia was ready to tear her hair out by lunchtime and sprawled dramatically on the chaise lounge as Elea set the tray of delicate sandwiches down on the table, flinging her arm over her eyes.

"I refuse to see one more person today. You're all awfully determined to have me as your queen, and it's absolutely not going to happen."

There was an odd silence, thick with tension, in the wake of her statement. Wondering if Elea had gone, she lifted her arm, only to find her handmaiden looking at her with an unexpectedly fierce expression. And then the girl seemed to... erupt, for lack of a better word.

"Forgive me for speaking out of turn, Your Highness, but I think you're being extremely childish about all of this and particularly unfair to His Majesty. The iron king has been alone since he was just a boy, with none but servants and guards for company, and you have no idea what sort of man he is at all. I'll leave you to your meal."

Alexia was stunned by the passionate, if brief, lecture. So much so that she could do little more than watch in silence as Elea hurried out of the sitting room, ostensibly to tend to some task or another, when it was clear she just didn't want to be around the princess. She didn't understand it. How could all of these people be so loyal to him, when he was such a beast to her? She had to be missing something.

But what?

"How could this have happened?" Although Benji stood at his side, the king spoke only to himself, his words soft and full of a deep melancholy. The jagged gouge in the ground before him, nearly fifty meters distant but exuding enough heat to make sweat bead upon his brow, was a scar on the face of Ironhold. Already, not the most beautiful of planets, this was nonetheless a malevolent wound that would change the face of his world for innumerable months, if not years.

"From what I understand, Your Majesty, the residents of this outpost were unaware of a pocket of methane beneath them. They were mining and…"

Benji trailed off, leaving the unspoken end of that sentence hovering between them. They both knew what happened when an errant spark struck methane. *This* happened. A violent explosion, and nothing left but ash and death. Although it had been nothing but a settlement of violent offenders, sent to Ironhold to work for the rest of their lives, they were *his* charge, the iron king's responsibility. And they'd died on his watch. Clenching his jaw, he inhaled sharply through his nose and whirled away from the horrific sight of the magma-filled pit.

"I want all mining activities halted until more thorough geological surveys can be performed for the other outposts.

I'll not have more lives wasted." His gaze fixed on Benji, and he tried not to resent the sympathetic look on his steward's face. The older man knew his king's mind and heart, although he kept the latter hidden from all but his most trusted companions, and knew that Zavier felt like he had failed.

Failure was unacceptable.

"Of course, Your Majesty. I'll send out the proclamation immediately and have teams on their way as soon as the proper equipment can be assembled."

"Good. And… find out their names. Have a monument built." At Benji's questioning glance, he scowled and spoke more quietly. "They deserve to be remembered, by us, if by no one else."

"Yes, Your Majesty." Benji bowed, and Zavier nodded briskly in response, before beginning the trek back to where the shuttle waited. This hadn't been how he wanted to start his day. He'd hoped to share breakfast with Alexia and perhaps invite her to join him in the garden after lunch. But word of the explosion had arrived in the small, dark hours of the morning, and he'd left to see the devastation for himself even before the sun crested Ironhold's eastern horizon.

The day had begun poorly. But as he boarded the shuttle, his mind on his future queen, he prayed it would make a turn for the better. If only he could get her to smile, he felt certain that it would.

Lunch had come and gone, with Alexia largely alone. Elea had left her tray of food and, after inquiring if she needed anything, left without another word. It was true that on Greenwell, Alexia had preferred to spend the majority of her time in solitude. But she was quickly discovering that there was a large difference between being alone and being lonely. The only thing that kept her from true misery was the data slate with detailed information about the galaxy. She was deeply engrossed in the history and political climate of the Golden Cloud system, the purported heart of galactic society and influence, when she heard the door slide open. Her head lifted, and she turned with an inquisitive glance, expecting to see Elea.

Instead, she was confronted with the sight of Zavier. Despite the fact that he was clad in the same type of attire, what she could only think of as his uniform, and he was immaculately groomed, while standing in the usual rigid posture, something about him seemed... drawn. Tired. Perhaps even sad. Setting aside the data slate, she stood, unconsciously smoothing her hands across the skirt of the new dress that had been delivered to her that morning. It was long-sleeved, snug in the bodice, with a wide neckline and full skirts, all in silken indigo fabric. It was quite possibly the most elegant thing she'd ever worn, and she loved it. Even when she saw the king's eyes roving over her body in a most inappropriate fashion.

"Forgive me for disturbing your reading."

He was being so polite. It wasn't at all what she expected, and for a moment, she was too caught off guard to respond. She wanted to tell him that he should be apologizing for abducting her, infringing on her personal space, and manhandling her. But then she remembered the words of the unnamed communications officer aboard the *Nightfall*, and those of Elea that very morning, and realized that perhaps they were right. Maybe there was more to him than she understood, and maybe she should give herself a chance to know him before making any true judgements about his person. So she ventured a hesitant response.

"It's quite all right. I've had nothing else to do with my time today. What brings you to my chambers?" She felt a flash of guilt when he seemed taken aback by her polite response. Had she truly been that awful to him? Admittedly, she'd had reason, in her mind, but that was hardly the point.

"I had intended to ask if you would share lunch with me, but I see you've already eaten." He paused, clearly intending to continue, and wondering what else he had to say was the only thing that kept her from speaking. "Would you... perhaps be willing to take a walk in the garden with me?"

He wanted to walk in the garden with her? That was a positively normal request. Perhaps even one might expect of a man attempting to woo his intended. She bit back on the urge to throw a snarky comment at him. Only because she wanted to see the garden again, but had no confidence in her ability to find them herself. That was the sole reason.

"I would like that. Thank you." His obvious relief, and the tiny smile that claimed his lips, made her feel strangely buoyant. And when he held out his arm in silent offer of escort, she hesitated just a moment before crossing to his side and tucking her hand into the crook of his elbow.

It was too easy. Zavier kept waiting for her to whip out that spear, or a shortened version of it, and stab him. Yet with every step they took, nothing happened. In fact, there was a nearly peaceful silence between them. He glanced down at her, unable to help but admire her appearance and how fascinated she seemed by every little thing she saw. When they finally arrived at the doors to the gardens, she visibly brightened, her obvious delight bringing a tiny smile to his face. The guards opened the doors for them, and they moved inside.

He couldn't look away from her, even when she let go of his arm to approach one of the flowering bushes. She seemed completely enamored with its fragrance as she leaned over to inhale the scent of the bright blue trumpet-shaped blossoms. What made his eyes narrow in puzzlement, was either a hallucination, or an overactive imagination, as he could've sworn the plant seemed to puff up beneath her gentle touch to its leaves.

No. That simply wasn't possible. Dismissing it as a flight of fancy, he followed her, more amused than anything, as she strolled down the path. Every few steps, she stopped to examine something that caught her eye, and he couldn't contain his amusement at her childlike excitement. He uttered a quiet chuckle, but apparently it was loud enough to capture her attention, as she straightened and turned to face him, a warily questioning expression dominating her features.

"What's funny?"

"You take such pleasure in little things. It's... refreshing." She blushed, his response clearly not what she'd been expecting, and he felt his smile return, slightly wider than before. Did she not understand what a rarity she was? She was... Ah, there were so many cliches he could use to describe her. A breath of fresh air. A ray of sunlight. A rose in a field of daisies. Yet none of them came even remotely close to truly expressing just how much she both stirred his desires and soothed the perpetual ache of loneliness inside him.

"If Ironhold's sun is so distant that it keeps normal plants from growing outside, how does the garden survive without artificial illumination?"

He blinked. Well, that was a far more specific and in-depth question than he'd been expecting. Then again, it was obvious just how intelligent she was, so he probably should've seen it coming. Clasping his hands behind himself, he strolled past the large fruit tree currently blocking their view of the trio of domes far above, and once they were visible, he gestured toward the structures with an upward tilt of his head.

"The domes are comprised of a special kind of crystal that refracts the sunlight in such a way that it's stronger, enough so as to provide the amount of energy the garden requires. That, in conjunction with a carefully derived soil composition and a steadfastly devoted garden staff, keeps them thriving. Although..."

He trailed off as he noticed that the tree he'd just passed under seemed to be sporting an unusually large number of blooms and budding fruits. His brow furrowed as he pondered what could have possibly caused this, immersed deeply enough in his consideration that he didn't notice she'd moved closer until she spoke again.

"Although what?"

His gaze dropped from the branches and to her upturned face. She was close enough that he could count every eyelash if he was of a mind to. Instead, he found himself staring into her eyes. The irises were almost over-whelmingly green, mostly a brilliant shade of emerald with bits of jade scattered through, but the coloration of her dress brought out something he'd not anticipated. Something that was, although small and seemingly unimportant, nonetheless utterly fascinating.

"The color of your gown brings out the blue in your eyes." He murmured the words absently, not truly realizing, until those very eyes widened, that he'd said them aloud. When she turned to him with an astonished look and reddening cheeks, he couldn't stop himself from lifting a hand to gently tuck some of her silvery hair behind her ear. His fingertips trailed lightly over the bare skin of her neck and collarbone as his hand fell away, eliciting a shudder from her that made him want to do it again.

"Why are you being so nice to me?"

That question was like being doused with snow. She sounded so suspicious, as though she expected him to violate her right there in the grass. Admittedly, he'd nearly kissed her twice and thrown her over his shoulder once, but hadn't she learned by now? If she was at least civil to him, he was nice in return. Resisting the urge to sigh, he stepped back, folding his arms across his chest.

"You're going to be my queen. I'd prefer it if you didn't despise me." Much to his amazement, she didn't protest and insist she wasn't going to be his queen. Was she coming around to the idea? Or had she simply realized that doing so in his presence tended to result in more awkward situations? Either way, he took it as a good sign and softened his tone as he continued. "Would you rather I acted the cruel tyrant? I'm sure you think that's my true nature, but I really despise behaving that way."

"No. I'm just… Never mind."

He tried to quell his disappointment as she cut herself off. What had she been going to say? And why did he get the feeling it was genuinely important?

He was disappointed in her answer. She didn't know how she could tell, but it was as plain as the sharp angles of his cheekbones. Turning away from him, she tried not to fidget as she began walking, heading in the direction of the pond she'd seen that first time here. When they rounded the bend and came to her destination, she paused, seeing an old man and a cluster of younger servants all chattering excitedly. She nearly jumped when Zavier came up behind her, his voice carrying toward the group. "Is something amiss?"

"Your Majesty!" The group broke apart as the older man exclaimed in surprise, and there was a ripple of curtsies and bows aimed their way. The bent old man hobbled their way, his wizened face creased with puzzlement. "Not at all, Your Majesty. We were just discussing something. It's the strangest thing. Half of the garden is the most robust I've ever seen it."

"I'd noticed it myself. But you're saying it wasn't your doing?" Zavier sounded thoughtful, and Alexia looked up at him, noting the furrow of his brow. She looked back to the old servant then, feeling almost like she was watching a game of grav-ball from mid-court.

"No, sire, we've changed nothing. It's quite a mystery. Especially since it's just this eastern side. The western half is the same as ever—healthy, but not... Well, you've seen it." The elderly servant gestured with a gnarled hand, and Alexia looked closely. Now that he mentioned it, she could see that the plants seemed particularly lush. Those with flowers were positively drowning in blooms, the shrubs and ferns were bursting with new growth, and the fruit-bearing species were overflowing with ripening blossoms.

"Only this half? I'll have the engineers do a check of the climate control. Perhaps there's been a malfunction."

"Can we see the other half? I know flora, I might be able to see if you have a problem."

Zavier and the servant both looked at her with confusion, as though they'd forgotten she was there. She was nearly offended by that, but then a tiny smirk tilted on the iron king's mouth as he explained to the servant. "Our guest is the Princess of Greenwell. She may well have an excellent point."

"Oh! The paradise planet! I'd be most grateful for your opinion, Your Highness." The elderly servant gave as deep a bow as he could manage, making Alexia smile. He truly loved his work, she could tell, which was why she didn't hesitate to step forward and help him straighten, then pat his shoulder once he was upright again.

"It would be my pleasure. Your dedication and love of this space is obvious, and I'd hate to see it go to waste due to an invasive species. Let's see what we have, hm?" And with that, she swept off, following the path around past the waterfall and pond to the other side of the garden.

She was something else, Zavier mused. While she examined the plants in the western half of the garden, chatting amicably with the servants and laughing at their jokes, he hung back and simply… watched. Any other lady of galactic society would've disdained kneeling in the grass next to servants, peering under leaves and at roots in search of unwanted pests or parasites. Yet there she was, her fingers in the dirt, even bringing small clumps of soil to her face so she could sniff at it.

But there was something interesting happening. Everywhere she went, the plant life seemed to… perk up, for lack of a better description. Where a shrub had been half-hidden in the shade of a tree, after she touched it, it seemed to thicken and lean toward the light from above. After observing her at this for nearly an hour, he became certain of it. Which was, in a word, baffling. He'd never heard of anyone who had such an effect on flora, aside from the old myths and legends of fantastic creatures that surely had never actually existed.

There was something different about Alexia of Greenwell, and he wanted to know what it was. Perhaps he could have some of his eyes and ears do a little digging in the empress's network. There had to be some hidden files with information about her daughter. Especially because no one knew who Alexia's father was. One day, Yvonne had simply been pregnant.

He was extracted from his thoughts by the princess rising to her feet and helping Warren to stand. She didn't seem to care that there was dirt under her nails and smudged on one cheek as she bade farewell to the servants and returned to him.

"I didn't see anything wrong, which is decidedly bizarre, but at least your garden seems to be healthy. Perhaps you were right and it's a fault in the climate control. You should run a soil analysis and make sure the moisture and atmospheric composition are within proper ranges, too."

Gods, she was knowledgeable about this sort of thing, wasn't she? It seemed like the women of his brother's court fell into two categories: Either they were brainless but friendly, or whip-smart and cold-hearted. Alexia was unlike any of the ones he'd met before, clearly intelligent, but not cruel or unfeeling. She'd been kind to everyone she met, from what he'd seen.

Except for him. And suddenly, that bothered him. He wanted her to look at him with warmth and give him her gentle smiles.

Without stopping to think of whether it was a wise decision or not, he lifted his hand and cupped her cheek. Although her eyes widened and her skin began to fill with a surge of pink, she didn't move away. And he didn't let go.

Instead, his thumb gently wiped the stain from her flesh, leaving it unblemished once more.

"You had dirt on your face." He could hear how husky his voice was and was unsurprised by it. Just having her so near, feeling the heat from her body, smelling that intoxicating aroma that seemed to come from her very skin, had him aflame with desire. Even knowing the servants could see, he yearned to crush her body to his and conquer her mouth. But he knew she would fight him right now. He could see the fear in her eyes. So he forced himself to drop his hand and take a deep breath.

"Oh. Thank you." She sounded uncertain, timid, and he only nodded briskly, before stepping back.

"I have matters to attend to. Will you join me for dinner?" Focusing on the administration of his planet should be enough to distract him from how badly he wanted her. Or so he hoped. All he knew was that he couldn't stay there, or he would lose his mind.

"Yes." With her agreement obtained, he nodded again and turned on his heel. But his hand burned with the memory of her soft skin beneath his touch.

The Iron King of Ironhold was an enigma. Alexia just couldn't seem to understand him. One moment, he was looking at her with a gaze so hot, she could almost feel it like the sun on her skin. The next, he couldn't seem to get away from her fast enough. She was tired of not knowing why he did the things he did.

Fortunately, she knew how to get the answers she sought.

"Warren?" She turned to the aging garden master as she spoke his name, pleased to see that he was still nearby.

He dipped his head in an approximation of a bow and shuffled to her side. "What can you tell me about the iron king?"

"Oh, Your Highness, I could tell you a great deal. I've known His Majesty his whole life." She followed him as he hobbled over to a pair of dark metal chairs, settling into one with a grunt of effort and leaving the other for her occupation. She sat eagerly, clasping her hands in her lap. "What is it you want to know?"

"Whatever you feel comfortable telling me. He seems to have no interest in speaking about such things, but since he's adamant I'm going to be his queen, I want to know about him." She felt a minor twinge of guilt even as the half-truth left her mouth. Surely, obfuscating the reality of it wasn't so bad as outright lying?

"Well then, I know you've lived a rather sheltered life, but what do you know about the King of Stars?"

"You mean Gerold the Conqueror? He waged an inter-system war to bring all inhabited planets under his control, before he was overthrown by his eldest son, Owen, the god-king, who now rules from the Golden Cloud system." All information she had learned just over the past couple of days, and was quite proud of herself for remembering. But the question seemed rather like a non sequitur, and she frowned. "But what does that have to do with the iron king?"

"It's not much of a secret, but no one likes to talk about it. Iron King Zavier is the younger brother of the god-king, and also of Aquis King Kade. Their mother, you see, the Star Queen Mariana, had been put aside by the King of Stars for one of his concubines, and she was living here in the Citadel when she birthed the iron king. His birth weakened her, and she lived only a couple of years more before she passed away. We all cared for him and raised him, saw to it he was protected from his mad father and got an education befitting a prince. So when the god-king overthrew their father and took the Star Crown for himself, he gave the aquis king rule of the Aqua system with Oceanis as its seat, and the iron king rule of the Ironstar system from Ironhold. Of course, most of the Ironstar system is nothing but asteroids and gas giants, so we're not nearly as popular as Aqua or Golden Cloud."

"I see." She spoke quietly, absorbing the information that had been given to her. She was starting to get a better picture of who Zavier was, and why he seemed so... cold, yet conflicted. And still, there were so many pieces of the puzzle that she was missing, each one she located seeming only to point out how many gaps there were.

It seemed the time had come for a true investigation.

"Warren, whom should I speak to if I want to learn more about who the iron king is, as a person? Without alerting him to what I'm doing, that is." Although the old man eyed her curiously, he didn't seem inclined to pursue the matter when she gave him her most brilliant smile.

"Well, let's see…"

***

By the time she was due to meet with Zavier for dinner, she had traversed what felt like the entire Citadel. She'd gone from the kitchens, to the guards' barracks, to the servants quarters, getting a different tale from every member of the staff she spoke to. And it felt like she'd learned more about the iron king than she knew even about her own mother.

Such as the fact that he loved cake with fresh berries and cream, and that he'd been a very studious, seriousminded child. That he had hand-chosen every plant in the garden, which had been his mother's favorite place in the

Citadel. That he had insisted on learning how to defend himself at a young age as he didn't like the idea of his guards dying for him. That he secretly loathed both of his brothers. That he made sure to attend every wedding, funeral, and welcoming of babes in the Citadel. That he refused to bed any of his servants and only rarely engaged in female company while visiting his brother's court.

And the list went on and on. A veritable novel of things that made one thing perfectly clear: Zavier was a good man. He simply had a hard time showing his emotions. Which she attributed to not receiving the love of a parent for the majority of his childhood. Of all the things she could say about Yvonne, she could never doubt her mother's love for her. Although she wished it didn't go hand-in-hand with a desire to control her in every way.

When she sat down at the table within his private study again, she was looking at him with new eyes. He'd greeted her silently and helped her into her chair, poured them both some pale yellow wine, and was now serving up plates of pasta with vegetables and strips of seared pink meat, covered in a light brown sauce. Once he'd finished, rather than eating, she just… looked at him, before finally speaking. "May I ask you a question?" His eyes met hers, and he nodded but didn't speak. He seemed more interested in spearing a forkful of food and sliding it into his mouth, but at least he wasn't trying to silence her. "Are your servants natives of Ironhold?"

That seemed to give him pause, as he hesitated with his fork between his lips and looked at her with obvious confusion. No doubt he was wondering why that question had come about, but she had to know. The answer was very important, somehow. Finally, he lowered the fork and answered in a solemn tone, "There are no natives of Ironhold."

She barely even waited for him to finish before asking another question, "Then where did your servants come from?"

He narrowed his eyes at her, a frown appearing on his lips, and leaned back in his chair. "Alexia, I hardly see how—"

"Please. Just answer me." Interrupting was rude. She knew that. But right then, she didn't care. She suspected she knew what he was going to say, but she had to hear it from him. Her heart was thundering in her chest as she waited, and waited.

Just when it seemed he was going to ignore her, he heaved a weary sigh, and rubbed his cheek with a thin hand. "I told you Ironhold is a prison planet. Those who live in the mining settlements are the violent offenders. Murderers, rapists, and the like. But some planets have... far more strict laws. People get arrested, banished, sentenced to life imprisonment, simply for stealing loaves of bread, or speaking out against their rulers. Those people also get sent to Ironhold. And those are the ones who work for me in the Citadel."

So she was right. A sense of triumph filled her as her suspicions were confirmed. He could just as easily have made everyone sent to his planet live outside the Citadel and work the mines until they died. Instead, he gave them protection, clothing, food, a safe place to live. It was the act of a kind-hearted man.

"I've come to a decision." The words left her almost before she knew she was going to say them, and they surprised her nearly as much as they intrigued Zavier, who leaned forward to fold his arms on the table and look at her curiously.

"Really? And what decision is that?" His eyes were sharp on her, but there was a hint of a smirk playing at the corners of his mouth. She found that infuriating, but also somehow amusing, and her own impish smile appeared.

"I've decided to let you properly court me, and assuming you don't do anything to horribly offend, injure, or otherwise alienate me, I'll marry you without argument in two weeks." Oh, to see his jaw drop and eyes widen was purely delicious. Still, she forged ahead, lifting a hand to point at him warningly. "*But*, I refuse to let you kiss me until you apologize for abducting me, rather than pursuing me in a proper manner from the start."

He was speechless. This was a rarity for the Iron King of Ironhold. Not to say he was a talkative man to begin with, as the opposite was true, but he usually *chose* not to speak. Being so thoroughly shocked that his mind was literally devoid of even the potential for words wasn't something that happened... ever, in truth.

Yet this friendly, mischievous, alluring princess had surprised him so greatly that he couldn't think up a single thing to say in response. The closest he could come to that, was wondering what had changed her mind. Just last night, she'd still been insisting she'd never marry him. Now she was willing, albeit with conditions. And there it was, something he could finally say.

"And what, pray tell, is your definition of 'properly' courting you?" He was amazed his voice came out as calm as it did, considering the disarray his thoughts were in. In truth, he was interested in her answer. He wasn't expecting to receive a list, though, as he watched her tick off points on her fingers.

"I want us to spend more time together. If we're going to be married, we should know each other as people, in addition to knowing each other as rulers. I want you to tell me more about Ironhold, and to learn what's involved in its management. And perhaps most importantly, I want to thoroughly discuss what my part as your queen will be. Because I absolutely will *not* be just an ornament that you have children with." It took every ounce of will he possessed not to gape in amazement at her specific demands, and apparently, she took his staring as reason to continue. She pressed her hands to the tabletop and fixed him with a determined gaze.

"My mother has kept me secluded my whole life, rarely even allowing me to leave the keep. Aside from the usual lessons—excluding galactic history, of course—I received instruction on comportment and etiquette. But nothing on how to rule. She never meant for me to ascend the throne, and I suppose I was meant to live my days simply existing. I won't let that happen as your wife. I'd sooner die than go from one prison to another."

That was shocking, to say the least, and Zavier sat back as the true depth of her words hit him square in the chest. Although it did explain why Yvonne had never brought her to the court in Golden Cloud, if she didn't mean her daughter to take the crown when she died. Although that did beg the question of who she *did* mean to rule Green-well. Perhaps that was something else he could have his agents look into…

Making a mental note to do something about that later, he began pushing bits of food around his plate while he mulled over everything she'd said. Barely noticing when Alexia began to eat, he weighed each point carefully in his mind. Spending time with her wouldn't be hard, as he found her fascinating, and of course, she was beautiful. It was something he'd never admit to anyone, but he was relieved. He'd seen his servants fall in love, of course, and had always wanted that for himself. Perhaps if they got to know each other, their marriage really *could* be more than just a political union.

He was somewhat surprised that she wanted to learn more about Ironhold and what it took to keep the planet running smoothly, but that, too, was a comfort in its own way. It showed that she was truly invested in the idea and wouldn't just be an idle body taking up space. In the end, he concluded that she hadn't said anything he objected to... except for the demanded apology, that was. His eyes narrowed on her as he finally speared a bit of meat on the tines of his utensil and pointed it at her.

"I agree to all your terms. Except for the apology. That will never happen." Sliding the bit of food off his fork and into his mouth, he watched her closely, wondering what her reaction would be. His lips twitched with mirth as she raised her chin in a haughty manner and glared at him.

"Then you'll never kiss me."

Zavier grinned. Gods, but he loved her fire.

"We'll see about that."

The shuttle of the Verdant Empress descended through the rain-filled clouds of Greenwell, swooping in an arc toward the landing pad of the imperial keep and landing lightly upon the steel surface. Almost as soon as the struts touched down, the door swung upward, and the empress herself emerged, looking drawn. Her steward and Guard Captain were waiting for her, and both stepped forward to greet their ruler as she swept toward the keep, her golden robes whipping in the pre-storm winds.

"What news?"

"The princess wasn't found at any of the nearby plantations or settlements, Your Majesty, but apparently several people did see her riding on her moss-deer, headed west. She disappeared into a stand of old growth trees, and that's where her trail ends. It's like she disappeared into the ether." Portia explained the situation as plainly as she could but flinched under Yvonne's sharp glance.

"My only child and heir can't just *disappear*. Someone must have taken her. I want every single plantation, farm, and warehouse on this planet searched, and I want it done immediately." She ignored the look exchanged by Portia and Harald as she entered the keep and made her way toward her private chambers, the two still steps behind her.

"Your Majesty, an operation of that size will take a great deal of time to put together, let alone to accomplish."

"I don't care!" She whirled on the pair, making them step back in the face of her frantic fury. Which was truly just a mask hiding her terror and panic. Who would want to take her daughter, and why? Was she safe? Would she ever get her Alexia back? "My only child is missing, and I want her back!"

"Of course, Your Majesty. I'll begin assembling the guard right away." Harald nodded and, after a brisk salute, turned on his heel. The steward lingered, eyeing her empress worriedly for a moment.

"I'll speak to the orbital monitoring crew. Perhaps there was a satellite in orbit with surveillance capability that picked something up. We'll do everything we can, Your Majesty." Portia bobbed a curtsy, then hurried away to do just as she'd said, leaving Yvonne alone. Silently distressed, she entered her chambers, her mind churning.

Where was her daughter?

Chapter 5

Alexia dreamed of paradise.

Not Greenwell. As much as she loved her home planet, it wasn't the untamed forests and endless plains she saw in her dreams. A planet of rainforests with towering trees, and an entire ecosystem thriving in the damp that filled the space below. Vast expanses of grassland where herd animals grazed and ran and raised their young. Wildflowers of every shape and color imaginable waving in the wind.

And not a farm, plantation, or settlement in sight.

"Your Highness?"

The voice of Elea penetrated her slumber, and the princess jerked awake, sitting upright in her bed. It took a few moments for the lingering image of the dream to fade, and then she blinked at her handmaiden, who was eyeing her curiously. She wondered if word had already spread among the servants about her change of heart?

"Sorry. I was… dreaming."

"It seemed to be a very pleasant dream, at least. The iron king sent a message for you." Withdrawing a bit of paper from her skirt pocket, she handed it to Alexia, who broke the wax seal and unfolded the paper. Zavier's penmanship was nothing exciting, but it was plain and somehow sturdy. Fitting, for someone like him, who seemed to disdain unnecessary frippery.

Princess,
> *I would be honored if you would join me for breakfast.*
> *Zavier*

Although the note was extremely short, she couldn't help but smile at it. He really was a man of few words. Folding the paper again, she glanced at Elea, who was waiting expectantly. Did the girl somehow know its contents?

"It seems I'll be sharing breakfast with the iron king, since he asked politely. Have any of my other dresses been finished?"

Elea's beaming smile was all the answer she needed.

She'd agreed to share breakfast with him. Apparently, she really did just want to be asked, rather than having her presence demanded. Despite receiving confirmation from Elea that she'd consented, Zavier still found himself pacing as he waited. Rather than choosing the dark and cozy comfort of his study, he'd decided that the chart room would be more fitting. This was because of the wall of windows that filled the room with light, illuminating the various holo-displays that would throw up detailed holographic renderings of star charts. He just hoped Alexia would agree it was better suited for such an early meal.

Just as he was beginning to regret his decision, the door opened, and he whirled around to see who had entered. Much to his pleasure, it was indeed his intended queen, who looked utterly resplendent in a sleeveless, high-necked gown of rich amethyst. She was smiling as she approached him, which, while unexpected, warmed his heart. He moved toward her, reaching out his hand when she came within range, and when she placed her delicate fingers in his, he raised it to his lips, brushing a kiss against her knuckles.

"You came." The words were murmured as his mouth lingered against her skin, pale eyes searching her verdant ones for signs of second thoughts or apprehension.

"You asked nicely." Her playful response and teasing grin had him smiling before he truly realized it. Lowering her hand, he tucked it into the curve of his arm as he moved to stand beside her, watching her while she looked around the room they were in. "What is this place?"

"This is the chart room. After we eat, I'll show you some of the star charts if you'd like." She looked so utterly delighted by the prospect as she turned back to him that he knew her answer, even though she didn't say a word. And he realized in that moment, he'd do whatever it took to keep making her look so pleased.

Guiding her to the small, round table placed by the windows, he helped her into her seat and gently pushed her closer, before settling into his own chair. The energy dome on the table deactivated, revealing a tiered platter filled with baked goods, fruit, and various flavored butters, along with a carafe of fragrant tea. While she began to fill her plate, he poured cups of the sweet, pale green drink for both of them.

"I have to confess, I was a little surprised you'd want to see me again so soon." He glanced at her, watching as she bit into a vivid blue fruit, topped with honeyed cream, and arched a brow. Setting down the carafe, he tilted his head as he selected a bit of fragrant, nut-filled bread and gestured with it.

"I want you as my queen. If I can convince you to marry me before your two weeks is up, that's only to my benefit. And since part of that means spending time with you, a prospect I already find quite pleasing, I decided there was no point in wasting time." He took a bite of the bread, feeling a surge of satisfaction as she blushed and smiled shyly. She really never had been the object of male attention, had she? It was utterly charming, and he was suddenly quite grateful Yvonne had hidden her away from the rest of the galaxy.

They chatted about nothing in particular as they ate their breakfast, Alexia sharing a few amusing anecdotes of her childhood mischief, and Zavier urging her along. He didn't really want to talk about his youth, after all. It had been largely devoid of joy. When they were both done, he stood and offered her his hand again and, once she took it, led her toward the nearest holo-display. With the touch of a few buttons, he darkened the glass of the windows, plunging the room into darkness, and activated a chart.

Stars leapt into view in front of them, the Aqua system and its planets in the very center, and he smiled at hearing her gasp of wonder. Her free hand reached up, likely just in curiosity, and touched the star at the center of his second-oldest brother's territory. The pale yellow star suddenly grew bigger, as did the planets orbiting around it, which made her squeak in surprise. He only barely bit back a laugh and cleared his throat instead.

"What is this?" He glanced at her and saw her wondering expression lit by the glow of the holo-display, wide-eyed and fascinated.

"This is the Aqua system, ruled by the aquis king." He reached out and touched the fourth planet from the sun, making the display zoom in. The planet was covered with water and only a few land masses. A large portion of its surface was dominated by a floating fortress city, visible even from space.

"It's covered in water. I'd never imagined such a thing." She hesitated, her expression growing both grim and thoughtful, which had Zavier wondering what she was thinking. Then she looked at him, her voice soft and uncertain. "Can we... see Greenwell on here?

So that was it. She wanted to see her home world. Her timidity was touching, and he nodded, reaching down to tap a few more keys. Stars sped by before their eyes, until suddenly, the agricultural paradise of the Verdant Empress appeared before them. Large swathes of green, interrupted by squares of plantations and farms, the occasional mountain range, river, and lake. He'd seen it countless times, but now, with her staring silently, he remembered the first time he'd viewed the planet from a distance and imagined how she must feel. Turning to face her, he realized he was still holding her hand and gently drew her closer, until her gaze turned from the hologram to his face.

"I know Ironhold isn't lush and beautiful like Greenwell, but it's got potential to be so much more than what it is. I feel certain that with you by my side, we can make it something wonderful." His voice was soft, earnest, and he gave her hand a gentle squeeze. Though she didn't say anything, she did smile back at him.

It wasn't a promise, but it was good enough. For now.

"I want you to meet someone."

Zavier had deactivated the holo-display and set the windows back to their crystal clear brilliance, allowing her to see the excited gleam in his eyes. Alexia was surprised by how boyish it made him seem. Surely, something that could elicit such a response within the normally stoic iron king would be worth seeing. And it was certainly enough to get her to agree.

"I'd like that." She smiled as she responded, and then gasped in surprise when he began pulling her along at a brisk pace. Soon, they were nearly running through the halls, her skirts held up in her free hand, and she found herself laughing. She had no idea where they were going as they descended stairwells and emerged into an outdoor portion of the walled Citadel that she wasn't familiar with, before finally stopping in front of a fenced-off area with an energy dome overhead.

She could see a wide variety of vegetation through the metal links and wondered who could possibly be living in such a place. He unlocked the paneled door with a touch of his hand, then led her inside. Immediately, she was struck by the humidity of the place and felt sweat beading on her brow. Still, she didn't voice a question or a complaint as he guided her deeper inside, until they came to what must have been the Citadel's barrier wall, although she couldn't be certain. Especially since she was facing what looked to be the side of a mountain instead, as a large cave mouth loomed in front of them, emerging from a wall of vines.

"Kal! Abe! Lan!" Her brows curved upward in puzzlement as the iron king called out those three words, or perhaps they were names. What in the world was he doing? There didn't seem to be any sort of response or reaction, until he whistled shrilly. Then, suddenly, she heard a scrambling from the cave, and out poured a mass of what looked to be... fur? The mass soon separated into three quadrupedal beings, each about as tall as her waist, covered in brindled black fur. They had long necks and nearly serpentine tails, with vaguely lizard-like heads that bore wickedly sharp raptor beaks and triangular ears, reflective black claws glinting on their four-toed paws. Zavier released her hand with a laugh as the animals barreled toward him, uttering soft, rasping cries as they went.

Her hands flew up to cover her face when the trio of creatures jumped on the iron king, knocking him down and beginning to lick his face with abandon. It was only his laughter that assured her they weren't attacking him, but it was still slightly alarming to see. And it only became more so when they seemed to realize a new person was there. All three froze, fixing her with brilliant green irises and slitted pupils, their bodies sinking low to the ground.

"Don't even *think* about it." Her tone was gently chastising as her hands dropped to her hips, fixing the three animals with a stern glare. She certainly didn't expect them to listen, and no one was more surprised than the princess herself when they trotted close and flopped down onto their rumps in front of her, looking up at her adoringly. After a moment of hesitation, she leaned down and petted the head of the one directly in front of her, who uttered a rumbling purr.

"I've never seen them take so quickly to anyone." She glanced up at Zavier as he found his feet, dusting grass and dirt from his clothing. She flashed him a grin, reaching out to begin scratching under the chin of the animal on her left.

"They're so soft. I've never heard of any creature that looks like this. What are they called?" The one on her right, that she didn't have a hand for, was nudging its head under her elbow with a whine, eager to get attention as well. She giggled, crouching down so that it could rub its head against her bare shoulder, which it seemed quite content to do.

"They're from a planet called Firen, on the far reaches of known space, and I couldn't even begin to pronounce what they're called in the local tongue. I just call them furred lizards. I rescued them as pups when one of my guards accidentally killed their mother. It seemed... cruel, to leave them to fend for themselves. They've been with me for fifteen years now."

He crossed his arms, watching as the furred lizards vied for her attention, seeming hesitant about confessing his act of kindness. Alexia was touched. Many a nobleman, let alone a king, likely would've left the young animals to die. But he'd chosen to bring them back to his home and treat them as pets. Rising from her crouched position, she gently pushed past the furred lizards and approached him. He was eyeing her with trepidation, until she reached up and laid her hand over his heart.

"I've learned in the past two days that despite the hard face you put on, you have a gentle and caring heart. It's what made me decide to give you a chance. You treat your people like family instead of criminals, and you even took in these orphaned animals. You are a good man, Zavier." Her voice was gentle, and the smile she gave him was warm. But she was watching him, and saw something hot and wild flash in his gaze.

That was all the warning she got before his arms abruptly unfolded, and the next thing she knew, they were around her waist. She found herself hauled against him, able to feel the hard muscle of his body against the softness of hers, his hands splayed against her back. The heat between them was palpable through the soft fabric of her dress, and her breath hitched as she stared up at him.

"Say it again." His voice was husky with something she couldn't identify, but whatever it was, it sent a shiver rushing through her. She licked her lips, uncertain what he meant, and struggled to find her voice, a task that became even more difficult when she watched his eyes following the path of her tongue.

"Say... what?" He pulled her even closer, and she gasped, both of her hands now pressed to his chest. Whether to push him away or not, she wasn't even sure. This was terrifying, but also thrilling.

"Say my *name*, Alexia." He growled the words, his head steadily lowering toward hers. *Oh.* That was the first time she'd said his name, wasn't it? She hadn't even truly realized it until just now, but she had the abrupt understanding that he liked hearing her say it. Ignoring the hammering of her heart, she swallowed thickly and did as he wanted.

"Zavier."

That heat surged to life in his eyes again, and his head dropped toward hers. He was going to kiss her! For a brief moment, she thought she should let him... But no. She didn't want him to think he could just walk all over her when she'd decided about something. So at the last possible moment, she lifted her hand and thrust her fingers between their faces, pressing her fingertips to his mouth.

He froze, eyes narrowing at her, and muttered against her skin. "What do you think you're doing?" The words were slightly muffled, just enough to make his utterance comical, drawing a wicked smile to her features.

"I told you, you're not allowed to kiss me until I get an apology." His gaze smoldered at the reminder, and she allowed herself a moment of silent gloating... until she felt him smirk, and then his lips were moving down to her palm.

———

Zavier watched her eyes go round and her cheeks fill with color, as his mouth dragged over the satin smooth skin of her hand. He didn't stop at her palm, however, and kissed his way down to the inside of her wrist, where he could feel her blood rushing beneath the skin. Her heart was thundering, a fact that filled him with masculine pride. One of his hands left her back, moving instead to gently grasp her hand as he murmured, his breath and words coursing over her flesh, "It's clear you don't mean to let me kiss you properly... but I believe this falls outside the bounds of your proclamation."

Her breath hitched as he tugged her hand upward and turned her arm slightly, baring more of that pale limb to his ministrations. He was very eager to give it as much of his attention as she would allow, and considering she seemed too dazed to stop him, he was going to take every opportunity he could.

His mouth moved along the inside of her forearm, leaving a trail of hot, open-mouthed kisses along the path of blue veins that stood out so clearly against her fair skin. When he reached the crook of her elbow, he paused, his gaze very intentionally capturing hers, and darted his tongue into that tender hollow. The sound she made, somewhere between a whimper and a stifled moan, shot straight to his groin. Gods, how did she do that? Did she know what effect she had on him?

"Zavier..." She breathed his name in a way that made him picture her laid out on his bed, her pale body and silver hair shining like moonlight against his dark sheets.

He knew she wasn't trying to entice him, but everything she did filled him with desire. The tip of his nose brushed over the tender flesh of the inside curve of her upper arm as he straightened, moving up her body, and mentally, he cursed the high collar of her gown. He wanted to taste the skin of her throat and feel her pulse thundering beneath his mouth.

It was only as his lips brushed against her jaw that he realized she was trembling. He didn't know if it was from arousal or fear, and that was enough to make him understand that he needed to stop. He wanted her to want him and to articulate it clearly, without doubt, before doing anything that she might otherwise regret. Stifling a frustrated groan, he stepped back from her and let his hands fall away from her body.

"I'm sorry. It was wrong of me to take advantage of your innocence." She looked shocked, her lips slightly parted as she stared up at him, and he felt a powerful rush of guilt. He'd not been with someone so inexperienced since he was just as clueless, and he needed to remember not to overwhelm her. It would be hard, but he would do it. Because he wanted her for the rest of his life, not just for a tryst of a few nights.

"Do you want me?" She blurted the words so swiftly that he very nearly missed them, and he blinked. Did she really need to ask? Was she so innocent that she couldn't tell? Or was it insecurity? He pondered how to answer that, wondering if he could do so without being too forceful and frightening her, before admitting he wasn't prepared for her reaction no matter what he said... and no matter what her response might be. So he bit back a sigh and turned away, offering her his arm for escort instead.

"We should go back inside. I have a great deal of work to do.

It was inescapable. Even though the footage was captured at a distance and was somewhat grainy, there was no mistaking what she saw. Alexia riding on her moss-deer into the stand of trees, and the dark figure running from a shuttle into the same patch of forest, soon followed by that figure's reappearance carrying her daughter and boarding the waiting shuttle. It took less than two minutes, but to Yvonne, watching that little bit of video felt like it took a year.

"Whose shuttle was that?" Her voice was just as cold as the rest of her as she stared at the still frame, frozen on the pure black vessel just as it was about to take off. Her Guard Captain cleared his throat, but she didn't look away, knowing he would retrieve the information from the data slate in his hand.

"Ah… it was registered to… the *Nightfall*, Your Majesty."

Her fury was abrupt and frigid, twined with shock at the knowledge. The *Nightfall*? What had that damned Zavier been doing on her planet, and why had he taken Alexia? Her gaze snapped from the holo-display to Harald, who was waiting with a grim expression for her orders. Rising from her seat, she started toward the door with a simple command.

"Ready my shuttle and have the *Bountiful* prepare for immediate departure to the Golden Cloud system."

The Golden Cloud system was the undeniable center of galactic politics and society, and that was just the way Owen liked it. He thrived on the attention, the fawning of men who wanted to be him and women who wanted in his bed—or vice versa, as the case may be. His only stipulation was that his bed partners had to be beautiful—and discreet. The latter was only marginally less important than the former, as his queen was the definition of a shrew, and a jealous one, at that. Thankfully, the witch was off visiting one of their children somewhere else, leaving him to a lazy day in the palatial space station he called home.

"Your Majesty?"

Owen groaned at hearing the voice of his steward, his head dropping back onto the rim of his bathtub. Of course, a rare moment of peace and quiet, and the man had to go and ruin it. But Grayson was smart and, more importantly, ambitious. He would never bother the god-king unless it was extremely important. So the monarch rolled his blue eyes up toward the sensor in the ceiling.

"What is it, Grayson?"

"The Verdant Empress wishes to speak with you, and she says it's extremely urgent."

His golden brows furrowed. Yvonne? She'd left the system just a few days ago in a tizzy, refusing to explain what was wrong, aside from some vague statement about needing to attend to a vital matter back on Greenwell. Why was she calling him now?

"Well, then, patch her through."

"Er, I'm afraid I can't do that, Your Majesty. She's here. At the station."

That was enough to have Owen sitting bolt upright. She'd hurried back without even sending a warning ahead? Yvonne was nearly as much of a witch as his queen, but she wasn't prone to rash decisions. If she was here and insisting to speak to him personally, it must be a dire matter indeed. Scrambling out of the tub, he grabbed a towel from the stack nearby and was already drying himself as he strode toward the door to his bedroom.

"Show her into the sitting room and tell her I'll be there presently." Within minutes, he was dressed, if not formally, and entering into the sitting room. Yvonne was pacing back and forth restlessly, twisting her hands in front of herself, although there seemed to be some sort of object clasped within them. "Empress, what brings you back to Golden Cloud so soon?"

The golden-haired woman stopped and turned to face him when she heard his voice and frowned. Her hands parted, and she thrust one of them toward him, allowing him to see the item she held. It was a small portable holo-display. He watched as it activated, and a bizarre scene played out before him. He watched as a girl on a moss-deer rode into a small tract of forest and a man bypassed a shuttle—

Wait. He recognized that shuttle. That was the vessel that served as ship-to-surface conveyance for Zavier's flagship, the *Nightfall*. What was his brother doing on Greenwell? He watched with growing bewilderment and a sense of dread as what he could only assume was his brother emerged from the trees, carrying what looked like the girl who'd been on the moss-deer, and boarded the shuttle with her. Then the video cut off, and he glanced up at Yvonne, arching a brow in silent question.

"I'm sure you recognize that shuttle, considering it belongs to the Iron King of Ironhold." Yvonne's voice was clipped, strained, as she tucked the holo-display into a pocket of her dark green robes. Owen crossed his arms, eyeing her as he nodded.

"Yes. What does that have to do with me?" The look she leveled at him was one of barely contained rage, and had he been any less than the god-king, he would've stepped back out of fear for his safety. Even before she spoke, he knew whatever words came out of her mouth were going to cause him a terrible headache.

"The girl he took was my daughter, Alexia. Your brother *abducted* my heir."

He couldn't stop thinking about her. No matter how hard he tried to focus on the data slates Benji handed him, he couldn't read more than a few words before his mind began to stray. Remembering the way she'd felt in his arms, how her skin had felt under his lips, the sound of his name on her tongue. It was enough to drive him to distraction, making the small list of items that required his attention take twice as long as it should have. Just when he was about to check the hour, praying it was time for dinner and he could see her again, the holo-comm on his desk flashed red, indicating an urgent message... from the Golden Cloud system.

"Why the hell is that bastard bothering me?" Zavier frowned, as he saw the digital signature of Owen attached to the signal, and grumbled as he pushed the data slates aside, reaching out to tap the holo-comm and open up the direct line. His brother's haughty face, more square of jaw and bright where he was dark, appeared in the air above the device, grim and frowning. "What do you want, Owen?"

"Nice to see you, too, Zavier. You really should visit Golden Cloud again soon. Calla misses you."

Zavier scowled at that. He'd always been friendly with his oldest brother's queen and had even had a brief infatuation with her when he was younger. Bringing Calla up was a low blow and did nothing to decrease his irritation with Owen.

"You didn't call just to badger me to visit your wife. Tell me what you want, or I'm deactivating the transmission." His voice was cold, words terse. It was disrespectful to someone he'd technically sworn fealty to, but then again, he hated his brother, so he didn't much care. And it would make even Owen unpopular if he killed his own flesh and blood.

"I had a visit from the Verdant Empress an hour ago. She showed me some... unsettling footage and made a very disturbing claim... that you abducted her daughter, Princess Alexia."

Zavier felt his heart plunge all the way to the soles of his feet. He'd hoped to have a little more time before Yvonne found out her heir was missing, but it seemed he'd used up his small store of good fortune. Now he had to come up with something that would divert his brother... and hopefully, by extension, the empress. Settling back in his chair, he steepled his hands in front of himself and let a dark brow curve upward in a disinterested expression.

"Is that what this is about? That's ridiculous. I met a common girl and took her for myself. It's nothing you haven't done countless times before, Owen. Now, if that's all you had to say, I have work to do." He watched Owen ponder his words, while his heart returned to its proper place and began to pound furiously. Would his brother buy the lie?

"Well, that settles it, I suppose. I'll speak to the empress and inform her there's been a misunderstanding. Sorry to have bothered you, brother."

Waving his hand in dismissal, Zavier waited for the transmission to deactivate, then slumped in his chair with a weary sigh. Dammit. He didn't know Yvonne well, but he knew the woman was like one of his precious pets with a bone. She wasn't going to let it go that easily. He would need to speak to Alexia about this. But he was afraid to mention it, for one simple reason.

What if she chose to go home?

Owen turned away from the holo-comm to face Yvonne. If he'd thought the empress looked enraged before, she was beyond livid now. Apparently, she didn't believe the story his brother told.

"You heard it yourself, Yvonne. He said the girl he took wasn't your daughter." Her attention turned from the air above the holo-comm to the god-king himself, and he felt his hackles rise at the murderous look in her eyes. Gods help whoever she decided to unleash her fury upon.

"He's lying. He took her, and now he's holding her captive. And if *you* don't do something about it, I'll have no choice but to take her back myself."

There was a clear threat in that statement, one that had Owen rising from his chair and rounding his desk, to loom over the empress. To her credit, she didn't flinch beneath his domineering presence, but rather, squared her shoulders and looked up at him with a scowl. He could respect that... if she wasn't so blatantly threatening his youngest brother.

"Are you threatening to declare war because of my brother, Empress?" Despite the flat tone of his voice, he felt anger bubbling away within him. He'd sworn not to intervene in intersystem affairs when he took the title of god-king, but this was his *brother*. There was no love lost between him and Zavier, and yet, he felt the strong urge to protect his sibling.

"Yes. Consider this an unofficial declaration. The official one will be announced as soon as I return to Greenwell."

She whirled away and stalked out of the room, leaving Owen to rub his hand across his face with a sigh. Dammit. Leave it to his brother to finally take interest in a woman of royal blood and cause a galactic incident. Letting his hand fall, he left his study and moved into the hallway preceding his personal wing of the space station, where Grayson stood waiting and watching calmly.

"Get me Calla."

Chapter 6

While Alexia was used to Zavier being quiet, there was a sort of dire tension about him that night as they met for dinner. He wasn't short with her, but his responses were quiet and brief. It was only after a meal full of stilted conversation and awkward silences that she finally broached the subject, hoping he would open up to her.

"Did something happen this afternoon? You seem... tired." She spoke gently, hesitantly, somewhat apprehensive that he would return to the way he'd treated her before. After seeing him open up, that would be truly distressing. When he glanced up at her from his nearly empty wine glass, she gave him a warm smile and was relieved to see one corner of his lips quirk up in response.

"I received a call from my brother. Talking to Owen is always... trying."

She sensed there was more he wasn't telling her, but she didn't want to pry and simply accepted it with a nod. She watched as he drained the wine from his glass, then stood and rounded the table to offer her his hand. She took it without pause and let him tug her gently to her feet, her gaze meeting his.

"Do I have to go back to my chambers? I'd like to spend more time with you." He seemed surprised by the admission, and then a glimmer of pleasure entered his gaze. Her breath caught as he lifted her hand to his mouth and kissed her knuckles lightly.

"Far be it from me to refuse such a request. What would you like to do?"

Her gaze skimmed the room in answer to his question, alighting on the rows upon rows of books and the plush sofa in front of the archaic fireplace. Then she looked back at him, a shy smile spreading across her lips. "It may sound silly, but could we sit in front of the fire and read together?"

He didn't seem quite sure what to make of her desire, but he clearly wasn't willing to deny her, either. Especially not when she fluttered her lashes at him in a decidedly exaggerated manner, just to make him smile. "I... Yes. That sounds... very pleasant."

They parted ways to select books and let him start the fire burning, then reconvened on the soft cushions of the sofa. She toed off her shoes and tucked her feet underneath her body as she settled in beside him, nestling herself into the warmth of his body while she opened the book she'd picked. Soon enough, she was drawn into the words on the pages and lost in a tale of worlds far beyond the ones she knew.

He wasn't entirely certain when it happened. All he knew was that at some point, he looked over and realized Alexia had fallen asleep. The book was still open and sitting on her thighs, her hands lying limply atop the pages, and her head was resting against his shoulder. He could barely see her face at this angle, but what he *could* see was achingly lovely, especially with the silver of her hair painted in shades of gold by the fire. Closing his own book and setting it aside, Zavier reached up and tenderly pushed a few loose strands back from her face, looping them behind her ear.

He knew it was wrong to touch her like this without permission, but he couldn't seem to stop. He found himself stroking her cheek, tracing the gentle slope of her nose with his fingertip, brushing it in the little hollow beneath her full lower lip. Something inside him twisted at the possibility that he might lose her. Already, she'd begun to work her way inside him, breathing life into the heart he'd long thought dead. Would she go back to her mother if given the choice? Or would she stay with him?

"Choose me, Alexia. That's all I want." His words were barely a whisper, a desperate plea that he'd never dare to voice when she was awake. Almost as though she heard him, she shifted and murmured softly, nuzzling her cheek against his arm. Knowing that if he didn't get her back to her own rooms soon, he'd do something for which she'd never forgive him, he decided it was time she left. But he couldn't bear to wake her.

Instead, he scooped her carefully into his arms, much like he had the day he'd first taken her. She stirred slightly but didn't wake, only tucked her face into the crook of his neck with a soft sigh. Reveling in the feel of her in his embrace, he carried her slowly through the halls and down the stairs until he reached her rooms. Elea was waiting inside, and she watched them with a misty gaze as he carried the sleeping princess to her bed and laid her down on its soft surface.

Then he ran, because the urge to join her was too strong.

"Your Highness?"

Although she'd been pretending to read the data slate in her hands, Alexia's mind was far from the words on the screen. She'd been thinking about Zavier, not obsessively, but he seemed to have thoroughly invaded her mind over the past few days. When they weren't in each other's company, he was in her thoughts, but she found they'd been together more often than not, sharing meals, walks through the Citadel, and their new evening routine of reading in front of the fire. It was all a little unsettling, so she was grateful when Elea interrupted her, and she looked up at her handmaiden with a small smile.

"Yes?"

"I've received word from both the seamstress and the jewel smith. They've finished their work and would like for you to approve it when you have time."

Her eyes widened. That must mean… her bridal gown and the crown she would wear as the queen of Ironhold. It would only be polite to see the work that had been done, but the idea of actually doing so filled her with a powerful nervous energy. As though seeing the items would make it all real and confirm that she truly meant to marry Zavier.

"I see." Setting the data slate aside, she considered. Then she nodded and stood. "Well then, take me to them."

"Yes, Your Highness."

Elea turned and led her out of her chambers, through hallways and toward where both the seamstress and the jewel smith had their workspaces. It was as they were passing through the entry hall that they heard a commotion and paused, turning to face the main doors just as they opened and Zavier went hurrying outside. Though she wondered what he was doing, she decided she would ask him later and continued on her way.

The room they entered was full of dress forms and fabrics, tables covered with patterns, boxes and baskets overflowing with buttons and ribbons and other items. It was cozy, and the organized chaos reminded her of the kitchens back in the keep on Greenwell. While Elea spoke with the seamstress, she wandered around, looking at other garments in various stages of completion. Catching a flash of white in a mirror before her, she turned around and was confronted with the most beautiful thing she'd ever seen.

It seemed to shimmer like moonlight reflected on water. The form-fitting bodice and full skirts were a brilliant, pure white, simple and unornamented. But overlaying the entire garment, comprising long sleeves and a high collar, was the finest pearlescent mesh that gave it that celestial shine. Tiny green and silver crystals had been sewn onto the sleeves and the lower half of the skirt, forming delicate patterns of vines and flowers. Unable to help herself, she crept closer to the gown being held up by the seamstress and her assistant and reached out to touch it. Even the mesh was silky soft, and she inhaled sharply.

"It's... *beautiful*. I've never seen anything so lovely. You've truly outdone yourself." The words were thick with emotion, and she smiled as the seamstress curtsied deeply, clearly delighted by the compliment. Turning to face one of the room's tall windows, she put her hands over her cheeks and tried to rein in her emotions, while they returned her bridal gown to the sealed container it was being kept in. She was staring out into the stone of the courtyard when Elea came up behind her, reaching out to gently touch her shoulder, at which Alexia turned and looked questioningly at her handmaiden.

"Do you still wish to see your crown, Your Highness?"

Unable to find her voice, Alexia nodded and once again followed the younger girl out of the room. To her surprise, they didn't venture deeper into the servants' wing but, instead, returned to the entry hall and up the main flight of stairs. She soon recognized that they were entering the area where Zavier had his rooms, and she felt a twinge of anxiety as well as curiosity. Why were they there?

The answer became obvious when they approached a door that was being held open by the jewel smith standing in its way, keeping the panels from sliding shut. He stepped back as they came closer, allowing them into the room, which she soon realized had to be some sort of vault for the royal jewels. Sealed drawers and cabinets were interspersed with mirrors, but there was one thing that caught her eye.

At the far end of the room, in a shallow alcove and illuminated from above, there sat a crown. It appeared to be made of a shining black metal, formed into a series of blade-like points, the tallest of which was set front and center, with each matching pair on either side growing gradually shorter, until they were less than an inch high at the back. The base of the largest, most prominent point was set with a single gem of dark blue, its facets catching the light. She approached it, mesmerized, and reached out to brush a fingertip over that lone jewel.

"This is his crown, isn't it?" The words left her almost unconsciously, and she turned to glance at the jewel smith, who nodded in confirmation. Looking back at the crown, she could so easily see it resting atop his head. Elegant yet dangerous, like the man it belonged to. A small smile tilted her lips as her hand fell, and she stepped back. "It suits him. You do wonderful work."

"I hope you find the one I made for you as fitting, Your Highness."

That's right. That's why they were here. She should've noticed the identical alcove beside the one that held Zavier's crown. It was clearly meant for hers. But where was it? That was when she realized the jewel smith was holding a box of dark wood, offering it to her. Filled with a sudden twinge of anxiety, she forced herself to reach out and lift the lid.

Resting on a silken pillow, was a beautifully intricate circlet. It was made of the same black metal as Zavier's crown, but there, all similarities ended. Where his was a single thick band, hers was several delicate looping swirls; where his had a single blue gem, hers was studded with small smooth-cut opals, their veined white surfaces shifting in shades of blue and green depending on how the light caught them. Her hands itched to reach out and touch it, and she almost stopped herself before remembering that it was meant for *her*.

Carefully lifting the crown out of its box, Alexia turned to the nearest mirror and set it on her head. The face that looked back at her was familiar, but not. For so long, she had only seen a girl, desperate for freedom and to be treated like an adult. Now, a powerful, elegant woman was gazing out of the mirror. Was that really her? Could she actually be that woman, that wife, that queen?

And perhaps more importantly, was that who she wanted to be?

Hearing that Calla's ship had manifested in orbit above Ironhold, had filled Zavier with a cold fury. No doubt she was there at the behest of his meddling brother, intending to persuade him out of his madness. So when he was informed that a shuttle had departed the *Pyxis* and was requesting permission to land in the Black Citadel, he'd agreed, if only to give Calla a piece of his mind. His long strides were full of ire as they carried him out of the keep and up to the landing pad, just as the shuttle's bay doors slid open and let the god-king's wife step out onto the durasteel surface.

Once upon a time, the sight of Calla would've made him ache with desire. She was all lush curves and tanned skin, with a long mane of rich auburn hair and stunningly blue eyes. But having been feasting his senses on the beauty of Alexia for nearly a week, he found the woman who had once been the object of his near obsession to be lackluster. Alluring, of course, but it was like comparing the sun and the moon; while both were lovely, they were so different, so there could be no true juxtaposition. And he had wholly devoted himself to worship of the moon, so there was no room in his life for the sun.

"What do you want, Calla?" He snapped the words and felt a brief surge of remorse when she frowned at him. She'd done nothing but listen to her stupid husband's commands, after all, and he couldn't take that out on her. Taking a deep breath, Zavier sighed and offered his hand to his sister-in-law. "Forgive me. I know why you're here, and I don't appreciate Owen sticking his nose in my business."

Placing her hand in his, Calla stepped closer and rose up on her toes, to press an affectionate kiss to the iron king's cheek. Her eyes narrowed at him, but her tone was gentle when she replied. "When your 'business' angers the leading exporter of agricultural products in the galaxy, it becomes the god-king's problem, Zav."

It seemed she was willing to let his rudeness slide, which was uncharacteristic, to say the least. Calla had a vicious temper and was known for holding grudges, even against him. There was something more going on here, and he didn't know what it was, but he was suspicious.

"Then you should probably come inside so I can explain this mess." He drawled the words as he placed her hand on his forearm and turned to escort her into the Citadel.

"Yes, I believe that would be best."

When Alexia entered his study, she pulled up short. Zavier wasn't alone. There was a voluptuous woman with sun-darkened skin and a riot of auburn hair sitting at the table with him. There was no third chair for her, so she didn't approach, instead standing there in shock while she looked back and forth between the two of them. Almost immediately, Zavier stood and hurried across the room to her side. The other woman was slower to stand, her crystal blue eyes assessing her in a highly discomfiting way.

"Alexia, this is Calla of Crystal Spire, wife of the god-king. Calla, allow me to introduce Alexia of Greenwell, daughter of the Verdant Empress."

Almost without thinking, she put her hand in Zavier's offered one and felt a surge of relief when he squeezed her fingers reassuringly. Glancing at him, she was pleased to see him smiling faintly, her own lips curving in response. Her gaze darted back to Calla as the older woman approached, tension filling her body. Why was the god-king's wife here?

"I can see why you took her, Zav. She's absolutely stunning."

Alexia inhaled sharply, turning an alarmed look on Zavier. The iron King looked more amused than anything, which only heightened her bewilderment.

"How did you know Zavier took me?" She tried to ignore her apprehension. If the god-king's wife knew about the circumstances of her arrival here, did that mean the god-king did, too? And if so, how had he been informed?

"Because your mother stormed into my husband's chambers and demanded your return. Owen, in his infinite wisdom, sent me to persuade Zavier to send you back and forestall a galactic incident."

There was a ringing in her ears as all of this information processed in her brain. Her mother knew she was gone and, somehow, knew Zavier had taken her. Was she going to be forced to go back? To return to her verdurous prison and her wasted life? She didn't realize she was swaying until Zavier's arm suddenly encircled her waist, and she glanced up at him gratefully before looking back at Calla. For reasons she couldn't even begin to fathom, the royal woman had a grin on her face.

"Calla, you know where your usual chambers are. Would you mind letting me have some time alone with Alexia?" Zavier's voice was firm, making it clear that despite phrasing his words as a request, it was anything but.

Calla's smile only widened, and she inclined her head in a nod. "Certainly. But I'll be wanting to speak to you before you retire, Alexia."

Dumbly, Alexia nodded and remained silent until after she heard Calla leave the room. Then, all at once, panic flooded her. Her heart began to race, and her respiration started to come in a cycle of rapid, shallow breaths. Her hands were trembling as she turned to face Zavier, looking up at him with wide eyes set in a face that had gone almost bloodless with terror.

"I can't go back to Greenwell. Mother will stifle me even more. I'd rather die than live as a prisoner in my own home!" She nearly choked on the words and realized she was on the verge of sobbing, her eyes stinging with tears.

Zavier's gaze was blazing with anger, and at first, she thought he was mad at her. Then he reached up and gently carded his fingers through her hair. "I won't let that happen. I promise."

His voice was calm and soothing, but with a steely undertone. His promise was as good as a blood oath, she sensed, and knowing that he would fight for her, wouldn't let her be subjected to a life of meaningless captivity, was undeniably reassuring. Wrapping her arms around his waist, she buried her face in his chest and felt pure warmth suffuse her body when he enfolded her in a tight embrace.

Dinner was a subdued affair, during which neither Zavier nor Alexia seemed inclined to speak much. Afterwards, he started toward the fire, intending to stoke it for their usual nightly ritual, but on impulse, she laid her hand on his arm and stopped him. When he turned a questioning gaze on her, she knew what she wanted more than anything. Her hand slid down until it found his, and she laced their fingers.

"Can we go to the garden instead?" Her voice was almost pleading, although she wasn't sure why. Ever since they'd come to their agreement, he hadn't denied her anything, but everything had changed today. She'd been confronted with the trappings of a choice she wasn't sure she was ready to make but which seemed inevitable, given her mother's knowledge of her whereabouts.

Zavier seemed to understand that she needed comfort, and he offered a small smile. "Of course."

Hand-in-hand, they proceeded through the hallways and down the stairs. The guards opened the doors to the garden for them, but once they were inside, Alexia froze, her eyes widening at the sight before her. Even in the pale light of Ironhold's two moons, she could see that the garden was overflowing with life. The perfume of flowers was thick in the air, intoxicating in its mélange of fragrances, trees and bushes almost struggling under the weight of their own fruit.

"The garden… you haven't figured out what's making it do this?" She looked at him questioningly, and the sight of uncertainty on his face filled her with worry. Why did she get the impression he was afraid to answer that?

"I have a few theories, but nothing solid yet."

He was hiding something from her. But why? And what was it? Unable to bring herself to ask the questions, she simply nodded, and when he began to walk, she kept pace beside him. Their stroll was slow and leisurely, wending in a different direction than they normally went. When they passed under an arch festooned with a flowering vine, clusters of vibrant red blooms hanging down to brush against their heads, she stopped and tilted her face up, letting silken petals caress her cheeks and nose.

"Alexia?"

She lowered her head just enough to look at him, and her heart thudded powerfully in her chest. He was striking enough during the day, but with his face partially obscured in shadow and barely illuminated by patchy moonlight, it only enhanced the dramatic details of his features. The hollows of his cheeks were more pronounced, and a shaft of wan silvery light made his eyes seem to glow in the dimness. She felt him move more than actually seeing it happen, and then he was shifting his grasp of her left hand. Something cool and metallic slid onto her fourth finger, urging her to look down out of curiosity.

He'd slipped a ring onto the thin digit. Moving her hand into a ray of celestial light, she gasped at the sight of it. It was made of that same shining black metal as both of their crowns, which had been molded into a delicate fili-gree pattern. A single marquise-cut opal dominated the center, with tiny silvery crystals studded to either side. The band encircled her finger perfectly, and it was clearly made just for her. Looking up at him with a questioning expres-sion, she noticed that he was visibly concerned. The vulnerability in his eyes made him look years younger.

"I know your familiarity with galactic customs is... minimal. It's traditional for someone seeking to marry to present their intended with a betrothal ring. In a normal situation, I would've asked for your hand, then given this to you. Our courtship has been far from normal, but I still wanted you to have a ring."

It took her a moment to realize he was afraid she was going to reject him. Even for all his bravado and insistence that she *was* going to be his queen, he was leaving the deci-sion up to her. She found that remarkable, considering his promise not to let her return to a stagnant and unfulfilling life on Greenwell. He was so much more than the stub-born, heartless kidnapper she'd first encountered aboard the *Nightfall*. Reaching up, she placed her hand against his cheek and murmured softly, "You should really apologize to me now."

He'd never been so scared in his life. Putting that ring on her finger and explaining its importance, had taken more courage than he'd expected it would. And when she just stared at him for several long moments, he fully expected her to refuse him. But when she finally spoke, he was admittedly bewildered. Why would she bring up that apology now? It was hard to think with her hand on his face, the touch of her soft skin utterly electric.

Her lips were slightly parted, and she was looking up at him with an intensity he wasn't expecting. All at once, it hit him. She *wanted* him to kiss her. She just didn't want to say it so plainly. His lips twitched into a smile as relief chased away his anxiety, although desire was hot on its heels. His hand curled over the back of her neck as he dipped his head, his hair spilling forward to form a curtain around their faces, while the tip of his nose brushed lightly against hers.

"I'm sorry for taking you. If things had been different and I'd met you in my brother's court, I would have pursued you relentlessly, despite Yvonne's protests. Because in a galaxy full of women, you are the only one who makes me feel alive, and I would overcome any challenge to make you mine." His voice was rough with need and an emotion he didn't dare name, and he burned with the desire to kiss her. But he wouldn't until she admitted it was what she wanted.

"It'll do."

He blinked in surprise. *It'll do?* Just when he felt his anger start to stir, he saw her lips curve into an impish smile, and it struck him that she was just... being herself. A mischievous, playful woman. He barked a laugh, threading his fingers into her hair, and grasped her waist with his other hand before pulling her firmly against himself.

"You're going to be the death of me, woman." He

heard her laugh in the heartbeat before he took her mouth with his, and then her mirth was silenced by the press of his lips.

It was true that he'd had his fair share of lovers. He was in his fortieth year of life, after all. But even when in the throes of passion, no woman had ever made him feel as vital as he did in that moment. Almost as though he'd been going through life with a barrier between him and the world that had suddenly been ripped away. He could feel the eddying currents of air against his skin, sense the plants nearby, even became aware of every inch of his own body. Then she sighed and melted into him, and he lost all ability to be aware of anything except Alexia. Tilting his head, he coaxed her lips open with his own, his tongue darting in to taste her. There were lingering traces of the spices that had flavored their dinner, but they were pale in comparison to the taste of her. He wanted to devour her, drink from her, fill himself up with her, and knew that even if he did, it would never be enough. Every cell in his body was screaming at him to lay her out on the grass and make her his.

"Save it for your wedding night, Zavier."

Calla's voice hit him like pure ice. He jerked away from Alexia and instinctively moved to put himself between her and the threat, his eyes narrowing at the thoroughly amused woman standing nearby. He adored his sister-in-law, really, he did, but in that moment, nothing would've given him greater satisfaction than throttling her.

"Oh, don't give me that look. I need to have a talk with your bride-to-be, preferably *before* you ravish her. Come with me, Alexia. Zavier needs to cool off."

Unable to find his voice, he turned his head to look at Alexia, who was delightfully flushed. She gave him a shy smile with kiss-swollen lips, then slid around him and approached Calla, who looped their arms together before leading her off. As they departed, he sagged against the arch with a groan, rubbing his hand over his face. In hindsight, it was probably a good thing Calla had intervened when she did, but he would never admit it.

Now he just needed to take a very cold bath.

***

Zavier looked so frustrated and disappointed, standing there alone in the garden. But Calla's deceptively strong grip made it clear she had no intention of letting the imperial princess go. Although annoyed by this turn of events, she was also curious about what the god-king's wife wanted from her. So she allowed herself to be towed along, casting a questioning look at the older, shorter woman beside her.

"I imagine you have a lot of questions, so go ahead. Ask away, and I'll answer them as best I can."

Alexia was surprised by this. How had Calla known what she was thinking? And why was she allowing her to share her thoughts, instead of simply proceeding with whatever it was she wanted? The urge to ask was strong, but she had more pressing inquiries that needed answers.

"How did my mother know I was taken by Zavier? Why did the god-king send you? Why do you want to talk to me?" She bit back the rest of the questions that threatened to fly out of her mouth. She didn't want to overwhelm Calla after all.

"Apparently, there was a satellite in orbit that managed to catch surveillance footage of your little adventure and Zavier taking you onto his shuttle. Owen sent me because Zav and I have always been friendly, and my husband is hoping I'll be able to persuade him to send you home before Yvonne does something stupid. And I want to talk to you because I'm very tired of kings thinking it's their right to decide everything for everyone—especially for strong, independent women."

Calla looked directly at her as they emerged from the garden and into the hallway, her eyes filled with clear meaning. All at once, Alexia understood. She was going to be given a choice. To decide if she wanted to stay here with Zavier, go home to Greenwell, or perhaps... even something else. And *that* was something she really needed to consider. Although there was one thing she knew for certain.

"I don't want to go back to Greenwell. Not if Mother is just going to keep me hidden away again. I've only seen Ironhold, but Zavier has assured me that if I marry him, he'll take me to see any planet I wish." It was more than her mother had ever offered, she thought ruefully. Besides, being married, being a queen, couldn't be all that bad, could it? Look at Calla. She was powerful, confident, and clearly had at least some freedom. Could that be her life, too?

"That's not the only option that would let you see the galaxy, Alexia. I could take you under my wing, and you could learn the ways of the court as my guest. Yvonne could hardly refuse me, not without causing an incident."

Something about her tone was sly, and Alexia narrowed her eyes at the queen. Her expression seemed to amuse the older woman, who laughed.

"What's funny?"

"I get the feeling you wouldn't want to be my ward, either. You care about him, don't you?"

The question was wholly unexpected, and the soft tone it was spoken in was such a change from her prior teasing mirth that Alexia felt like she had whiplash. She was so caught off guard that she blurted out her answer before she could think better of it. "Yes."

That answer appeared to please Calla, as her smile warmed and she patted the princess' hand fondly, like they were old friends. She didn't know why, but Alexia felt like she'd just passed a test she hadn't been prepared for.

"Well, then, I think that's all that really needs to be said on the matter. I'll inform Owen that you intend to stay, and hopefully I can persuade Yvonne away from whatever idiotic course of action she's intending to pursue."

Unable to find words, Alexia simply nodded, her mind awhirl. This was not at all what she'd been anticipating to come of her talk with Calla, but after a few minutes of silent contemplation, she decided it felt... good.

Chapter 7

Alexia dreamed of Paradise.

It was the same planet she'd seen before, but something was different this time. Although she didn't consciously recognize any of the landmarks, the mountains seemed oddly familiar. The landscape spun around her as she turned, blending into an ill-defined blur of gold and green, until she came to a stop with a dark structure visible in the near distance. She placed it after a moment: The Ebon Citadel. But how? Was this Ironhold, as it had once been?

"It's beautiful, isn't it?"

Zavier was suddenly there, behind her. She felt his arms wrap around her waist, his nose nuzzling into her hair before his lips brushed over her skin. His hands curved over the swell of her belly, which was what made her realize that she was heavy with child, and yet this, too, seemed perfectly natural. Just as natural as the warmth in his voice as he murmured against the shell of her ear.

"You've done the impossible."

Her mouth opened, but no words came out. She didn't understand. What had she done? Had she somehow brought life and greenery to Ironhold?

"Your Highness, are you well?"

Alexia jerked awake with a strangled gasp as Elea's voice penetrated the dream, yanking her out of sleep and into wakefulness all in one moment. The girl was at her bedside, looking concerned, and with good reason. Her whole body was sticky with sweat, perspiration soaking her nightgown and even dampening the sheet beneath her. But she didn't feel ill.

What was happening to her?

"No, Elea. I'm… fine. Just a dream. Have I overslept?" She pushed her slick hair back from her face and grimaced. She would need to bathe before she met Zavier, but the idea of food turned her stomach. Maybe she would just have some tea.

"No, Your Highness. It's still early. Queen Calla asked me to give you her warmest regards and a promise that she'll handle everything. Her shuttle just left. The iron king has urgent business he's attending to first, but Benji assured me he'll send word as soon as he's available. Would you like me to fetch your breakfast?"

Zavier was already busy at such an early hour? That was strange. Idly, she hoped everything was all right but satisfied herself that she would see him within a few hours at least. Dismissing these thoughts, she slid out of bed and disrobed as she moved toward the bathing room.

"No, I'm not hungry. Just some tea." She paused at the doorway, thinking deeply for a few moments, then looked at Elea over her shoulder. "And any information you can get me on the atmosphere and soil composition of Ironhold."

"Um… as you wish, Your Highness."

"Are you certain?" Zavier knew that he sounded tense, and he didn't care. He'd had his people working around the clock for days to analyze everything about the garden. Soil samples, atmospheric conditions. He had even ordered the domes cleaned. Everything seemed normal. But he'd received a message from his lead scientist informing him that they'd found an unusual chemical in the examination of a flower petal.

A flower that Alexia had touched just a few days before.

"As certain as I can be, Your Majesty. I've never seen anything like it. We're still trying to identify the molecular composition. I'll alert you as soon as we find anything else."

"Good. This needs to be your priority." He pushed away from the holo-display showing the microscopic image of the chemical and strode out of the laboratory at a swift pace. Things were starting to come together, and it seemed the theory he'd spoken of last night with Alexia was proving accurate. Now he just needed information from his agents investigating Yvonne's network. He suspected the key lay in whatever files she had hidden away.

He wanted to see Alexia. Having a heated discussion with Calla before she left, trying and failing to reach his agents on Greenwell, and then this information from his science team, just made him tense and stressed. He *needed* to see her, hold her, hopefully kiss her again... Bypassing the guards at her door, he stepped into her sitting room and stared in consternation.

Where was she?

"Alexia?" A sudden surge of panic filled him. Was she ill? Had she been injured? She had to be here—her guards wouldn't have been outside the door otherwise. Hurrying toward the door that led to her bedroom, it whooshed open at his approach, and he blinked at the sight of her seated at her vanity, Elea dressing her hair while she was deeply absorbed in the contents of a data slate. She glanced up, spotted him in the mirror, and smiled brightly.

"Good morning, Zavier. Is something wrong?"

She was fine. Perhaps she'd simply gotten a late start this morning? Feeling the tension slowly leach out of his body, he crossed the room to stand beside her, looking down at the data slate she held. Upon seeing the words on the screen and realizing it was a comprehensive assessment of Ironhold's atmosphere data and soil composition, his brow furrowed.

"Good morning. What are you reading?" Had she perhaps figured out what he was starting to suspect? It was obvious she didn't know what she could do, or at least she wasn't consciously aware of it. But that begged the question of the reason for her reading material.

"I've had the strangest dream twice now since I arrived. Last night, I realized I was dreaming about Ironhold, except it was covered in plains and forests. It occurred to me, there must be some reason other than distance from the sun that keeps it from being fertile. I thought perhaps I might see something your scientists missed, and... well... maybe, I could help."

His mouth nearly fell open in shock, and had Elea not been standing right there, it likely would've done just that. She'd dreamed about an Ironhold covered in plant life? And, more importantly, had decided to theorize about terraforming the surface to see it become reality? Unable to find words, he waited only long enough for Elea to step back from his future bride, then grabbed Alexia's arm and gently hauled her to her feet.

When she looked up at him, her expression a blend of confusion and irritation, he silenced the protest starting to form on her lips by kissing her. It wasn't the tender but passionate kiss of the night before, but was no less intense, simply briefer, and almost bruising. Only when she began to lean into him, did he break away to grin down at her, thoroughly pleased and amused by her flushed cheeks and dazed look.

"You're amazing. Come, let's go sit; we can discuss what you've learned." The way she lit up made every harsh word he'd exchanged with Calla that morning completely worth it. This woman was better than he could've dreamed, and in less than a week, she was going to be his.

"So let me see if I understand this correctly. Ironhold's soil isn't precisely unfertile, but due to the combination of the rocky terrain, the Ironhold ore, the distance from the sun, and the high moisture content, the majority of Ironhold's plant life is along the lines of fungi and night-blooming flowers. Things that thrive in dim and damp environments." Counting off these points on her fingers, Alexia glanced at Zavier, who was sitting at the opposite end of the chaise, looking at her intently.

"Correct. Finding plants that produce anything useful is difficult, but because of the precise conditions needed to form Ironhold ore, it only grows in certain locations. This means there's a great deal of surface area that's going to waste, and we have settlements that are overcrowded. I don't have to tell you what problems crowding of a violent populace leads to."

He looked grim, yet she found herself powerfully attracted to him at that moment. He'd removed the dark jacket of his habitual attire, revealing the long-sleeved grey shirt he wore underneath, and had rolled the sleeves up to just below his elbows, displaying his leanly muscled forearms. They were littered with scars, a fact that she was quite curious about, but she wasn't going to ask. That seemed... oddly personal, and she wasn't prepared for that. Yet. Maybe after their wedding night... a thought that had her blushing.

"Greenwell has places very similar to Ironhold, the closer you get to the poles, and we produce a great deal in those zones. All it would take is a sample of seeds and bulbs from those regions, and with a little genetic engineering, we'd easily be able to tailor them to grow on Ironhold. The trees would take years to grow, of course, but the grasses and grains would be viable within one growing cycle." It was intuitive to her, but she knew he was unfamiliar with the complexities of these things. If only she could get those samples from Greenwell, but with her mother's apparent anger about her departure...

"I don't know when, or if, we'll be able to get samples out of Greenwell. But Owen has resources, of course. You could reach out to Calla and see if she can facilitate something." His comment made her blink, although he didn't seem to realize the import of what he'd said until he realized she was staring at him. Then his brow wrinkled in confusion. "What did I say?"

"You would trust me with an off-world communications link?" She knew she sounded suspicious, but she couldn't help it. Considering how cut off she'd been from the galaxy since she'd come here, she hadn't expected him to grant such a thing. Then, again, their relationship had changed drastically since her arrival. She felt a considerable amount of guilt when he winced in reaction to her question and moved closer to him.

It appeared Zavier had much the same idea, as he was already leaning in and reaching for her. They met halfway, his hands encircling her slender waist while hers came to rest on his chest. She could feel the heat of his skin all the more intensely, without the thick fabric of his coat in the way, and it was as soothing as it was enticing. His brow pressed to hers, fingers stroking her back through her gown, as he murmured quietly, "You're not a prisoner, Alexia. Not anymore. It was wrong of me to treat you like one in the first place, but I should hope by now, you know that's not how I see you."

His voice was so soft, filled with such genuine remorse and other sentiment, that she couldn't stop herself from smiling. Tilting her head just a fraction, she brushed the tip of her nose against his. "I know that now. We've both grown since you first brought me here."

He was looking at her with a powerful intensity. The force of that gaze was almost like a physical caress, and it sent a shudder up her spine. His hands followed the path of that shiver, smoothing up the length of her back until those long, thin fingers were splayed between her shoulder blades. It took only the slightest pressure of his hands to have her leaning toward him, her arms moving to encircle his neck.

Their lips came together. Nothing felt more natural than for Zavier to kiss her, she realized. He was skillful, she assumed, but didn't attempt to pressure her or go farther than she was willing to allow. He gently coaxed her mouth open, and she breathed a hushed moan as his tongue dipped into her mouth, stroking against hers in a way that was utterly tantalizing. It stirred a heat low in her body that she was quite familiar with, but which had never been inspired by another person before. It made her want to be closer to him. So she gave in.

His hands shifted down to her hips as she rose onto her knees and moved toward him, guiding her while she settled astride his thighs. He groaned when she pressed into him, her body lowering onto his, the husky sound inspiring a thrilling tingle that spanned all the way from the tips of her toes to her middle. His grip tightened, pulling her down against him, and she was struck firmly by the proof of his desire, tangible even through the layers of their clothing.

They were both breathing hard by the time she pulled away, her eyes slowly sliding open to look at him. His grey eyes had gone dark and almost steely with arousal, and she could see how badly he wanted to lay her out and explore her body. That knowledge was heady, filling her with a sense of empowerment she'd never before experienced.

Sifting her fingers through his hair, an impish smile curled on her lips. "How many days until we're married?"

His eyes narrowed at her, and he purposely rolled his hips up against hers, making her gasp as arousal spiked within her. She was playing with fire but had no fear of being burned, even when his response held a threatening growl, "Keep teasing me, and it will happen tonight."

"Promises, promises."

Her sing-song tone and faux disappointed expression made his eyes narrow. She was challenging him. He couldn't let that stand, now could he?

"You *minx*."

She gasped when he suddenly leaned away from her, perhaps assuming he was genuinely displeased and about to leave, but he had something far more pleasant in mind. His hands slid around the dip of her waist and upwards. He watched the heat rising in her face as his long fingers moved to cup her breasts, gently massaging the sensitive mounds. She whined, a throaty sound that went straight to his groin, and tilted her head back as her eyes closed.

With the lovely expanse of her neck bared to him, he didn't pass up the opportunity presented. His focus moved to that pale skin, dragging hot, open-mouthed kisses over her flesh and up to where he could feel her heart hammering beneath his lips. His tongue swept out then, sampling the flavor of her in that little hollow where her essence was strong, that heady floral fragrance egging him on. She breathed a sigh that threatened to be a moan, and he knew then that he couldn't leave this room until he heard her say his name in a voice thick with pleasure.

His hands hadn't ceased moving, and now they shifted upward, abandoning her breasts only so that he could hook his fingertips in the low neckline of her gown and tug it downward. Creamy expanses of flesh were bared by the motion, until finally, the pale green fabric slid off her shoulders. He watched with undeniable desire as two perfectly pale pink nipples emerged, their tips standing proud as proof of her need. He couldn't have stopped himself if he wanted to when his left hand returned to cradling her breast, his thumb circling that tender peak, but it was the other that he swept his tongue across, before suckling it into his mouth.

She tasted just as delicious as she looked, and he groaned as she jerked against him with a breathless cry, the hidden apex of her thighs rubbing against his clothed hardness. Was she as slick with lust as he was rigid for her? The urge to know was overwhelming. Driven near unto madness by the way she was gripping his hair and panting above him, his free hand fumbled its way down to her skirts, hurriedly pulling them out of the way until he felt soft, bare skin beneath his fingertips. Unerringly, his hand moved up, skimming over the flesh of her inner thighs, until he met hot, damp fabric.

"Zavier, stop!"

He froze. Although he'd wanted to hear his name from her lips, that single word was enough to kill all his amorous intent, even if it didn't stifle his ardor. Immediately, he snatched his hand away from between her legs, let her nipple slide out of his mouth, and looked up at her. He couldn't hide the fear in his gaze if he tried, even if his voice was deep and hoarse with need. "Are you all right? Did I hurt you?" The thought that he might have inadvertently done something to cause her pain tore at his heart, and nothing else could have made him soften more quickly, except perhaps being dunked in the snows atop Ironhold's mountains. Before she even had a chance to reply, he was tugging the bodice of her dress back up to cover her bared skin, looking at her flushed but terrified face with a welling self-loathing. "Forgive me. I didn't mean to frighten you."

"I-I'm sorry. I don't…" She sounded confused and more than a little afraid, and he acted on instinct. Gently shifting her so that she was no longer straddling his lap, he urged her to settle sitting on his thighs, with her legs draping off the side of the chaise, and wrapped his arms around her. Tugging her close, he was relieved when she tucked her face into his neck and nuzzled him. At least she wasn't angry.

"Don't ever apologize to me. You haven't done anything wrong. I let my desire for you get the better of me, and I'm ashamed of myself for being so weak." The words were muffled as he pressed his mouth to her hair, lightly rubbing his hand over her upper arm. She didn't seem too upset, but he was still kicking himself for letting his hormones rule him. That hadn't happened since he was in his twenties. Perhaps it was just proof of how powerfully she affected him.

Much to his dismay, if the past few days were any indication, he was going to be in agony by their wedding night.

It pained her to let him walk away after their passionate interlude in her sitting room, but he was a king and had affairs that required his attention, ones that didn't involve her. Not yet, anyway. He'd given her an idea of what she'd be expected to do as his queen and, more importantly, what she would be *capable* of doing if those things weren't enough. He'd had the list sent to the data slate in her hands, as well as approving a communications uplink for her.

She could reach out to her mother now, she mused. Zavier clearly trusted her, and she suspected any messages she might send would go unobserved by him or his communications officers. But even as she pondered sending something to Greenwell, to her mother, she knew that she had no desire to do so. Yvonne would do as she had always done when things happened to her daughter—she would smother in an overbearing attempt to protect, believing that the only way to keep Alexia safe was to separate her from everything dangerous. She had freedom here, with Zavier, that she'd never had on Greenwell. Even the guards were there for her protection and to guide her around the Citadel, not to keep her contained... not anymore.

It was true that she hadn't been outside the Citadel yet, but she wasn't terribly interested in doing so, either. And she knew that if she requested it of him, Zavier would agree. The time was coming, she knew that, but not yet. Perhaps tomorrow, or after they were married. For now, she needed to focus on what was in her hands and the tasks she had assigned herself. Namely, asking Calla for her husband's assistance in acquiring what she needed to help Ironhold develop the means to provide agricultural products for its own sustainability.

Despite her great interest in what she was reading, her mind kept wandering back to what had transpired between herself and the iron king on the very chaise where she was still sitting. Blood filled her cheeks as she remembered the feel of his mouth on her skin, his fingers and lips touching places no one but she had ever explored, and the burning ache it had brought to life within her. She'd been afraid of how powerful that feeling was and hadn't known how to react, although in hindsight, telling him to stop was *not* the correct choice.

She wanted more.

Admitting that, even just silently to herself, filled her with excitement. Her mother would've been mortified, which was all the more reason to do it. Besides, did she want to go to her wedding night completely ignorant?

No. That night, she would ask Zavier to show her what she'd been missing. She felt certain he'd agree and returned to her reading with a grin. But with her resolution now set in her mind, it felt like the hours dragged, through her lunch and the quiet afternoon, until Elea entered and informed her Zavier was waiting in his study. Familiar with the route from her rooms to his, she practically flew through the hallways and up the stairs and entered into his room without preamble.

As soon as she saw him, she lost all urge to eat, even though the table was set up for their evening meal. Instead, as he rounded the table to pull her chair out for her, she caught his sleeve and pulled him gently to a halt. His confusion was oddly endearing, and she grinned up at him, her face warming with the knowledge of what she was about to say... and, hopefully, *do*.

"I'm not hungry." She watched his face transform from an expression of mild bewilderment to one of extreme concern. His hands moved to rest on her shoulders as he searched her features with pale eyes, his voice suffused with worry. "Are you not feeling well? Should I call the doctor?"

Her smile widened, her heart thudding in response to his questions. His solicitude really was quite touching, but she hastened to reassure him. "No, I feel fine. There's just something else I'd rather do first."

His brows drew together, and she could positively see the thoughts running through his mind as he tried to discern what she was talking about. Something flashed in his eyes as he apparently considered a possibility, but his hesitance was plain, as though he were afraid to believe there was even a slight chance of his notion being feasible.

"And… what might that be?" His voice had gone thick, and his hands glided upward, letting the tips of his fingers ghost over the bare skin of her neck.

She shivered at the touch, inhaling sharply, and was shocked by how breathless her own voice was. "I want you to finish what you started earlier."

His reaction was instantaneous. The hue of his irises darkened, filling with desire, and his hands roamed down over her back, coming to rest on her hips. They gripped her tightly, and she could tell he wanted nothing more than to pull her against him, but he held back. Likely out of fear she'd stop him again, as she had that morning.

"Think very carefully about what you're asking of me, Alexia. I'm a patient man, but even I have my limits, and I don't appreciate being teased."

"I'm not teasing you, Zavier. Earlier, I… wasn't expecting it, and it frightened me. But you stopped when I asked." Although still with a breathy quality, her voice was gentle and filled with warmth as she lifted her hand, settling it on the curve of his jaw. He turned his face into her touch, obviously reveling in the display of affection, though his gaze never left hers. "I want to learn. Please?"

It was apparent that words were beyond him, as his jaw clenched and he swallowed convulsively. There was no hesitation in him when his hands lowered, curving over the backs of her thighs, and easily hoisted her up, parting her legs so that he could settle her against him. Her eyes widened at the unexpected display of strength, her arms quickly winding around his neck to stabilize herself as he carried her over to the lounge in front of the fireplace, which was already crackling quietly in the stillness.

He laid her out on the soft cushions and moved to brace his weight on his arms as his hips settled in the vee of her legs. The way he looked at her, his face cast into shadow by his hair tumbling forward, made her feel like the most beautiful woman in the universe, because the intensity of his gaze said she was the *only* woman in the universe to him, at least in this moment. Then his lips found hers, and all ability to think was lost.

His kiss was passionate but not fierce, as it had been that morning, in the desperation of their mutual need. He was going slowly, easing her mouth open and tasting her in slow, tender motions of lips and tongue, as though the taste of her was the rarest of delicacies to be gradually savored. Drowning in sensation, her body moved instinctively, curling her legs over his hips and rocking her pelvis up against the hardness she knew was forming in his trousers. She felt him jerk toward her, seeking some kind of relief, and he groaned into the melding of their lips, before breaking the kiss to mutter against her jaw in a strangled voice, "Thank the gods you're not asking me to bed you. I wouldn't last long enough to be worth anything if you kept doing things like that."

She felt a surge of feminine pride, knowing how powerfully she roused his desire for her, and uttered a muted laugh. It faded into a hum of pleasure when his mouth roved over her skin, his teeth nipping playfully at her clavicle as he descended down to the valley of her breasts. Her breath hitched in eager anticipation when he shifted his weight fully onto one arm and reached up with his other hand to tug down the neckline of her gown. She moved her shoulders to ease its passage, and then she was shivering as the cool air of the room met her sensitive peaks.

She watched through half-lidded eyes as he nuzzled his way farther down, the faint rasp of stubble on his jaw delightfully abrasive against her tender skin, until he reached one of those pale pink tips. Brushing his lips over it, she gasped, then whimpered when his tongue circled the rapidly hardening center. His gaze darted up to ensnare hers just as he drew her nipple into his mouth, suckling on her firmly and grazing his teeth across her flesh. The act seemed to pull on the very core of her, her hips rolling toward his while the heat of arousal flared into life between her legs.

"Zavier." She moaned his name, her hands fumbling their way across the expanse of his shoulders and upper back until she found his hair. Her fingers twined into the night-dark tendrils as she writhed beneath him, aching for some kind of relief. He let her nipple slide out of his mouth with a wet sound that was delightfully debauched, then pursed his lips and exhaled. The shock of cold air against her wet skin made her squirm, her eyes closing as sensation swamped her.

Which was, apparently, just what he wanted. She was entirely unaware of his hand moving down until she felt his fingers on her bare thigh, gliding slowly upward. Rather than the fear and anxiety she'd felt this morning, she was decidedly eager, even a little impatient, and was panting with anticipation by the time she felt the heat and pressure of his touch against her undergarments.

And there, he froze. Her eyes flew open and fell to him, wondering why he'd stopped. He was staring at her, his gaze intent, though the skin around his eyes was tight with strain. Keeping himself from going farther was plainly hard for him, but he didn't move. The reason why became clear a moment later, when he rasped a question against the swell of her breast. "Tell me you want this, Alexia. There's no stopping once you say it, but I won't go any farther until you do."

Her heart swelled with emotion. Even as much as he wanted to touch her, to please her, he wanted her to be absolutely certain of this course of action before he crossed the point of no return. Shifting her hands, she brought them forward to cup his cheeks, her thumbs lightly stroking the sharp angles of his cheekbones as she replied, "I want this. I want *you*."

He groaned as he turned his head, just enough to press a heated kiss to the inside of her wrist. Then he was pulling her other nipple into his mouth as his hand finally began to move. She once more twisted her fingers into his hair as he pressed more firmly against the fabric covering her opening, rubbing her hidden flesh in a circular motion. She'd done this to herself many times, but having his larger, stronger fingers doing it, made it so much more intense. And still, it wasn't enough. Whining with need, she wriggled beneath him, bucking her hips in an attempt to get him to touch her where she wanted it most.

There was the sudden sense of something electric in the air, as though he'd had a rapidly fraying rope tied to his control and it had just snapped. A growl rumbled in his throat as his hand fled quickly upward, grasped the top of her underwear, and pulled it down several inches. The next thing she knew, she felt the rough pads of his fingertips against her bare, hairless skin, traversing the span from her pubic bone to her slick petals. His thumb slid over the top of her sex, and her breath caught as he unerringly located her hidden bud.

His thumb began to circle around that hooded nub of flesh, and Alexia felt such a powerful bolt of lust, she was surprised she didn't come apart right then. He was flicking his tongue against her nipple in time with the circling of his thumb, the synchronicity enough to have her seeing stars as her eyes slid shut. Had she been capable of coherent thought, she would've been thoroughly embarrassed by the wanton way her hips were moving toward his hand, craving more.

Maybe it was just his experience, or maybe he was so in tune with her, but Zavier knew just what she needed. She felt one of his fingers press between her lower lips, rubbing back and forth and spreading her arousal, before it slipped fully into her channel. Her inner walls clamped down on that single digit as it began to move in and out of her, then gradually, he introduced another. She'd only ever felt her own fingers in her core, and his were larger, longer, *so* much more satisfying. He began to pump them into her in earnest, and his thumb shifted, pressing fully to that tiny bundle of nerves as it emerged fully from its sheltering hood.

She'd begun exploring her own body and pleasure when her breasts first formed, and she was no stranger to climax. But how she was feeling now put all those other experiences to shame. She was panting, arching and trembling beneath him, clawing for her release as her world shrank down to his mouth on her breast and his hand moving so vigorously between her legs. Then her mind exploded into pure bliss, waves of heat rushing through her body while she cried out and lost herself to climax.

When she returned to a semblance of reality, it was to

the realization that she was tingling from head to toe in the most delectable fashion, and that Zavier had gone still on top of her as he had his hand between her thighs. He was breathing hard, his face pressed to the skin just above her breast. She smoothed some of his hair back from his brow and sighed with a sense of loss as he drew his hand from between her legs, tugged her underwear back up, and lifted himself off her slightly. It took her a moment to understand he was righting her appearance as best as he was able, by pulling her skirts down and then drawing her bodice up over her breasts.

When he lifted his head and looked at her, his disgruntled expression made her heart sink. Had she done something wrong? Licking her lips, she noted the hoarse quality of her voice as she murmured hesitantly, "Are you all right?"

He huffed a derisive chuckle but, rather than settling on top of her again, leaned back until he was sitting upright. She mourned the loss of his warmth, although she didn't reach for him as he ruffled a hand back through his hair and grumbled. "Aside from the fact that I just popped off in my trousers like an untried boy, I'm fine. You are…" He trailed off, and she unconsciously tensed, until he looked at her with a gaze so adoring, it made her chest fill with warmth. "You are the most beautiful and sensual woman I've ever met, let alone touched. That makes any discomfort worth it. Thank you, for letting me bring you pleasure."

In that moment, she lost her heart, wholly and irrevocably, to the Iron King of Ironhold.

By the time he returned from changing out of his uncomfortably damp trousers and into a fresh pair, Zavier no longer felt ashamed by his lack of control. Alexia hadn't seemed to mind, and indeed, if he'd judged her response accurately, she'd been quite flattered by the knowledge. He only hoped he could hold out longer on their wedding night and grimaced at the thought as he stepped back into the study. The sight before him made him pull up short, brows curving upward in surprise.

During his absence, she'd apparently summoned Benji or another servant and had called for blankets. They were now spread out on the floor in front of the fire, along with some cushions, in a space that had been formed by the sofa being pushed back several paces, until its back was flush with his desk. The platter with the energy dome that held their dinner was sitting on the floor near the pile of padding, clearly waiting for them. Her eyes were sparkling when she smiled shyly up at him, something that made his heart surge with a blend of desire and possessiveness.

"I hope you don't mind. I wanted to do something a little less formal."

He hesitated briefly, then shrugged out of his jacket and draped it across the back of a nearby chair, before toeing off his boots and crossing to where she sat. She was visibly pleased by his silent acquiescence, which made his mild discomfort worth it.

"I can't exactly begrudge you the impulse. I'll admit, the intimacy is… pleasant." Reaching over, he deactivated the energy dome, and the scents of their dinner filled the room. It was then that he remembered what they were eating that night, and he bit back a groan. His cook was skilled and enjoyed making cuisine from other systems and planets, although one of her favorites was the spicy-sweet finger foods of Oceanis, a blend of sea creatures and aquatic plants with a subtle but inherently salty flavor to them. The thought of seeing Alexia eating the fare made his already tired length twitch with interest, and he knew it was going to be a long night.

"Oh, this is… I've never seen food like this before. There aren't any utensils. How are we supposed to eat it?"

His eyes rolled toward the ceiling, and he bit the inside of his cheek. It was official. The gods were trying to kill him. Swallowing thickly, he leaned forward and picked up the steamed flesh of a small, shelled creature stuffed with a crunchy seed, dipped it in a dish of reddish sauce, and offered it to her. Her eyes widened, and her cheeks flushed, as though him feeding her was far more exotic than what they'd done less than an hour prior.

"It's from Oceanis, and they prefer to eat with their fingers. If you'd like, I'll send for utensils." Zavier was surprised by how smooth his own voice was. He'd expected it to be rough with building desire. He could only pray she'd take him up on the offer, but his prayers went unanswered, as she shyly leaned forward and parted her lips.

He watched with growing hunger as she delicately pulled the morsel out of his grasp with her teeth, her lips brushing against his thumb and forefinger, before she leaned back and began chewing with a soft hum of approval. Her tongue darted out to capture a droplet of the sauce which had lingered on her lower lip, and he grunted as his stomach clenched with arousal. It seemed his earlier embarrassment wasn't the only way he was hearkening back to his youth tonight.

"That's delicious. I want to learn how other cultures do things, so I'll eat as they do on Oceanis." She smiled at him, then visibly hesitated. He knew the moment the color in her face deepened that he was going to be in danger of perishing from blood loss to his brain the moment she opened her mouth. "Should I... feed you in return?"

"No." He could tell by the way she recoiled that he'd been a little too quick in responding and a little too firm, to boot. Rubbing his hand over his face, he inhaled deeply and tried to calm himself. Then he chuckled as his hand fell, leveling a heated look on her as his lips quirked into a crooked smile. "That's not the custom, and if you tried it, I can't promise I wouldn't try to ravish you."

Her lips parted and formed an 'O' of surprise, before she lowered her eyes and smiled.

Leaning forward, he gently grasped her chin in his fingers and drew her gaze up to meet his. There was something uncertain lurking in those rich, emerald eyes, and it tugged at his heart. As he moved closer to her, his hand shifted, fingers brushing lightly along her jaw until he was cupping her cheek. "You truly have no idea how absolutely stunning you are, do you? I've seen many women in my time, because they flock to Owen's court, and he loves to summon me there just to make me uncomfortable. And I won't lie, I've bedded several of them. But none of them have ever made me half as mad with desire as you do just by being near."

Her eyes gleamed with a suspicious glassy sheen, but before he could think to question it, she was cupping his face in her hands and pulling his lips to hers. Kissing Alexia made him forget everything except her, and he was glad to spend the next few hours doing nothing but tasting her lips, talking, and occasionally remembering to eat.

Chapter 8

S he was starting to hate sleeping alone. It wasn't that she didn't like her bed or her rooms. But she woke up wanting to see Zavier, and when he wasn't there, it immediately put a damper on her good mood. Elea entered to find her already dressed and braiding her own hair, and the young handmaiden was visibly surprised by the eagerness of her lady's movements, not to mention the fact that she was wearing trousers and a femininely cut jacket, rather than a dress.

"Your Highness? Is something the matter?"

"No. I've made a decision about something, is all. Is Zavier ready for me?" She tied off the end of her braid and sat on a bench, where she pulled on the boots that had been made for her. Sturdy and comfortable, they would be perfect for an outing beyond the Citadel, which was exactly what she had in mind.

"Um, yes, Your Highness, he's waiting in his study. Is there anything I can do to help with this… decision you've made?" She stepped back as Alexia stood, the princess flashing her a mischievous smile.

"Yes. Have the cook prepare a simple meal for lunch and put it aboard the shuttle." Without explaining and completely ignoring Elea's stammering surprise, she hurried out of her room and through the keep. She ended up nearly bounding up the steps, and her cheeks were flushed with exertion by the time she entered Zavier's study, where he was pouring cups of tea for both of them. He was smiling when he looked her way, but as he noticed she was slightly out of breath, he arched a brow.

"Did you run here?"

"You could say that. I want to go outside the Citadel. As soon as we finish breakfast." His surprise was obvious, as he quickly set down the teapot and turned to face her. She crossed the room to where he stood, reaching out to put her hands on his chest, and rose up onto her toes to press a quick kiss of greeting to his lips, which were slightly slack with shock.

"This is… unexpected. What made you decide to do this today?" His hands fell to her hips as she dropped back onto her heels, looking down at her with a crooked but confused smile.

"Reading my duties as Queen. I want to see the planet I'm going to help rule, and if I'm going to help figure out a way to form a self-sustaining agricultural ecosystem, I need to get my hands in the dirt." She expected him to question the statement, which she didn't truly understand herself. It was more voicing an instinct she couldn't pinpoint. But he seemed to accept it at face value, something that had her eyes narrowing slightly. Why wasn't he more surprised by that resolution?

"Then that's what we'll do. I'll have the shuttle prepared for takeoff and guards readied to accompany us."

She would question him about his odd reaction—or

rather, lack thereof—later. For now, she was simply glad he'd agreed… and she was hungry.

An hour later, Zavier was aboard the shuttle with Alexia and a handful of guards, as well as the shuttle's pilot and copilot. He'd decided that the best spot for them to visit was about an hour's flight away, in one of the few places on the planet that he believed would be the best spot to begin their terraforming attempts. There was a spring, and it was somewhat sheltered from Ironhold's occasional storms by a semicircle of mountains. He spent their flight time hunched over a data slate with her, discussing the contents of the message she'd received from Calla that morning, with offers of seeds from planets other than Greenwell for their venture.

When the shuttle touched down, the guards stood, weapons in hand. The nearest settlement was barely within view, but there was always the chance some of the village's denizens had left. There were occasionally deserters, people who grew tired of mining Ironhold ore for a living and thought they could survive by raiding other settlements. They usually didn't last long, but they were always violent and often less than sane. Once the guards had given the all-clear, Zavier exited the shuttle and offered his hand to Alexia.

He watched her as she peered curiously at their surroundings. The ground was hardly visible past the grey-blue mist, which was thick and hovered at about the height of his knees. Much to his surprise, she tugged her hand out of his and approached the spring, which was bubbling up into a stone hollow a few paces away. He followed her, wondering what she was doing. The mist thinned near the banks of the spring, and it was there that she stopped and knelt, burying her hands in the loose, damp soil.

The sudden intense scent of something akin to the sharp tang in the air after a lightning storm assaulted his senses, and although he couldn't be certain, he thought he saw the color of her eyes become more brilliant. He couldn't tell for sure, as she was half-turned away from him, but there was no denying what happened next. Little green shoots emerged from the earth near her hands, the effect rippling outward for half a dozen feet, before it finally stopped. She inhaled sharply and stood, her body wavering.

"Alexia?" Zavier reached for her, grasping her elbow to steady the wobbling princess, before pulling her gently closer and sliding his arm around her waist. She looked dazed as she tilted her head back, her eyes meeting his.

"I feel... strange. Did something happen?" He glanced down at the ground, noting that where the tiny sprouts had come up, the mist was thinner. She followed his gaze and blinked, then frowned. "Were those there before? I feel like I dreamed about seeing them grow."

"I think we should get back to the shuttle." His voice was calm, but his heart was hammering. He'd suspected something like this, what with the changes in the garden and the findings by his scientists, but seeing it confirmed before his very eyes, was another matter entirely. When she didn't protest, he led her back to the shuttle and eased her into a seat.

She put her hand to her forehead, uncaring of the dirt she left behind on her fair skin, and met his eyes as he settled beside her. "Zavier... what did I just do?"

"...and then they just sprouted from the ground."

Alexia couldn't believe what she'd just heard. The story seemed too fantastic to be true. Not just what had happened at the spring, but the changes in his garden and what his scientists had found in their molecular scans. Zavier was in the process of cleaning the dirt from her hands, and embarrassingly enough, off her face, with a damp cloth as he told her everything. Yet as he fell silent and sat there holding her hands, she remembered something. The flash of a distant memory, faded with time and repression.

She was just a child, just barely in her third year. Her mother doted on her, and she adored her, the goddess with the golden hair and the green eyes. She didn't understand yet how important she was, or what place her mother held in the galaxy. All she knew was that her mother smelled like sunshine and rain, and her favorite thing was to be out in the gardens with her.

Her mother was distracted, speaking to one of her handmaidens, and Alexia was wandering barefoot through the grass as she often did. She was always on the search for plants that were struggling, tiny blossoms that were lost in the shade beneath bushes or tangled in the roots of trees. Today, she found one, a tiny purple flower that was fighting to get to the sunlight and being held back by a berry bush.

Uncaring of the sharp twigs that scratched her fair skin, she dug her hands into the soil around the little flower and carefully scooped it out, being sure to gather all of its roots. She didn't realize her mother had seen what she was doing and was now watching her intently as she carried the little bloom over to an open patch of grass near a trestle and set it down. She dug a hole, deposited the flower in it, then covered up the root ball before cupping her hands around the stem.

This was her Big Secret. She'd been doing it for a while now but had always been sure not to let anyone see, not even her mother. She wanted to perfect this Big Secret before showing it to Mother, wanting nothing more than to make her proud. She felt the energy flow into her hands, and then from her hands into the leaves that were touching her skin. All at once, the flower burst into vivacious life, sprouting numerous stalks and blossoms until it was a massive, flourishing vine, climbing up the trestle.

"Alexia, what have you done?"

She looked up at her mother, alarmed by the anger and fear within her voice. Before she could voice a reply, Mother had knelt and grabbed her shoulders, whipping her around so fast, it hurt her neck. Then Mother shook her, something that had never happened before, and had her eyes filling with tears.

"You must never do that again, Alexia. Swear it to me. Swear it!"

"I swear, Mother, I'll never do it again."

As she surfaced from the memory, Alexia looked at Zavier, bewildered by the unexpectedly cool air on her cheeks, until he swiped his thumb across her face, and she realized she was crying. Her voice was little more than a whisper as she confessed what she'd just remembered, after nearly twenty years of forcing the memory down deep into her subconscious.

"She knew. Mother knew and made me promise never to do it. I forgot. It was so long ago..." She didn't understand. How was this possible? Confused and more than a little scared, she allowed him to pull her close and laid her head on his shoulder as he stroked her back.

"I don't know how this is possible, but I have agents on Greenwell trying to find answers to questions I have. Once I can make contact with them, I'll have them look into this, too."

His words made her brow wrinkle, and she lifted her head, looking at him questioningly. He appeared to anticipate her confusion, although he said nothing, only nodding his head to silently indicate she could ask what was on her mind.

"What other questions do you have that you think my mother has hidden answers to?"

He was visibly discomfited by the question and inhaled slowly, as though to brace himself before answering. "Alexia... Did your mother ever tell you who your father is?"

He could see that the question stunned her, which was perhaps a good thing, as there was a sudden commotion in the cockpit. He turned just as the co-pilot emerged into the passenger area, the young man's face marred with worry.

"I'm sorry, Your Majesty, but we're going to have to make an emergency landing. An electrical storm has formed between us and the Citadel."

He bit back a curse and nodded briskly, then turned back to Alexia, who was clearly concerned. Taking her hands in his, he urged her to lean back into the nano-gel of their seats, which changed shape to conform to their bodies in response to the turbulence they began experiencing.

"Electrical storm? Are we in danger?" She clutched his hands tightly and glanced toward the cockpit, where she could just barely catch glimpses of the exterior world through the screen. He knew she wouldn't be able to see much of anything, and it was easy to draw her attention back to him.

"Not if we land quickly and shelter outside the shuttle. The lightning strikes are drawn to metal and energy sources, so taking cover in the rocks will keep us—"

The mild shuddering of the shuttle was interrupted by an abrupt and violent jolt, and everything went dark as it felt like the world had dropped out from under them. He grabbed hold of Alexia when it became clear the shuttle was plunging from the sky, tucking her face into his chest. The last thing he heard was her scream before pain blossomed in his head, and the world went dark.

"Your Highness, we need to get away from the shuttle!"

The voice was muffled, and at first, Alexia couldn't figure out why. Then the heavy object on top of her was lifted away, and the crashing of lightning and thunder roared into her ears. She realized that it was Zavier's unconscious body that had been sprawled over her, and she gasped at the sight of blood staining his pale skin.

"He's hurt! We can't move him with an injury!" She struggled to sit up then saw the figure who'd been speaking to her. It was Kit, the dark-skinned head of her personal guard. The woman had lost her helmet at some point during the crash, and her brilliant orange curls were whipping violently in the wind as she grasped Alexia's arm and pulled her to her feet.

"If we leave the iron king in the shuttle, he'll die for certain. Better to risk moving him and get him in the safety of the rocks."

Very shortly, Alexia found herself sheltered in the sturdy curve of Kit's arm, being hurried toward the side of a mountain, which she could barely see in the flashes of lightning. They squeezed through a jagged opening and into a grotto. One of the guards had managed to retrieve a survival kit from the shuttle before escaping, and she saw with relief that a few glow-packs had been hung from rocky protrusions. Even better, the co-pilot was tending the wound on Zavier's head. Breaking away from Kit, she hurried to the unconscious king's side, kneeling next to the co-pilot.

"Can I help?"

The co-pilot glanced at her, offering a small, tight smile, then shook his head. "I've got the bleeding stopped and the wound covered, so now we just have to make sure he doesn't go into shock. Keep him warm; that should help."

Alexia nodded and didn't hesitate to stretch out beside Zavier, laying her head on his chest while her arms wrapped around his body. The co-pilot dug a thermal blanket out of the survival kit and spread it out across them, immediately engulfing both of their bodies in warmth. Though she tried to watch as the pilots and guards talked among themselves, the exhaustion of her earlier actions and the stress of the crash soon took their toll on her. Light flashed against her closed eyes as she drifted into slumber.

She had no idea how much later it was when she suddenly snapped awake, but she was relieved to see that the electrical storm had passed. There was no strobing lightning or rolling thunder, even after several minutes of lying there, listening.

Zavier was breathing easily beside her, and when she shifted against him, his hand moved to rest on the curve of her waist, making her jump and look up at him. His eyes remained closed, but a faint smile appeared on his lips as he muttered, "Not how I'd hoped to sleep beside you for the first time, but it seems nothing goes to plan where you're concerned."

"You're awake. Are you in pain?" She pushed herself up into a sitting position and leaned down to look at him, his features barely visible in the thin light of the glow-packs. She did see his eyes flicker open and look up at her, a fact that made her smile.

"I feel like the shuttle landed on my head, so, yes, I'm

in pain. You weren't injured, were you?"

She shook her head, eliciting a sigh from him, and she could veritably feel the tension seep out of him. He'd been that concerned for her, when he was injured? She reached up and gently stroked his cheek, watching as he slid calmly back into unconsciousness.

"The iron king woke up?" She glanced up to see Kit looking down at them and nodded. The big woman's shoulders relaxed in response to the news, and she sank down to sit on a rock beside the royal pair. "That's a good sign there's no lasting damage, but I'll still feel better once we get him back to the Citadel and seen by the doctor."

"Me too. He was hurt because he was trying to protect me." She felt a powerful welling of guilt and swallowed thickly as she looked down at the peacefully sleeping king.

"People do things like that when they love someone."

Her head snapped back up, eyes widening in astonishment at the words that left Kit's mouth. She floundered for a moment, trying to think of anything to say in response.

"What? He... the iron king doesn't love me. Why would you think such a thing?"

Kit's red eyes flicked in her direction, her expression one of amusement, as though she knew a secret Alexia didn't. It made her feel like a child again, which had her frowning as she raised her chin in a haughty manner.

"Anyone with eyes can see His Majesty is stupidly in love with you, Your Highness. I just don't think he's willing to admit it to himself yet. He's been without love for so long that I'm not sure he recognizes it anymore."

The words bounced around inside her head as she looked back down at Zavier. Did he love her? Would he ever say so if he did? Even though she'd never been in love before, she knew she loved him. Would he push her away if she told him how she felt? The thought made her heart ache, so she extricated herself from his grasp and wriggled out from beneath the thermal blanket, then moved to the grotto's exit to look outside.

She could vaguely see the pilot and co-pilot working in the shuttle, trying to fix whatever systems had been damaged by the lightning strike. From what she could gather, it wasn't going well. Curious about what Ironhold looked like at night, with both of its moons high overhead, she slipped out of the grotto and climbed up the rocks that surmounted the rocky hollow. She had just pulled herself up onto a flat stone when she heard the shuffle of movement in front of her and looked up.

A handful of men in tattered clothing, holding rugged mining equipment, stood before her. They seemed just as surprised by her appearance as Alexia was by theirs, but they reacted first. One of them stepped toward her, hand outstretched. She quickly pushed backward, then screamed as she half-slid, half-rolled down the slope, landing hard on the ground beside the shuttle. She heard scrambling from above as they made to follow her, but even worse, she could see more of the rough men approaching the grotto entrance. The guards, having heard her scream, poured out of the opening, where they clashed with the intruders.

One of them figured the princess would be an easier target, though, and lunged toward her. Without thinking, Alexia rolled out of his reach, lurched to her feet, and began to run. Her side ached from where she'd landed, making breathing difficult, but she didn't care. She needed to get away from those men. She could tell just by their collective demeanor that if they got their hands on her, she'd wish she were dead.

It didn't occur to her until she stopped running, several minutes later, that she had no clue where she was, let alone where she could go. And by that time, the mist that covered Ironhold's surface had grown so thick around her, she couldn't see anything. Sounds were muffled and distorted, and due to the rocky ground, she couldn't see which direction she'd come from. Suddenly, a figure moved through the mist toward her, and she screamed, backing away.

"Your Highness, it's all right! It's me." Kit appeared, reaching out to take her arm and haul her along. Alexia gasped but stumbled along after her guard, struggling to keep up with the big, muscular woman.

"Where are we going? Shouldn't we head back toward the shuttle?" She glanced over her shoulder, fruitlessly as it turned out. She couldn't even tell if that was really the direction of the shuttle. She couldn't hear fighting, or anything.

"The others are defending the iron king. I know a safe place where we can hide until the rescue shuttle from the Citadel can retrieve them, and then us."

A safe place? What could be safer than the hollow where they'd been hiding out? She tripped over a large rock, and nearly went sprawling, only to huff and pull her arm out of Kit's grasp.

"What is this safe place?"

Kit looked back at her, her expression oddly grim.

"It's Haven. The only settlement on Ironhold composed solely of women."

How Kit could tell where she was going, Alexia couldn't even begin to imagine, but after an hour or so of walking, she saw lights breaking through the mist ahead. Very shortly after that, they almost walked into the wall surrounding the settlement, and she saw the lights were rudimentary torches, thrust into brackets around the wall top. Stepping back, she looked up, trying to discern movement, and jumped when Kit called out, "I am Kit, sister of Sasha, and I request right of entry for myself and the one I protect!"

There was a flurry of conversation and activity above them, the muted rumble of conversation, before she heard the sound of something scraping against the earth to her right. Looking in that direction, she could just barely make out a large gate swinging open in the wall, and the fact that people were hurrying out. It was a group of about seven women, all clad in armor or carrying weapons and eyeing the pair warily as Kit urged her in their direction. The women began to mutter among themselves when Kit came closer, and the woman in front, short and pale-skinned, grimaced.

"You know Sasha isn't going to like this."

"I get the feeling she'll forgive me when she hears what I have to say. Just get us inside and wake her up." Alexia glanced curiously at Kit, wondering what was happening here. Who was Sasha? Why would she be mad about Kit being there? How did Kit know these women? She didn't get a chance to ask any of these questions as she and Kit were hustled inside. In the light of the torches, she could see surprisingly sturdy and well-made houses of stone with wooden roofs, all of them shuttered up tight for the evening. It was to the largest house at the center of the village that they were led and then left.

"I thought I heard your name, but I didn't think you'd actually be stupid enough to come back."

Alexia turned to look for the source of the voice and saw a woman standing in a nearby doorway. Much to her amazement, this female looked exactly like Kit, except she had far more scars, and her hair was woven into tight braids across her scalp. The two glared at each other, before Kit cleared her throat and gestured toward the imperial princess.

"I know you want to throw us out, Sasha, but before you do, I should probably tell you that this woman is an imperial princess. More importantly, the iron king is due to marry her in five days. I get the feeling he'd be more than ready to reward anyone who protected her in this time of need."

The woman known as Sasha stared at Kit for a moment, then glanced at Alexia herself, her scowl deepening. Finally, she grunted and pushed away from the doorframe she was leaning against.

"Fine. You can stay. But I want an explanation of how you ended up at my settlement."

Sasha, it turned out, was Kit's older sister. Far more interestingly, Sasha was the one who had founded Haven... more than a century ago. They were of a race she'd never even heard of before; an extremely long-lived people from the space beyond the Golden Cloud system, who called themselves something she couldn't pronounce. Roughly translated, it meant Fire-Eyes. Sasha and Kit had been arrested for killing a group of men on Oceanis and exiled here. The story was enthralling, and Alexia didn't even realize her tea had gone cold as she listened, fascinated.

"When I realized the men were going to beat any woman who got with child until she lost the babe, I decided it was high time I made a safe space for the women of this planet. Just because we've done violent crimes, doesn't mean we deserve that kind of treatment."

Sipping at her tea and realizing how chilled it was, she

absently set the cup aside and leaned forward, her hands clasped in her lap.

"So, why did you leave, Kit? And how did you come to be serving Zavier? I thought he only let non-violent offenders work in the Citadel."

A look flashed between the two sisters, and Kit turned away first, lowering her eyes to the wooden floor with a frown. Well, it looked like she wasn't going to get an answer from her guard. Sasha seemed more ready to reply, even if she was scowling at her younger sibling.

"Kit didn't actually kill anyone. She just got arrested and sentenced alongside me because we're of the same species, so they assumed she'd been involved. I want no part of working for that iron king of yours, so when she said she was tired of struggling to eke out an existence with the rest of us, I told her never to come back." Sasha's vivid red eyes snapped toward her so quickly that Alexia jumped, unconsciously leaning back in her seat at the intensity of that gaze. The woman was certainly intimidating, she'd give her that. "So, you're going to try to terraform Ironhold, eh?"

"That's the plan. Greenwell is a very rich planet in terms of plant life, and I think I can find a way to make Ironhold's soil more receptive to growing things." Nodding, she fiddled with the hem of her jacket, watching as Sasha turned the information over in her mind.

"Well, isn't that something? Tell you what. I'll treat you like a queen until your precious Zavier comes to get you, on one condition." That was said in such a way that it sent a prickle of alarm zipping to the base of her skull, but a quick glance at Kit told her that she didn't have much choice. Dammit. She really hated being backed into a corner.

"Name it."

Sasha's grin was crooked, baring sharpened teeth that did nothing to soften her menacing appearance. Alexia straightened her shoulders and raised her chin, meeting the other woman's gaze head-on, and blinked when Sasha cackled.

"I like your moxie. Here it is. If this plan of yours works, I want the women of Haven to be allowed to do any harvesting or other jobs of that sort that need doing, in exchange for a little more lenient treatment and some upgrades to our basic necessities. Better housing, better food, you get the idea."

That was... surprising. But as she pondered it, Alexia could understand. Mining was a hard life, and the women burned out much faster than their larger, more muscular masculine counterparts. And someone would have to harvest and process the grains, fruits, and other products that came of her agricultural endeavor if it was successful. After considering this, she nodded.

"Very well. I'll see to it Zavier puts something together formally, once we're safely back at the Citadel."

Chapter 9

His head was killing him. Though the wound hadn't broken open, it was throbbing terribly, and he had a headache behind his eyes that was threatening to drive him mad. But all the outcasts who'd attacked them were dead, and the shuttle was still being worked on. None of that mattered to him at the moment, though, as he was too busy glaring at the senior guardsman standing in front of him.

"What do you mean, you can't find her?" His voice was frigid with rage as he snapped the words, and some part of him was proud when the guardsman failed to flinch beneath his obvious anger. It was a very small part, however, as the majority of him wanted someone to quail in the face of his fury.

"Just what I said, Your Majesty. The princess and Guard Kit were lost in the fray, and we haven't been able to discern which way they went. The terrain is too rocky for them to have left any tracks."

Turning away as quickly as he could without making himself dizzy and collapsing, Zavier cursed luridly. Had

Kit betrayed him and kidnapped Alexia? Or had his bride-to-be gotten panicked and run off, and Kit had done her duty in following? He paced for a few moments as he tried to decide what to do, then turned back to the guard who was waiting for his response. "Are there any settlements nearby?"

"Just one, Your Majesty. Haven is a short distance northwest of here."

Haven. Of course. Kit's sister was still there. If they had been in any kind of danger, he didn't doubt Kit would've taken her to safety at the settlement. Approaching the shuttle, he peered inside, looking at the pilot and co-pilot as they bent over the exposed wires behind a panel in the cockpit.

"How much longer until you get this thing working again?"

Both men looked up and shared a guilty glance, before the grizzled pilot frowned at him. "The shuttle is little more than scrap now, Your Majesty. But we've almost managed to get the communications array functioning again. Once it's in working condition, we'll hail the Citadel and get them to send a rescue shuttle."

His frown could've melted the entire shuttle with the sheer force of his displeasure. That was not what he'd wanted to hear. He couldn't in good conscience leave the two men undefended, but if he was going to go looking for Alexia, he wanted his full complement of guards with him. Slamming a hand on the side of the shuttle, he turned away and began to pace.

He needed to find her.

Sasha had fed them and shown them a place where they could sleep, for which Alexia was extremely grateful. It had been a harrowing day, and she was exhausted. The moment she curled up under the warm blanket, she was asleep. She dreamed again of an Ironhold made lush and verdant, with the singing of women in the air, and Zavier standing beside her while they surveyed what they had made. It was a pleasant dream, and she was disgruntled to be awakened from it by Kit shaking her shoulder.

"Your Highness, the iron king has come for us."

That was all it took to have Alexia flying up from her pallet and out of the house. The women of Haven were clustered near the gate, peering out at the shuttle sitting beyond their walls and the men who had emerged from it. Her heart swelled at seeing Zavier standing there, his gaze searching the crowd avidly for her. As soon as their eyes met, she saw the relief that filled him, and a smile spread across her face.

Before she could run to him, however, a hand clamped on her shoulder, and she glanced up to see Sasha staring at her. "Remember your promise, Princess."

It was more a threat than a reminder, and Alexia didn't want to know what Sasha would do if she reneged on the deal. Nodding her understanding, as soon as the woman let her go, she started toward Zavier. The women of the settlement parted before her once they realized someone important was coming through, and she heard whispers about her hair color and the vivid greenness of her eyes. Come to think of it, she hadn't seen a single person since arriving on this planet who had coloring even remotely close to her own. Was it something to do with the strange ability she had?

When she finally reached Zavier, he offered his hand to her, and she took it willingly. He squeezed her fingers gently, silently asking if she was all right, to which she returned the squeeze and nodded. His attention shifted to Kit as the guard approached, kneeling before the noble pair and bowing her head.

"Kit, why did you bring Princess Alexia here?"

"She was frightened by the outcast attack and ran, Your Majesty. I didn't want to risk taking her back to the shuttle, fearing she might get injured or captured. Haven seemed like the safest place to bring her."

He glanced at Alexia, and she nodded. "It's true. She kept me safe. As did Sasha, after our arrival."

That bit of information caused him to narrow his eyes at her, then look toward Sasha, who had moved to stand at the front of the crowd, her arms crossed. The leader arched a brow, jerking her chin toward them in a vague gesture of acknowledgement, which had Zavier growling.

"Then it seems I owe Sasha a great debt. What reward would you have for this good deed, Sasha?"

"Your future queen knows what I want. Ask her, once you're back safe in your stone prison, Iron King."

As she gestured to the women around her, the crowd dispersed, returning to their various tasks with whispers and curious glances. Kit stood as Alexia touched her shoulder, and then the trio were joining the other guards at the shuttle. The moment they were inside and seated, Zavier pulled her close, burying his face in her hair. She clutched at him almost desperately, the fear she'd been trying so hard to ignore ebbing away in the face of his warmth.

"I was afraid I'd lost you. You weren't hurt?" His voice was soft and warm, and she shook her head as she burrowed closer to him. She just wanted to go home.

It took her several minutes to realize that she now thought of the Ebon Citadel as home.

The *Pyxis* dropped out of lightspeed a short distance from Greenwell, just as Calla entered the bridge. All news from the agricultural planet had been uncomfortably quiet since Yvonne's flurry of back-and-forth between her home world and the Golden Cloud system. It gave the wife of the god-king a sickly feeling. Her eyes turned toward one of the crewmembers to her right, a young woman who had her hands pressed firmly over her ears, shutting out the noise of the bridge as she listened to the sounds coming through the small devices in her ears. The girl's expression only made Calla's sick feeling grow as she approached her station.

"Anything, Lieutenant?"

The communications officer glanced up at the queen, letting her hands fall with a grimace as she shook her head. "Nothing, Your Majesty. No outgoing comm chatter, and all our hails are going unanswered, regardless of frequency."

It wasn't what she wanted to hear. They were still well beyond range of orbiting the green world, and to move any closer, would be to risk an attack. Not that she thought Yvonne was far enough gone to actually fire at the *Pyxis*. Or at least, she hoped not. Exhaling slowly through her nose, she turned to the ship's captain, who was sitting in her chair with a grimly thoughtful expression.

"Captain, what do you recommend?"

The grizzled captain glanced her way, then straightened from her ponderous slouch and pursed her lips. "Something tells me they're not experiencing a comm malfunction. The smart course of action would be to hang back and keep hailing, but that's likely to get us nowhere fast. Approaching orbital range, would likely provoke a reaction, although there's always the chance it will be a violent one. How patient are you feeling, Your Majesty?"

The answer was about what she'd expected, but having her suspicions confirmed did nothing to alleviate her concern. Finally, she gave her head a brisk shake. "Not at all. Move us into orbital range."

"You heard Her Majesty. Helm, move us into orbital range, *cautiously*. Shields at the ready, and I want all hands prepared to move to battle stations."

There was a flurry of activity as people rushed around, settling into chairs of nano-gel that conformed to their bodies while they prepared for a possible attack from the planet. Truth be told, she didn't know much about Greenwell's defenses, although there were rumors of a powerful satellite defense network. She hoped that wasn't true and watched as the green world gradually grew larger on the viewscreen.

When the *Pyxis* was about to reach orbital height, the lieutenant on her right sat up sharply. "Your Majesty, we have an incoming transmission from the Verdant Palace. Audio only."

"Patch it through." Calla clasped her hands behind herself to keep from fidgeting as the speakers clicked faintly.

A moment later, a crisp, professional voice resonated through the bridge. "This is Greenwell high command. You are infringing on the sovereign space of Her Royal Majesty, the Verdant Empress. You have two minutes to reverse course and depart. Failure to comply will be met with force."

Her heart seemed to freeze in her chest. Had Yvonne really closed Greenwell's borders? Surely, she hadn't taken such a drastic measure so quickly.

"This is Calla of Crystal Spire, wife of God-King

Owen. I insist that you put me through to the Verdant Empress immediately." She paused and heard the comm officer inhale sharply, no doubt preparing to tell the wife of the galaxy's most important man to sod off. If politely. "Tell her I have news of her daughter."

There was a beat of silence, followed by the click of the comm link closing. She waited, outwardly calm, and even while certain that Yvonne wouldn't refuse to speak with her, she was inwardly wrought with nerves.

After less than a minute, the large holo-comm in the center of the bridge flickered, and the projected image of Yvonne appeared. "I heard you took a little trip, Calla. Tell me, how is Ironhold this time of year?"

Dammit. Yvonne knew about her trip to Ironhold? Did the woman have spies in Owen's court? Or perhaps even on the *Pyxis*? She would have a thorough investigation conducted… later. Right now, she needed to deal with Yvonne's madness. "Misty and vaguely unpleasant, as usual. What's this about vessels entering Greenwell space being met with violence?"

"I'll answer that depending on how you answer my question. Do you have my daughter?"

She wasn't going to answer. That was doubly concerning. Especially since Yvonne's cold demeanor made it clear she suspected the truth. A truth that Calla conveyed with a small frown. "She's on Ironhold. I spoke to her myself. She doesn't want to return to Greenwell, and she refused an offer to become part of the god-king's court as well."

Yvonne's face screwed up into an expression of pure wrath, and she seemed almost to lunge toward the holo-comm, pointing an accusing finger at the image of herself Calla knew was displayed before her. "I refuse to believe such lies! Zavier is holding her hostage, and you and Owen are helping him do it!" She slowly settled back in her chair, taking advantage of Calla's dumbstruck silence to continue in a far calmer manner, albeit with a seething rage underlying her tone. "There will be no trade with Greenwell until my daughter is returned to me. Let's see how quickly your story changes when the galaxy is starving."

Without even a word of farewell or warning, the holo-comm cut off. Everyone on the bridge was staring, stunned, at where the empress' image had just been.

Even the captain was staring, until the scarred older woman gave herself a shake and turned to look at her queen. "Orders, Your Majesty?"

There was a ringing in her ears as she processed Yvonne's threat. Greenwell was the largest exporter of agricultural goods in all the known systems, and without their constant stream of supplies, the galaxy would struggle to feed itself. Her face paled as she realized that the empress had backed them neatly into a corner. This situation needed to be handled, swiftly and brutally.

She just wished it wouldn't have to be at the expense of Zavier's happiness. Maybe... just *maybe*... they could find a way around this.

"We return to the Golden Cloud system. Immediately. Patch me through to the god-king, and send the transmission to my quarters."

Chapter 10

The days after their return were a flurry of activity. Aside from their usual dinner in the evening and the occasional moments of stolen kisses in the garden, Alexia rarely saw Zavier. If she'd known that preparing a royal wedding was going to be such a hassle, she would've insisted they do something a little smaller. And she wasn't even really doing anything! Although there were a lot of formalities to learn, since she was, apparently, going to be meeting two kings after the ceremony.

Who knew?

When the day finally arrived, she was roused by Elea shortly before the sun rose and glared blearily up at her handmaiden as the girl smiled.

"It's time to get ready for your wedding, Your Highness. Although, I suppose I should go ahead and start calling you 'Your Majesty', shouldn't I?"

Not awake enough to do more than grumble a half-hearted response, Alexia allowed the younger woman to hustle her out of bed and into a bath. Several hours later, after much primping and pampering, she stood at the door to her rooms, waiting. For what, she wasn't sure, but Elea had insisted she was supposed to wait. To her surprise, the door slid open, and she saw Calla standing there.

The wife of the god-king inhaled sharply, her fingers pressing to her mouth as a smile spread across her lips. "Alexia, you look absolutely stunning."

"Oh, um, thank you, Calla. Why are you here?" She tried to make her smile more genuine, but she felt extremely out of place in such a fine gown. She would be immensely glad when all this was over and she could stop feeling like some strange creature with unnecessary plumage.

"If you mean in the Ebon Citadel, do you really think I'd let Zavier get married without me being here? If you mean at your rooms, I'm here to escort you to the ceremony. Usually, a woman's mother would do it, but, well..."

Alexia's chest ached. She had no idea her mother would've been the one to do such a thing. Did Yvonne even know she was getting married today? Forcing a smile, she stepped forward and linked arms with the red-haired queen. "Then I suppose we'd better get going. I know Zavier's patience has limits."

Calla's laughter made her smile more real, steadier, and the two proceeded through the halls together. When they entered the main hall, they turned toward a set of tall, ornate doors that Alexia had never been through, which turned out to lead to the throne room. Its vaulted ceilings, gleaming black stone columns, and patterned glass windows gave the room a sense of majesty that was only heightened by the pair of thrones on the dais at the far end.

She was surprised to see there were two, then realized Zavier must have had one made for her after their arrival on Ironhold. One of the two chairs was large and commanding, made of dark wood, with thick legs and a high back, topped by what looked to be some sort of dark-feathered wings holding a nine-pointed star. The other chair was smaller, daintier, carved of pale grey wood and surmounted with woven vines cupping another nine-pointed star. They were opposite, but united, clearly a pair. And sitting on the cushion of the smaller one, was her circlet.

Standing at the foot of the dais, she saw Zavier, wearing his crown and looking stately in rich blue attire, and a seemingly ancient man in ornate red robes. Off to one side, she saw two men, both older than Zavier, but with the same drastically sharp facial features that there could be no mistaking who they were. His brothers. One had golden hair and blue eyes, the other dark brown hair and green eyes, with a thick goatee. She didn't know which one was Owen, and which was Kade, but had no doubt she'd be finding out once this was all over.

As they came through the doors and proceeded up the intricately tiled walkway that ran through the center of the throne room, all eyes turned toward the two women. She had no idea what the reactions of the other two men were, because all she saw was Zavier looking at her with an expression of complete and utter awe. It was enough to wash away any reservations she might have had, and by the time Calla put her hand in his, she was smiling.

She loved him. That made all the ruckus and anxiety worth it.

She was beautiful.

It was the only thing Zavier could think, from the first moment a shaft of Ironhold's weak sunlight slanted through one of the windows and lit upon her. He'd told the seamstress to make something that suited Alexia after their first meeting, and he made a mental note to give the woman a pay raise. She'd met the criteria, and then some. His bride was radiant, her hair twisted back and held in place with ornamental pins that had little silver crystals. The only thing she was missing was her circlet, but he had every intention of getting that on her gleaming silver mane as soon as she was his wife.

Their eyes remained locked together when Calla put Alexia's hand in his, and she came to stand before him on the lowest level of the dais. The holo-transmitters mounted in the ceiling flickered to life, displaying rows of people, who were all gathered on other worlds to watch this joining. He only barely noticed the motion in his peripheral vision, but Alexia jumped slightly and glanced that way, then looked back at him with wide eyes.

"Is this being beamed out to the whole galaxy?"

Her hissed whisper had a smile spreading across his face, and he chuckled as he gently squeezed her fingers and murmured a reply. "I've been a bachelor for my whole life, and you're the mysterious daughter of the Verdant Empress no one has seen before. You really think people wouldn't want to see this?"

His amusement seemed to settle her a little, and she afforded the holographic crowd one more sidelong look, before the officiant in his robes cleared his throat. This arrested her attention and had both the princess and the iron king looking at the aged man in his robes.

"Today, we stand witness to the union of Iron King Zavier of Ironhold and Imperial Princess Alexia of Greenwell. The god-king has given his blessing upon this joining, and I understand both parties come into this marriage of their own free will. Do you both so avow?"

He looked at Zavier, who nodded once, firmly, as he murmured an *'I do'*, before he turned his attention on Alexia.

She licked her lips, then spoke in a firm voice. "I do."

Zavier hadn't even been aware he was tense until those words left her lips. Thank the gods, she hadn't changed her mind. His shoulders sagged slightly in relief, which made a small smile appear on her face, and he flashed her a playful smirk. The officiant was saying something he was barely listening to, until the old man produced a large and ornate data slate.

"To seal your union, you must both sign the marriage contract."

He knew what it said. He'd been working on it since shortly after their arrival and over the past few days, had been consulting Alexia for her thoughts. It wasn't the normal way of doing things. Typically, the parents of the two parties would form the contract, with no input from their children. But Zavier's parents were dead, and Yvonne obviously wasn't going to consent, let alone be involved. But he liked it better this way. This made things a truly equal partnership, not just two people being told what to do, which was why he didn't hesitate to pick up the digi-pen and sign his name. After handing it to Alexia and allowing her to do the same, they both pressed their thumbs to the indicated spaces beside their signatures, which officially sealed the contract. The officiant withdrew the slate and handed it to Calla, then held his hands in the air.

"I present to you all, Iron King Zavier of Ironhold and his wife, Imperial Princess Alexia of Ironhold."

There was polite applause from the holographic audience, and the officiant stepped aside, shuffling down the dais.

In his stead, Owen ascended the few steps to where Alexia's circlet sat and carefully lifted it. Moving to stand where the officiant had been, he held up the crown and spoke in a commanding voice that had Zavier rolling his eyes. "I, God-King Owen and eldest brother of Iron King Zavier, say that she should be a princess no longer. It is my belief that she should be equal to her husband on all grounds and be Iron Queen of Ironhold. What say you, brother?"

Resisting the urge to glare at his brother, Zavier took the circlet and held it between himself and Alexia, who was looking a little pale and overwhelmed. Better to get this over with quickly, then. "Alexia, do you swear to rule with an open mind, a firm hand, and a pure heart?"

"I swear it." Despite the fact that she looked ready to fall over, her voice was strong, and Zavier smiled at her as he gently placed the circlet on her head.

It suited her perfectly, just as he'd thought it would. Taking her hand, they turned to face the assemblage together, and his heart swelled with pride when the image of the masses fell into bows and curtsies. Then, blessedly, the holo-transmitters shut off, and he exhaled a sharp sigh.

"Thank the gods that's over with." Pulling her closer, he wrapped his arms around her waist and ducked his head, sealing his lips to hers with passion. He didn't even care when Owen sounded like he was choking, and Calla and Kade laughed. He'd never thought to have a wife, a queen, and now he *did*, and she was beautiful, and kind, and smart, and—

Oh, dear sweet gods, he was in love with her.

It had all happened so fast, and Alexia was only dimly aware of things that weren't Zavier. She gave her answers by rote, not just because they were expected of her, but because she wanted to get everything over with. She hated all this pomp and circumstance, and she was starving. She'd skipped lunch and there was supposed to be a party after this, so she just wanted to eat. Until, that was, Zavier pulled her in and kissed her. She leaned into him, savoring the press of his lips against hers. Well, maybe the food could wait...

"Good grief, Zavier, stop kissing the girl and let us see her."

Oh, right. There were other people there. Her cheeks were hot with embarrassment as she pulled away, turning a sheepish smile on her husband—*husband*, that was a word that would take some getting used to—before she shifted to face their trio of observers. The one she now knew as Owen was gaping at them, Calla at his side with a mischievously pleased expression, and Kade was grinning. The bearded king barked a laugh, tromping over to clap Zavier firmly on the shoulder, much to the iron king's obvious displeasure.

"Well, I'll be. Who knew Yvonne's daughter was so beautiful? How did you convince her to marry you, you grumpy sod?"

Her brows curved upward in surprise. She hadn't expected a king to act so... normal. He reminded her of the guards in her mother's keep. Well, if he was going to make jokes...

"He kidnapped me, claimed I'd be his queen without asking permission, then gradually showed me he's not a complete and utter beast, so I agreed."

Calla bit her lip to stifle a laugh. Kade's eyes widened. And Owen's mouth dropped open.

Zavier shot her a stunned glance, then looked back to his brothers and sister-in-law, before shrugging as a crooked smile appeared on his face. "It's the truth. Let's eat. I'm famished."

Gladly, Alexia tucked her hand into his arm, and the group progressed into the formal dining hall. They entered to a raucous cheer, which took her aback, until she realized every denizen of the Citadel was in the room to share in their joy. The fact warmed her heart. They were the family Zavier knew, so it made sense, but not every man would open his wedding feast to his servants. It just reinforced what she already knew—that he was a good man with a good heart.

Now she just had to make him fall in love with her.

The sun had barely begun to set when they sat down to eat, and much to his surprise, even with his brothers there, Zavier was having an excellent time. He attributed that largely to the woman at his side, who made their presence bearable. She had a deliciously sharp wit, which she used to verbally fence with both Owen and Kade, parrying their jabs and redirecting them expertly. This allowed him to converse mostly with Calla when he wasn't utterly enraptured by his bride. She was charming and had the most wonderful laugh, and he just wanted to sit there and marvel at her all night.

It was this hyperfocus on Alexia that allowed him to see when she attempted to hide a yawn in her glass of wine. Of course. She'd had a long day of preparing, and a glance at the chrono on the wall told him it was very late. Rising abruptly from his chair, he raised his hand in the air, and silence gradually rippled down from the high table where the royals sat.

"I thank you all for coming to celebrate my wedding. It brings me joy to see my family welcoming my queen without inhibitions. I hope you all continue to enjoy the feast, but it's time we retire for the evening." He offered his hand to Alexia, and her gratitude was obvious as she took it. He deftly ignored the suggestive whistles from his brother Kade, even if he was thoroughly charmed by the fetching blush on Alexia's face when she stood. Leading her out of the hall, they proceeded quietly through the Citadel until they reached the door to the royal treasury.

It slid open when Zavier pressed his hand to the security panel, and they ventured inside, proceeding past the rows of closed drawers and cabinets until they reached the spot where their crowns would rest. He carefully removed her circlet and laid it on the cushion there, then lifted his own off his head and placed it alongside. Touching a small drawer nearby, it slid open, revealing two dozen shallow divots in a bed of soft fabric. She looked confused, even as he started gently pulling the pins out of her hair and laying them in the drawer, so he answered her unspoken question in a soft voice. "These were my mother's. She would've liked you. It seemed only fitting that you should wear them today."

Her eyes softened, and she turned so that he could get to the pins in the back. This left them both facing a nearby mirror, a fact that didn't escape Zavier. Unable to help himself, he looked up. The sight of them both together like this was a striking one, what with her light coloring and vivid eyes and his own dark hair and nearly colorless irises. But what tantalized him at that moment was the graceful curve of her neck.

His lips found her skin, trailing kisses over that soft

expanse of creamy flesh, while his fingers dug gently through her hair, until he found the last few pins. Dropping them gently into the drawer, his hands settled on her hips, gliding up over the curve of her waist and stopping just beneath the swell of her breasts. She inhaled sharply, her head lolling back against his shoulder. The sight of her flushed cheeks and parted lips in the mirror was almost too much to bear. It took every ounce of willpower he had to lift his head and step back from her.

"Elea should be waiting to help you undress. Your rooms are through this door." He gestured in the direction of the door to his left, then proceeded quickly through the one to his right, leaving her alone in the room. He was in agony and knew that if he didn't get some relief soon, tomorrow, he was going to be the very beast that she'd said he wasn't. This called for a shower.

Zavier left her. Quite frankly, Alexia was stunned. How could he kiss her neck and touch her that way, and then just… walk out on her? At first, she felt hurt, wondering if she'd said or done something to displease him. But that was quickly replaced by anger. This was her wedding night, dammit, and she absolutely refused to sleep alone.

Stepping closer to the door he'd indicated, she called out without even looking into the room. She could explore this adjoining chamber tomorrow. Right now, she was a woman on a mission.

"Elea? Come get me out of this gown, please."

"Your Majesty? You don't mean to come into your rooms?" The girl's confused voice came closer as she hurried to the door and, after Alexia shot her a sharp glance, began hastily undoing the fastenings up the back of her gown.

"No. I don't. I'll see them tomorrow. In fact, take the night off. I don't plan on needing you until morning." She could positively feel the question radiating off her hand-maiden, but blessedly, Elea didn't say a word. Soon, she shed her gown and the undergarments beneath it, which she left crumpled on the floor. Striding determinedly across the treasure-filled room to the opposite door, she was pleased when it opened beneath her touch.

Zavier wasn't there. Her irritation grew, until she heard motion coming from another room nearby. Crossing to that door, when it slid open at her approach, she stopped cold. Well, she'd found Zavier. But he was mostly naked. And about to bathe, considering they were, apparently, in his bathroom. He whirled around when the door opened, his hands still gripping his unfastened trousers, and looked at her with wide eyes.

"Alexia? What are you doing in here? And why… You're naked."

That last bit sounded oddly strangled, a fact that filled her with a sort of malicious glee. Good. She wanted to knock him off his feet. Moving toward him, she was quite delighted by the fact that he couldn't seem to lift his eyes from her bare body and took advantage of his distraction to plant her hands against his chest and give him a shove.

"You left me alone on my wedding night. Clearly, you expected me to sleep somewhere other than in your arms. Which is utterly ridiculous, because how in the stars are you supposed to make love to me if we're in different beds?" She flung her arm in the general direction of the rooms that she assumed were hers, then propped her hands on her hips and glowered at him.

His jaw worked silently for a few moments, before he

finally managed to bring his eyes to hers. "I… you yawned. At the celebration. I thought you would… prefer to sleep, after such a long and trying day."

That was very considerate, she could admit. And his concern for her was deeply touching. It helped to soothe some of her frustration, but did nothing for the desire building in her body as she looked at him. He was charmingly disheveled, his hair in tousled disarray around his face and shoulders; his upper body was lightly muscled and scattered with scars, and there was a dusting of tiny black hairs around his navel that descended toward the opening of his trousers, as though beckoning her to see what was hidden beneath the fabric. She wanted to touch that line of hair and realized she could do that now. So she stepped toward him and reached out to lay her hand on his chest. "Zavier, that's very sweet, and I do appreciate the thought. But after nearly a week of barely being able to see you, I don't want to spend the night sleeping in another room. I want to spend it barely sleeping in your bed."

It was clear the words ignited a fire inside him, because his grey eyes began to darken. Forgetting himself, he released his grip on his trousers, which remained held up by his hips alone. She had a brief thought that she wished they'd fall, but her attention was wholly arrested by him placing his hands on her shoulders, which had her looking up into his eyes once more.

"Are you certain? Because if you change your mind mid-moment and ask me to stop, I can't promise I won't go mad and blow something up."

She stared at him, uncertain if he was serious or not, but when his lips quirked into a smirk, she grinned. A laugh tumbled out of her as she flung her arms around his neck, pulling her body up against his, and tilted her head back to look up into his eyes. "I'm absolutely certain. Now stop talking and kiss me, my king."

His hands dropped to her waist, then slid down over the small of her back to cup her posterior. She gasped when he pulled her pelvis against his, the feel of something hard prodding her stomach, making her heart begin to race. Just when she was wondering if he was going to ignore her demand, his lips crashed onto hers.

She was barely aware of what happened next, between the fierce passion of him conquering her mouth and the heat of his hands on her body. She only truly became cognizant of the fact that he'd shed his trousers when his hands glided along her thighs, cupping them and hauling her up so that her legs could encircle his waist. She distantly heard the door slide open behind her as he staggered toward it, then they were in a darker, warmer space.

Her back suddenly met with his bed as he tipped them over, and she landed with a sharp exhalation when he abruptly pulled away from her. She was only halfway on the bed, her legs dangling over the side, as she looked up at him with an expression of muddled curiosity. What was he doing? Her gaze drifted down his form and halted when it reached his length, which was proudly on display, jutting out from a nest of curly black hairs. Pushing herself upright, she reached out and trailed her fingertips over the line of hair that ran from his navel to his shaft, then wrapped her fingers gently around it.

He grunted, hips jerking toward her hand, and his hardness twitched against her palm. It was... hot, so hot, and felt like stone encased in the softest fabric. Fascinated by this part of him and enamored of his reactions to her touching it, she adjusted her grip and slid her hand from the base, toward the tip, her cheeks heating with arousal when he groaned and bucked into her touch once again.

"Stop." She froze as he ground out the word, her eyes flicking up to his face. Had she hurt him? He looked pained in the dim light that emanated from a small glow-lamp, but he also appeared very intent. She watched the knob in his throat move as he swallowed harshly, then explained in a rough voice, "Keep that up and I won't be good for anything at all. This is about you."

What did he mean, it was about her? Before she could ask, he was sinking to his knees, his hands falling to rest on her thighs, then sliding down beneath them. He grasped the backs of her legs and pulled her closer to the edge of the bed, forcing her to press her hands to the mattress behind her, lest she fall over. Her eyes widened as he insinuated himself between her parted legs and began to trail kisses up the insides of her thighs, switching back and forth between them with measured precision.

She'd read about this in *Essays* but had thought it was just something the man made up. Surely, no one would ever put their mouth... His eyes met hers, then his lips pressed to her slit, and she lost the ability to think. All she could do was sit there and watch, her fingers curling into the coverlet, while she both felt and saw him tasting her. His lips parted, his tongue sweeping out to dip between her petals, and that was the point when she realized that her arms were threatening to give out.

That worked, because as she flopped onto her back, she discovered that she could touch him now. Her hands shot downward and settled on his head, fingers twining into his hair. He took that as the encouragement it was and began to act in earnest. She closed her eyes, arching her back and unconsciously rocking her hips against his mouth as he devoured her. There could be no other word for what he was doing. He'd spread her apart with his fingertips, and his tongue was delving, swirling, lapping, plunging into her opening then darting up to flick and circle her sensitive bud. It was unlike anything she'd ever imagined, not as satisfying as his fingers inside her had been that night, but utterly electric.

She felt the muscles deep in her belly beginning to twist and clench as he worked at her, a powerful climax speeding toward her and threatening to engulf her at any moment. She didn't know how long they remained like that, nothing filling the air but her own labored breaths and panting moans, but then he shifted. His thumb moved to press against her pearl and rub it vigorously, while his tongue thrust deep into her channel. The release crashed into her, her vision going white as she cried out in ecstasy, every nerve ending alight with absolute sensation.

When a semblance of coherency returned to her, she felt his arms cradling her form, holding her against his chest while they moved farther up the bed. He laid her down, her head on the pillows, then sat beside her, tugging the covers out from under both their bodies and drawing them upwards. He scooted closer, though oddly kept his hips away from her, his arm draping over her waist while he looked down at her. Wan though the light was, she could see the strain around his eyes and the worry within those steely depths.

"Are you all right?" His voice was gravelly, but that wasn't why she stared at him in disbelief.

No, she was wondering if he'd lost all his senses. Something she made obvious as she sputtered before answering. "*All right?* Zavier, I've never felt anything so good. But I know that's not what happens in the marriage bed between a man and a woman."

"Alexia…" His voice grew tight as he said her name, and her eyes narrowed. She could tell he was about to say something she didn't like. "I'm not sure you're ready for that."

"You agreed to treat me as your equal in our contract. You do *not* get to decide what I'm ready for." She pushed herself into a sitting position so quickly that he fell back, which was just fine by her. It got her a step closer to doing what she wanted, which was to shift onto her knees, sling one of her legs over his waist, and straddle him. His hands moved to grip her hips, though whether to move her off him or not, she didn't know. She purposely moved herself backwards a bit, where she could feel the hot length of him pressing against her skin, and halted him on a sharp intake of breath.

"Alexia, please, you're killing me." His pleading tone was almost enough to make her stop. *Almost.* Instead, she rose up slightly, just enough so that part of him was now protruding from the space between her thighs. Looking down at it, she placed one hand on his stomach to balance herself and grasped his hardness with the other, making him wheeze.

She knew the basics of what was supposed to happen. Theory, it turned out, somewhat fell apart in the face of practice. It took her several long moments to figure out the angle, how to hold him without hurting him but also guide him to her entrance, how to urge the bulbous tip past her swollen petals and into where she wanted him. But finally, blessedly, it all came together, and he slipped into her. It felt… different. Not bad, not good. And with every gentle rolling motion of her hips, making him slide farther inside her, it felt better and better. Biting her lower lip, she looked up to see his eyes clenched tightly shut, an expression of utmost focus on his face.

Then she could go no farther. She felt… filled. Complete. As though she'd spent her whole life waiting for the moment he was hilted within her. Gasping a shuddering breath, she rocked her hips against his and moaned when he jerked up against her. Then he was shifting, his eyes open as he sat up, and his hands once again moved downward to cup her backside. His lips captured hers, tongue sweeping into her mouth, as he began to move her. Her stiff peaks rubbed against his chest, sending pleasant jolts of feeling through her body, down to where they were joined. He was struggling to thrust into her, bringing her down firmly upon his length as soft, keening whimpers left his throat.

A piteous growl escaped him as she felt him pulse inside her with a few final, firm motions of his pelvis against hers. He broke the kiss to bury his face into her neck, before they were suddenly toppling down into the bed, him pulling her along so she ended up sprawled out on top of him. She felt tense, on edge, knew what had just happened, and what *hadn't*. But she wasn't going to say anything. Instead, she propped herself up slightly so she could see his face, a smile slowly spreading across her lips. She was hot, sticky with sweat, and could feel something trickling down the inside of her thigh.

She'd never felt so wonderful.

It was a massive understatement to say that Zavier was humiliated. He got a few thrusts in, and he spent himself so quickly, it was like he'd never been with a woman before. Which meant he was really confused about why she looked so bloody happy. He'd made her climax once, of course, but wasn't she feeling unfulfilled now? It made no sense why she was lying there, smiling at him like she was the happiest woman in the galaxy.

"Alexia?"

"Hmm?" She sounded just as joyful as she looked, which only increased his confusion. His brow furrowed as he reached up and caressed her cheek, twirling his fingers into her silky silver hair.

"Why are you so happy?" He watched as she processed his words, her smile taking on a vaguely bewildered cast. Which probably should've irritated him, but instead, he found it endearing.

"Why shouldn't I be? That was wonderful." He blinked, his hand trailing down to begin caressing her back. She shivered beneath the touch, like a pet enjoying the display of its owner's affection, and the urge to see how far the reaction went led him to slide his hand down to her backside, stroking the pleasantly plump curve.

"But you weren't satisfied." Although considering how he was being affected by just fondling her soft flesh, he suspected it wouldn't be long before he could rectify that problem. He could already feel himself stirring and twitching. Something that she was all too aware of, judging by the way her cheeks flushed and her smile took on a decidedly wicked edge.

"No, but that's all right. It was more about the intimacy. Although... if you feel up to showing me how it can be?"

That was all the urging he needed, and Alexia's laughter rang in the room as he flipped her over onto her back and stretched out above her. They had a *very* long night ahead of them.

"Owen, we need to talk about this situation." The god-king looked up from the data slate in his hands as his wife spoke, their blue eyes locking across the room. The Ebon Citadel wasn't as luxurious as his own palace-cum-space station, but it was a pleasant enough spot for a night. Especially since Zavier was so fond of those archaic fireplaces. The flickering light caught in Calla's hair, shooting strands of gold and copper through the red waves and illuminating her curvaceous body through the thin blue fabric of her negligee. Owen felt a stirring of desire as he set the data slate aside and reached out for his wife. They'd been together for nearly twenty years, had six children to show for it, and they'd both had many lovers. But they always came back to each other, because something more lasting than lust bound them: Love of power.

"What situation might that be, my dear?" She rolled her eyes but took his hand anyway, allowing him to pull her into the bed beside him. His lips immediately began roving over the bare skin of her neck and shoulder, sampling her with playful bites and kisses. He was only halfway listening, which he knew she'd make him pay for later, but that was future Owen's problem.

"The situation with the newlyweds and Yvonne. What are we going to do if she doesn't lift this ridiculous embargo? I don't want to force Alexia back to Greenwell. It would break her heart, and even worse, Zavier's."

Owen grunted. Nothing killed his libido quite like hearing his brother's name, so he sighed and left off trying to tempt his wife so he could focus on what she was saying. Her concerned expression made him frown. He'd never liked how friendly Calla and Zavier were, but he couldn't deny he was concerned, too.

"What do you mean, it would break his heart?" The way she stared at him made his spine stiffen. She had that look that said he was being an idiot. He did *not* like that expression, and he glowered at her, until she huffed an exasperated sigh.

"He's clearly in love with the girl, and she loves him in return. She hasn't said as much, but it's plain as day to anyone who's watching."

That had managed to escape him, and being smacked in the face with the statement made him think back to the ceremony. It was true, his youngest brother had looked particularly enamored of the imperial princess, and their courtship had been very swift… Good gods, could it be true? Had Zavier fallen for the heretofore unseen heir of the verdant empress? If that was the case, then he was obligated, not just as the god-king, but as a brother, to try to mediate. Somehow.

"We'll give it a few months. Let them enjoy their happiness, while we try to persuade Yvonne to open her borders again. If she refuses, and things start to become dire… we'll inform them of what's happening and proceed from there."

The decision seemed to please Calla, who draped herself across him and captured his lips, which thoroughly drove away all thoughts of the newlyweds and the problem of Greenwell.

Chapter 11

The sensation of lips on her skin awakened her, and Alexia moaned softly as she indulged in a full-body stretch. It took her a few moments to remember where she was, and the knowledge that it was Zavier's mouth on her shoulder made her smile. She was deliciously sore in places she'd never thought of, and she was quite satisfied knowing how that had happened. Rolling onto her back, she turned her head and opened her eyes to the sight of her husband propped on one arm, gazing at her with a look she couldn't quite unravel in his eyes.

"Good morning. How are you feeling?" His voice was thick with sleep, or perhaps it was desire. His hand came to rest on her stomach beneath the sheet, stroking upward but stopping just beneath her breasts.

"Sore, in all the best ways. I don't think I've ever slept so soundly." She cupped his cheek, guiding him down so that their lips could meet. He kissed her hungrily, something she gladly reciprocated, and began giggling when he slid his hand up to her breast. Her laughter became breathless as he teased her nipple to hardness with his thumb, and she broke the kiss so she could murmur against his mouth. "Do we have time for that? Shouldn't we go to breakfast with your brothers and Calla?"

"We got married yesterday. It would be positively scandalous if we came out before lunch." He nibbled on her lower lip, his attention wandering down the slender column of her neck, to which she eagerly tilted her head back. When he caught her nipple between his teeth, she gasped, twisting her fingers into his hair.

"Well, we wouldn't want to cause a stir, would we? Carry on." She glanced down at him when she felt him smiling against her breast, and she shivered as his hand slid downward.

"As my queen commands."

To her delight, Zavier slid his hand between her legs, gently stroking her folds. She murmured a sound of pleasure and rolled her hips against his fingers, increasing the pressure and inspiring a tremble of delight in her body. She was already growing slick with need and parted her legs gladly to welcome his touch, her back arching as he promptly slid two fingers into her eager body. When his thumb pressed to her bud and began to massage it firmly, she moaned, her depths clenching around the two digits that were pumping slowly in and out of her body, while he teased her nipple with his mouth.

But it wasn't enough.

"Stop." The commanding tone surprised Alexia herself, but apparently no more than Zavier, who froze and looked up at her with wide eyes. Feeling emboldened by his reaction, she acted swiftly, reaching down to grasp his wrist and pull his hand out from between her thighs. "On your back, peasant."

His eyes flew wide at the words, then darkened with

both desire and what was obviously a threat. Although he was clearly wondering just what she had up her currently nonexistent sleeve, he complied, shifting slowly until he was reclining on the bed, his head resting on the pillows. Alexia thought fast as she sat up and eased herself over on top of him, straddling his hips so that the hard, hot length of him was pressed up against her backside. It twitched, and he reached for her, but she caught his wrists again, arching an imperious brow at him.

"Did I say you could touch me? You dare to lay hands on your queen?" It was impulsive. Perhaps foolhardy. But the way his breath caught and the feeling of his hardness surging against her skin, made her feel certain she was doing something right at least. She watched him swallow thickly, then shake his head and speak in a guttural tone.

"No… Your Majesty."

"I thought not. Now. Hands above your head. And no touching unless I give you permission." She almost felt like someone else was talking through her. This was unlike anything she'd ever imagined before, but she couldn't seem to make herself stop. More importantly, as he moved his hands to cross them above his head, resting on the pillows, she realized she didn't want to. Her hands pressing to his chest, she began to caress his skin with aching slowness and rocked her hips back against his shaft, reveling in the look of nearly pained arousal on his face. Tempted as she was to take him inside her already, rubbing her aching opening against the hard ridges of his pelvic region was doing delightful things to her, and she shivered as pleasure spiraled through her body.

"Very good. You can listen after all. Perhaps I'll reward you for your obedience. Would you like that?" She purred the words at him, leaning down slightly so her hair spilled forward, forming a gossamer curtain around her upper body and brushing against his chest and shoulders. She could feel him quiver beneath her, see his fingers twitch with the urge to grab her and fulfill both their needs. Then, suddenly, the world tilted and spun, and she found herself on her stomach, laid out across his thighs. His expression was a ferocious one, intent and almost animalistic, as he grasped her wrists in one strong hand and held them easily in place, his other hand moving to caress her bare backside.

Try as she might, she couldn't pull free, and her eyes widened as he leaned down to growl in her ear, "You may be queen, but I am and will always be your lord and king, Alexia. Don't forget that."

She gasped as his hand lifted away from her pale skin, then came swooping back down to crack loudly against her posterior. A squeal escaped her as pain radiated down to her upper thighs, but a pleasant and surprising tingling sprang to life between them. Unable to help herself, she squirmed, and although she was unprepared for the second smack, that tingle became a delicious ache that drew a whimper from her throat. The third blow turned the ache to an undeniably powerful pulse of desire, and there was no stopping the moan that fell from her parted lips.

"I think you've learned your lesson, wouldn't you say?" She looked up at him, flushed and dazed with desire, and nodded. He seemed to accept her acquiescence, and with a few movements that left her shocked by his strength, he hauled her up onto the bed, stretching her clasped wrists above her head and pinning them in place. When he ducked his head, he dragged his teeth harshly over her neck and down to her breast, where he once again pulled her nipple into his mouth. He teased it for several long moments as he settled himself between her willingly parted legs, his free hand grasping his length and guiding it to her wet opening. Without warning, he pressed into her in one firm motion, then began to thrust at an almost brutal speed, before his teeth bit down on that pebbled tip. The shock of combined pleasure and pain tightened deep within her body, her hips bucking almost mindlessly up against his, and she cried out as perfection swept through her. She distantly felt herself tightening around him in rhythmic spasms, moving her hips toward his as hard as she could as she rode out her climax, and was vaguely aware of heat blooming within her depths as he groaned heavily against her skin.

When a semblance of sanity returned, she gasped for breath, looking down at him with a dazed expression that was reflected back at her. Then she offered a small, unsteady smile, and huffed a soft laugh. "I think I can get used to this queen thing."

True to his word, it was well into the afternoon before they finally emerged, just in time to find the other royals preparing to board their respective shuttles and depart. Zavier shared a brief farewell with Calla, then left the two queens to converse while he spoke with his brothers. To her surprise, Calla embraced her readily, but Alexia returned the hug with warmth, and both were smiling as they parted.

"Being a queen suits you, my dear. Zavier can be a hard man to live with, but I suspect you'll have no trouble keeping him in line. He's already twisted around your little finger."

Alexia flushed at the words, causing Calla to laugh. "I don't know what I'm doing as a queen, but I have such high hopes for Ironhold. It can be a paradise just like

Greenwell, I know it. It may always be a prison planet, but the prisoners won't have to choose between dying in the mines or serving in the Citadel if I can make this work."

Something in Calla's manner shifted, although she couldn't tell what it was. But the older woman gripped her hands firmly, and her smile seemed a bit drawn around the edges. "With your determination and creativity, and Zavier's resources, I'm sure you can do anything you put your mind to. I've found a planet with plant life like you wanted and have arranged for a trade to get seeds, but it will take some time. If you need me, I'm just a holo-comm away."

"Thank you, Calla. Travel safely." They parted ways, with Calla joining Owen as they climbed into their shuttle. She had the feeling the older queen had wanted to say something but had held back. And that worried her, far more than she wanted to admit.

"That girl is a spitfire, and she's going to give you trouble. I look forward to hearing about it soon." Kade laughed uproariously at the glare Zavier shot at him, then ambled toward his shuttle. This left the god-king and the iron king alone, sharing an uncomfortable silence, before Owen finally cleared his throat and spoke in a subdued tone.

"I wish I could congratulate you on your nuptials, brother, but I'm afraid your happiness is going to be short-lived."

Zavier narrowed his eyes at his eldest brother, wondering if that was a threat, or a warning. They shared a bond of hatred for their deceased father and little else, but surely, Owen wouldn't turn against his own brother, would he?

"What is that supposed to mean?"

"It means your actions are going to have consequences, Zavier. I just hope you're prepared for them. You know Yvonne isn't going to simply let this stand."

Unable to find words, let alone speak them around the lump of dread in his throat, Zavier nodded briskly and briefly clasped hands with Owen. Once they parted and Owen joined his wife in the shuttle, he moved to Alexia's side, where they stood watching the pair of vessels depart, returning to the flagships in orbit. He turned to his wife when the shuttles were no more than distant specks against the pale sky and waited for her to face him.

"You know, it's customary for newlywed couples, and particularly royal ones, to spend a couple of weeks in an exotic locale, taking their ease and enjoying each other." She arched a brow at him, her lips curving into a smile that made his groin tighten with need.

"I don't think I could take being idle for that long, and I suspect you can't, either. Instead, I propose we spend as much time in bed as possible for the next month."

He blinked. Well, that was forward of her. And it was definitely a compromise he could get behind. Something he made obvious as he grasped her waist and hauled her against him, dipping his head to growl against her mouth.

"Our bed isn't the only place I mean to have you."

The promise clearly affected her, as she shivered in his arms before her own wrapped around his neck. Her eyes flashed with heat as she smiled and purred her reply, "It seems I have much to learn. We should start on that immediately... after we eat. I'm famished."

It became commonplace over the course of the next few weeks for the servants of the Ebon Citadel to check any room before they entered it fully. But none of them minded much at all. They were all delighted to see their iron king, who had been so lonely and dour, happy at last, even if it did take several instances of staff walking in on illicit moments between Zavier and Alexia for them to learn this caution and implement ways to avoid repeat performances.

But it wasn't all sensual rendezvous for the pair. Zavier still had a planet to run, and Alexia was fitting into her new role as queen more easily than she anticipated. That meant many hours spent with a data slate in her hands. Two weeks after their wedding, she barged into Zavier's study and stalked over in front of his desk, planting her hands on her hips. The iron king looked up at her with an impassive expression, and she ignored the amused sparkle in his eyes.

"Is something the matter, Alexia?"

"I want an office." She proclaimed the words firmly and felt a surge of vaguely malicious satisfaction when he seemed utterly blindsided by the request.

"An... office. I'll admit, that's not what I was expecting." He set down his pen and leaned back in his chair, crossing his arms while he looked at her. It didn't take long for his gaze to wander down over her body, and although she felt a thrill of excitement, she tamped it down. That could wait. This was important! To her, at least. "Just out of curiosity, why do you want an office?"

"If I'm going to be managing the affairs of the Citadel and taking a hands-on role in the implementation of the terraforming and the harvesting of the crops, I need some place quiet of my own to work." She could see him mulling it over and knew that she had good points, so she felt certain he'd agree. But that didn't prepare her for what he said next.

"Is there a reason why you wouldn't want a desk of your own here? In the study?"

It wasn't what she'd expected, and she took a moment to ponder it. While sharing space with him would be nice, this room was too dark and masculine for her to feel comfortable. That wasn't what made her stifle a laugh as she replied, "You know as well as I do that we'd get too distracted by each other, and as much fun as that would be, we have important work to do. Besides, I want somewhere a little brighter, that I can decorate to my own tastes."

She knew the moment his eyes flashed and began to darken that she'd said the wrong thing. Or, perhaps, just the *right* thing, depending on how one looked at it. Stepping back, she watched him as he stood and moved around the desk, slipping in between her and the sofa. Very quickly, she found herself pinned back against the sturdy wooden item, with Zavier's arms to either side of her body.

"Hmm. You make an excellent point. If you were in here, I'd be more interested in bending you over this desk than working." His warm breath washed across her pulse point, and she inhaled sharply as she shivered. *Oh.* Licking her lips, she couldn't seem to find words, which he took to his advantage, reaching down to ruck up her skirts as he murmured against her neck. "Pick a room. It's yours to do with as you will."

"Thank you. I should... go do that now..." She moaned when his fingers dipped between her thighs, and her head tilted back, his voice growling in her ear, "You're not going anywhere just yet, wife."

"Oh? And why is that?" She knew exactly why, as his wicked hands were already beneath her skirts and in the process of pulling down her undergarments. She eased up on to the edge of his desk as he pulled them off and tossed them aside, vaguely noting that the scrap of silky fabric and lace ended up coming to rest on the arm of the sofa. She arched a brow at him, refusing to part her legs as he attempted to step between them. "Just what do you think you're doing?"

"I believe I'm seducing my wife. Is it working?" His lips brushed over her ear, and she could feel him smirking as she shuddered, the curve of his lips against her skin unde-niable. Feeling mischievous, she tilted her head, a thoughtful expression forming on her face. "Hm, I'm not certain. Perhaps you should try a little lower."

He drew back, looking at her with eyes that flashed dangerously and slid his hands up over her thighs, hips, and waist, until he was grasping the neckline of her gown. This one wouldn't easily be pulled down, and she narrowed her eyes at him. He seemed to sense the threat, but also didn't appear to care as he yanked at the collar of her dress. She gasped as she heard the material ripping and then frowned. Mightily.

"I'll have another made just like it. You can't tease me and expect to walk away unscathed."

Before she could form a retort, Zavier grasped her waist and leaned down, his lips unerringly finding her nipple. Alexia moaned, tilting her head back as he began to suck on the stiff peak, his tongue twirling around it and causing it to harden more. She felt arousal between her thighs but refused to admit it, even just by squirming in an attempt to alleviate the pressure. He pulled away and moved to her other breast, giving its taut pink tip the same attention as the other, and she bit back a whimper of need. Looking down, she saw him watching her and forced herself to adopt an impassive expression. "Not quite what I had in mind. I was thinking... lower. You should kneel before your queen, you know."

His eyes flashed dangerously, and she suddenly found herself being whipped around and bent over the cushioned back of the sofa. Fabric rustled as he shoved her skirts up and out of the way, baring her backside to the warm air of the room.

"What do you think you're doing?" She looked over her shoulder at him, eyes wide, and was surprised to see him still clothed. He looked down at her heatedly, and the smirk that tilted on his lips was one that bespoke retribution for her behavior.

"Reminding you who your king is."

Before she could so much as utter a retort, his hand smacked down against the pale, smooth skin of her rump, hard enough to send a resounding crack through the room and sting more than a little. She yelped, instinctively trying to pull herself away from the act, and was rewarded with another strike to the other side of her posterior. This time, she felt that familiar warmth gathering between her legs and was unable to keep from moaning as her pleasure mounted. Where once she'd been trying to scramble away from him, she was now gripping the fabric of the couch and pushing back toward him, desperate to be filled. Uncertain whether or not Zavier was aware of what she wanted, she was relieved to hear the rasp of metal and shifting of material and groaned as she felt the hard length of him nudging between her thighs.

His hands gripped her hips tightly enough that Alexia felt certain there would be bruises later, something that didn't bother her in the slightest as he began to thrust into her with wild abandon. She arched her back and pressed back against him as much as she was able, reveling in the power of her husband and lover as he took her like an animal in heat. She felt her climax winding tighter and hotter, and she heard him growl her name as he slammed into her again. Satisfaction filled her at the response, and she cried out as pleasure crashed into her, her body tightening around his with every ripple of ecstasy that rolled over her. As it faded and sensibility returned, she turned her head to look over her shoulder at him, impishly delighted by the dazed gleam in his eyes and the way he was struggling for breath, just as she was.

"Well then. I believe I have an office to select and furnish."

The room she chose was near the garden, with wide windows that let in copious amounts of the admittedly weak Ironhold sunlight, and was further illuminated by glow-lamps perched on her desk as well as standing atop slender, fluted metal columns in two corners. A delicate desk of warm golden wood was matched by a chair with nano-gel cushions and several large bookcases that she was gradually filling with books. Some of which she'd pilfered from Zavier's study, much to his amusement, and others, she'd had Benji acquire for her.

Slightly more than two months after her wedding, Alexia had settled into her role and her office quite nicely and was looking over the most recent report sent to her by Zavier's science team. They hadn't yet identified the chemical that had caused the growth spree in the garden, nor had they deduced how she was able to create it, and she was growing frustrated, which meant she was exceptionally grateful for the interruption when Elea entered the room.

"Your Majesty, a ship from the Golden Cloud system is

in orbit, and we've received word a shuttle will be landing shortly."

Alexia looked up from the data slate with an excited expression. "From Golden Cloud? My seeds!" Before Elea could so much as speak, Alexia was on her feet and running out of the room, her skirts pulled up to prevent tripping. The shuttle had just touched down when she emerged from the Citadel, and she was delighted to see it was a sturdy and unornamented cargo shuttle, which meant it almost certainly contained the seeds Calla had promised. She watched the bay door open and saw the lev-sleds carrying sturdy stasis crates.

"I see your seeds are here."

She turned toward the sound of Zavier's voice, offering her husband a beaming grin. He smiled back, pressing a soft kiss to her brow as he came to a stop beside her, and both watched the crates being unloaded. Several of the Citadel's science team had emerged and were inspecting the cargo, making sure the seeds and bulbs were undamaged before ending the stasis and opening the crates. A few of each were extracted to be tested, and as per Alexia's instruction, some would be sent to her office, so she could test them in the field herself. She wanted to learn the limits of her odd ability.

"This is it, Zav. This is the start of making Ironhold fully self-sustaining. You'll be able to import species for meat and milk and build a thriving ecosystem." Her eagerness was obvious, and as the crates were moved into the Citadel, she faced him with sparkling eyes. Having a purpose, something to do other than simply existing, filled her with joy—almost as much as the warmth in her husband's grey eyes.

He cupped her cheek and leaned down to kiss her gently, his brow resting against hers as he murmured, "I'm so proud of you, Alexia. You've done something truly amazing."

"I haven't even done anything yet. You can be proud of me when the first crop starts sprouting." She grinned up at him, pressing a playful kiss to the tip of his nose, then laced her fingers with his. She had confidence that her venture would succeed, but his belief meant everything to her, even if she failed.

It was time. The science team had verified the seeds were unaltered and prime for planting. They were entering the calm season, when the powerful storms of Ironhold were dormant, and the days were gradually becoming longer. The morning after a heavy rain had fallen was the day Alexia chose to conduct her test. With Zavier at her side, along with a handful of guards and a trio of scientists to record the experiment, they ventured into the open land just outside the Ebon Citadel. It was a clear area, near one of the planet's smaller lakes, with rich soil and not too many rocks. They wouldn't get better circumstances than this.

Kneeling in the rocky earth, she dug a few small furrows and planted her bounty. Seven different kinds of seeds and five of bulbs that Calla had found for her. She'd thoroughly researched the plants after Calla had located their planet of origin, and while she wondered at the quality compared to what she knew on Greenwell, she had to hope it would suffice. With five of each type of plant nestled in the earth, she took a deep breath and buried her fingers in the damp soil.

Closing her eyes, she thought back to that faded child-hood memory, past the disapproval of her mother, beyond the terror of having done something wrong. She thought of the power, the emotion, the desire to make the plant thrive. Something she couldn't describe swelled within her, a sensation akin to the aftermath of a mild electric shock, the tingling in her arms and hands that grew almost painfully intense in her fingers. Unaware of the fact that her eyes were vaguely luminescent when she opened them, she watched with awe as sixty green shoots emerged from the ground.

But they didn't stop there. The gathered company could only stare as grasses elongated, flowers bloomed, tiny saplings sprouted equally minuscule leaves, and the mist that perpetually covered Ironhold's surface was pushed away. Rather than feeling disoriented and weak, Alexia felt energized. She'd done it. Intentionally, this time. And the plants were flourishing! They continued to grow, surging upward even without her influence, until the grasses were waving in front of her face and the tiny trees were even with Zavier's knees.

"Alexia... This is amazing. If you can just seed a few fields..." Zavier's voice was muted with wonder. When he offered his hand, she took it and stood firmly, unable to take her eyes from the little miracle in front of them.

"If I can seed a few tracts of land like this, Ironhold will be completely green within a year."

"What else is on the agenda today, Grayson?" Owen shifted restlessly in his seat while looking at his steward. Things had been blessedly quiet since his brother's wedding, but he knew it wasn't going to last. Yvonne's self-imposed embargo had begun to affect the farthest reaches of his empire, but not enough for any real problems to arise just yet. He knew it was a brief peace that wasn't going to last, and he dreaded the moment he had to reach out to Zavier. Looking at his young steward, he noticed the man's brow crinkling, in what he could only assume was confusion.

"We have Minister Ian of Darkrook, a last minute addition to your schedule, before you have the imperial budgetary meeting."

Darkrook? It took Owen a moment to remember the planet, and then he recalled it was the only habitable planet in a small system at the farthest reaches of his empire. One of the first to willingly bow to his father's rule and to bend the knee to him when he deposed the conqueror. It was barely a blip in the imperial codex, and he couldn't even remember what its exports were.

"Remind me what Darkrook is all about, and then let the minister enter."

Grayson tapped on the screen of his data slate, then projected an image of the planet on the audience chamber's holo-terminal. It was a dull, murky green-brown, splotched with blackish areas that he thought might be marshland.

He studied it as Grayson spoke, rubbing his chin thoughtfully. "Darkrook is the home planet of the butter frog, which is considered a delicacy in many parts of the galaxy." Anticipating Owen's curiosity, Grayson brought up an image of the strange, tentacled amphibian alongside the display of Darkrook, and the god-king remembered them.

The tentacles were a known aphrodisiac, and the creature's flesh was particularly delicious when cooked properly. With a sinking feeling, he nodded, indicating Grayson could admit the minister.

Into the gold and blue of the audience chamber, shuffled a wrinkled man with webbed fingers and a ridiculously tall green hat, wearing threadbare robes of the same color. That was all Owen really noticed about him, because as soon as the minister bowed and opened his mouth, the god-king knew his time of peace was over.

"Your Majesty, please forgive this impromptu appearance, but Darkrook desperately needs your help. My people are starving. We do not eat the butter frog, we breed and sell them and subsist upon the foods imported to us from other planets in exchange. Our ships have been turned back from Greenwell, the main source of our trade, and the farmers are rioting in the cities. Why has the verdant empress closed her borders?"

Zavier rose from his desk chair and loosened the buttons of his high collar in eager anticipation. He had elected to work through dinner in order to join Alexia in bed at an earlier time, and he was quite ready to see his wife. Before he could step away, however, the holo-comm on his desk blinked to life, displaying the communication code of the god-king. Attempting, and largely failing, to suppress his irritation, he dropped back into his chair and activated the comm with a fierce grimace. "This had better be important, Owen. I've got plans and you're delaying them."

"Bedding your wife can wait, Zavier. I was hoping to resolve this situation on my own and let your wedded bliss last longer, but things have reached an untenable point."

That was enough to make Zavier pause and truly take in his oldest brother's appearance. Normally immaculate, Owen was visibly worn and haggard, and he knew that something was genuinely wrong. He also had a feeling he knew what it was about. Flattening his hands on the top of his desk, he inhaled deeply before replying. "It's Yvonne, isn't it? What has that harpy done?"

"She has refused all trade and is turning ships away from Greenwell with threats of deadly force. The farthest reaches of the empire are feeling the effects, and riots are occurring in increasing numbers." Owen sighed, raking his hand back through his already tousled golden hair, and gave Zavier a sympathetic look. Even before he spoke, the iron king knew he was going to deny whatever his brother had to say. "She's refusing to open her borders until Alexia is returned to her."

"No." The word left his mouth immediately, and he was amazed at how calm he sounded, considering that his heart was thundering in his chest. He couldn't stand the thought of letting Alexia go, not now. Not after everything they'd accomplished, everything they'd shared. Not after he'd fallen in love with her. The taste of bile was strong in his mouth as he stared coldly at his brother's holographic image. "She doesn't want to go back to Greenwell, and I won't make her."

"You need to tell her about this, Zavier. I don't know your wife, but Calla said she has a tender heart, and she won't like hearing that people are starving because of her. She might agree to speak to Yvonne, or go back of her own will—"

"This is not up for discussion, Owen. I'll handle my queen and my planet as I see fit. If there's nothing else?" His tone made it clear that he wouldn't brook any further discussion on this front, and Owen sighed.

"Do something about this before I'm forced to take action of my own."

Before he could respond, the holo-comm went dark. Zavier was left staring at the dark wood of his desk as his stomach churned. He couldn't let her go, but he knew

Owen was as good as his word when it came to the health and happiness of his empire, and he would be forced to step in and make Zavier give up his wife if the situation persisted.

What was he going to do?

Alexia turned, when she heard the door slide open, and smiled at the sight of her husband. But that smile faded swiftly at the sight of Zavier almost running toward her. She rose from her seat on the edge of the bed, alarm filling her heart. Had something happened? Was he all right?

"Zavier? What's—" Before she could fully form the question, his arms were around her, then his lips were on hers. There was an almost desperate need in his kiss that she'd never felt before, and while she wanted to question what had him in such a state, she was unable to break the kiss long enough to breathe, let alone speak. His hands were on her body, tugging the straps of her nightdress down and pushing the fabric over her hips, to pool at her feet. She could feel his need pressing into the soft flesh of her lower belly, which drove all thoughts of discussion out of her head.

Between their combined efforts, he was just as bare as she within the span of heartbeats. His hands embedded in her hair as he leaned into her, until they both went tumbling back onto the bed behind her. His large body covered hers, her legs instinctively parting to welcome him into the cradle of her thighs. Then one of his hands crept downward, his fingers finding her heat. The expert motions of those long, thin digits drew a moan from her mouth, her hips bucking eagerly against his touch as tendrils of pleasure began to spiral upward and form into a pulsing knot in her pelvis.

Then his hand was gone, and instead, the head of his length was pressing between her folds. She bit his lip with a breathless murmur of desire as he pushed farther into her, until his pelvis was flush with hers. Normally, he waited for her to adjust to the penetration, but this time, he began to thrust immediately. There was a fervor to his motions that she'd never witnessed before, and it was enthralling. She felt herself scrambling quickly toward her peak as his thrusts came harder and faster, her nails dragging across his back. His hand fumbled its way back between their forms and found her nub, beginning to stroke it firmly with his thumb, and she came unraveled with a cry.

She returned to a shade of coherency shortly afterward, to find his face hidden against her neck and his body lying flush along the length of hers. Bewildered by this, she said not a word and only wrapped her arms around him. Something was wrong, but she didn't even begin to know how to broach the subject.

She would just have to wait until the moment felt right.

Chapter 12

Zavier knew that his unusually frenzied display had concerned his wife, but she didn't seem inclined to pursue discussion of the matter, which was concerning in and of itself, but for the time being, he was going to consider it a small blessing. He didn't know how to tell her what Owen had revealed and was resolved not to do so until he had no other option. Lying to her, even just by omission, felt wrong. It didn't feel as wrong as the idea of losing her, which meant that when he stepped into her office and found it empty, he felt a brief surge of terror. It was just before lunch, and they usually shared their meals together unless one or both were particularly busy, so where was she?

After stopping by her rooms and the garden with no results, he was on the verge of a full-blown panic attack. His steps were hurried as he proceeded toward the Citadel's security level, intent on haranguing someone until they found Alexia. But as he passed by the staircase that led to his science team's rooms, he heard the familiar tinkling of her laughter. A blend of curious and annoyed, he proceeded down the hallway until he located the room her voice was emanating from. The sight of his queen seated on a stool, one arm bared by a rolled-up sleeve and a bloodstained piece of gauze held to the interior curve of her elbow, made him see red.

"What is going on here?" The team of scientists froze and looked at their king with wide-eyed dismay, hearing the chill in his tone.

Alexia frowned at him, which made him feel much like a little boy throwing a tantrum. And that only made him angrier. "Maksim asked if I would be willing to give some samples, and I happily agreed. I'm curious to know how I can do… the things I do."

Her obviously uncomfortable tone eased a great deal of his ire, and he immediately crossed to where she sat, reaching out to take her hand. He guided it away from her arm so he could see the tiny pinprick on her skin where blood had been drawn. So that was it. Relief flooded his body as he exhaled a quiet sigh. "I see. My apologies. Would you like to remain here, or shall we adjourn for lunch?"

"Oh, I didn't even notice the time! I'll come back after we eat. Unless something interesting comes up, in which case, I expect you to send someone for me immediately." This last was offered as a gentle admonishment to Maksim as she slid off the stool, and Zavier stared as his usually dour lead scientist *blushed* beneath his queen's words.

"Of course, Your Majesty. Right away."

Their meal was spent suffering under the shroud of an awkward near-silence and a weighty sensation of tension. She kept opening her mouth to ask what was bothering him, but every time she tried, banalities emerged instead. When they finished eating, she was both surprised and pleased by his insistence on returning to the laboratory with her. They entered to the sight of Maksim surrounded by his colleagues, and they were all chattering quietly about something on the table in front of them.

"Maksim? Did you find something?" The group turned as one to face her, their expressions lit with excitement. Maksim was almost agitated with delight as he beckoned the royal pair over.

"I've never seen anything like it, Your Majesty. There's an unfamiliar organelle in your cells that none of us have ever witnessed before. It appears to create the chemical that we observed in the cells of the plants you affected, which stimulates their growth to amazing degrees."

Stunned by this information, Alexia leaned in to observe as a small drop of her blood was deposited on the leaves of a tiny potted seedling on the table. Almost immediately, it began to grow at rapid speeds and, soon, was filled with juicy white berries. She looked up at Zavier, who appeared both amazed and somehow dire.

"I have a feeling your mother has the answers to this. I'll reach out to my agents again and see if they've found anything."

All she could do was nod mutely. There could be no doubt that Yvonne had knowledge of what caused this unbelievable effect. The question was would the irate verdant empress be willing to share what she knew?

Zavier stepped out of the room, while Alexia was hunched over the various technological devices and chatting quietly with Maksim, and proceeded down the stairs to the security level. The door yielded at his approach, and he stepped into the dim room full of holo-comms, screens, and quietly conversing agents. Conversations that trickled into silence as they realized their king had arrived. One woman with a jagged scar across her cheek and mouth departed from the crowd and approached, her short grey hair bobbing as she nodded a brisk greeting.

"Your Majesty, what do you need?"

"Has Patrice reached the rendezvous yet?" The woman's eyes flashed, and she nodded once again, gesturing toward a nearby terminal. Glancing at it, he saw lines of communication and tracking of a cargo ship's progress on the screen.

"Yes, Your Majesty. She was picked up three hours ago and should arrive back at the Ebon Citadel before day's end."

A blend of relief and anxious eagerness suffused him as he inhaled deeply.

"Excellent. Debrief her upon arrival, see to it she's rested, and the queen and I will speak with her first thing in the morning."

Something was definitely going on. Zavier had again made love to her like it was the last time, and he'd been oddly quiet throughout breakfast. Just when she was about to begin pestering him for answers, the door slid open, and a face she found strangely familiar appeared. It took her a few moments to place it before she recognized one of her mother's personal maids, and her eyes flew wide with surprised alarm.

"Jenna? What are you doing here?" The slender woman grinned at her, then bobbed a quick curtsy.

"My name is actually Patrice, Your Majesty. I'm an agent in the service of the iron king, and I was sent to observe your mother many years ago. I've returned now at his command with information he requested."

The news was wholly unexpected and had Alexia staring, stunned, while the spy turned over a data slate and a small holo-display. Why had Zavier sent her to spy on Yvonne? What had she uncovered? And why hadn't she simply sent the information directly instead of coming all this way herself? She had so many questions running through her brain that she was only distantly aware of Zavier and Patrice talking, but she snapped out of her near-stupor when the woman departed. Without giving him a chance to say anything, she launched her questions at him in rapid succession. "Why are you spying on my mother? What did she find? Why did she come back, rather than send the information via holo-channel?"

Zavier gaped at her for a moment, then shook his head, scooping up the data slate and the holo-display in one hand as he rose from his chair. The other was offered to her, and Alexia took it without preamble, allowing him to lead her over to the nearby divan in her personal sitting room, where they usually ate in the mornings. They settled in together, and to her surprise, he laid the items in her lap.

"I have agents in every court, including those of both my brothers. I'm hardly a popular figure, after all, and it's important that I'm prepared for any potential hostilities, or can send information to deter outright conflict. As for why Patrice was here, Yvonne has cut off all communications and trade with Ironhold in protest of our marriage."

Dismay filled her, but she wasn't surprised. Her mother was a proud, stubborn woman, and no doubt took it as a horrible offense that her daughter had chosen a husband instead of her own mother. While she was briefly concerned about Ironhold being cut off from trade with Greenwell, she dismissed it. The planet would soon be self-sufficient in terms of feeding itself, so she knew there was no need to worry. Instead, she looked down at the items in her lap, then once again at her husband.

"And the information?"

Zavier shook his head.

"I haven't looked at it, but I assume it's about your parentage. That was what I had her looking into before her return."

Suddenly both anxious and excited, Alexia activated the data slate and began to read. Zavier moved closer and peered over her shoulder, reading the information it contained as she did. Though, apparently, he was a bit faster about it as she heard his sharp inhale of breath and, a few moments later, read something that struck her like a physical blow.

"Zav, I don't understand. What does this mean?"

He cleared his throat, took the data slate and holo-display from her lax grip, and stood.

"I think we should let Maksim look this over. Perhaps he can explain it better."

"This is astounding!"

Alexia looked up from the data slate as Maksim spoke, nearly bolting up from his seat at a nearby terminal within the laboratory. Zavier was quick to stand and intercept the plainly excited scientist, who was rushing in their direction. Both curious and oddly frightened by his reaction, she stood as well, clutching the data slate to her chest.

"Maksim, what has you so energized?" Zavier's voice was stern, commanding, but not harsh. It was enough to make Maksim calm immediately, though he fluttered a hand toward the data slate she held.

"It's the contents of that data slate, Your Majesties. It holds the secret of Queen Alexia's parentage, and also the knowledge of how she can cause flora to grow at such exponential rates."

Her heart twisted with anxiety. What did her father's identity have to do with the way she affected plant life? It didn't make any sense, but she wanted to know. Pulling the data slate away from her body, she held it out to Maksim, who took it eagerly.

"Please, Maksim, explain what you mean. And remember, we're not scientists, so try to keep it… simple." The scientist blushed at the admonition from his queen, then cleared his throat and swiped through the slate as he began to explain, apparently looking for something in particular.

"Well, you see, Your Majesties, Empress Yvonne is well known for disdaining men, which meant everyone was quite surprised when she announced she was going to have a child. I, myself, thought she'd simply made a drunken mistake, but in fact, your conception was anything but an accident. These files show that she'd had her scientists working on a very important project for most of her reign, one that would change the face of motherhood throughout the galaxy if it worked. And work it did, resulting in you, Your Majesty. They took one of the empress' ovum and manipulated it until it was capable of serving as the other half of the genetic material required to form a child.

"For reasons I can't explain, it seems there is something —some force, energy, whatever you want to call it—that is omnipresent on Greenwell. We've found minute traces of it in materials originating from the planet, and also in the residents, albeit usually in far lesser quantities. Whatever this is, during your creation, it built up in your cells and altered them. This is what allows you to affect flora the way you do. You are, in effect, a superior and slightly altered clone of your mother, Your Majesty. One with spectacular abilities that mimic the very life force of Greenwell itself, if on a smaller scale. As Greenwell is abundant in plant life, so, too, can you make plants grow wild, simply by your will."

For a moment, Alexia wished she hadn't told him to explain the matter simply. She'd understood everything he said, and the knowledge was enough to make her world turn on its head. It felt as though her legs went numb, and her fingertips grew cold, as she sank back down on to the chair she'd been occupying before, only dimly aware of Zavier's steadying arm around her shoulders. She was little more than a glorified clone, but one that had apparently been infused with some unknowable power by the very essence of her home world. How was that even possible? Had her mother known that would happen? What about the scientists who'd apparently created her? It was all too much to process, and she could feel all the blood draining from her face as she quietly addressed her husband.

"Zavier, I think I need to lie down."

At her subdued request, Zavier saw Alexia back to their conjoined rooms, where she retired to his bed and curled up beneath the dark sheet and blanket. She looked so small there, all pale skin and shining hair, and he felt a fierce urge to protect her. More than that, he wanted to raise an army and go straight to Greenwell, to confront Yvonne with what she'd done. How could she keep such a secret from her only child? Did the woman not understand, or care, how tender-hearted and emotional her daughter was?

He found himself pacing angrily in his study, trying to come up with an idea of what to do. Should he comfort his wife? Should he reach out to Yvonne and insist on answers? No, the witch was likely to demand her daughter back, and that would be enough to drive him to murder. As much as Alexia clearly struggled with her feelings for her oppressive and over-protective mother, he thought she would be quite displeased if he killed the verdant empress, so he should probably avoid that. Making another turn back toward the door leading to his bedroom, he froze at the sight of his wife standing there in nothing but a silken robe of jade green, watching him with a small smile on her lips.

"Please, don't let me stop you. You looked so serious, pacing around like that."

"Alexia." He knew he sounded absurdly concerned as he crossed to where she stood, his hands reaching out to her in a silent offer of comfort. She took it with an expression he could only describe as relief, her arms winding around his waist while his own enfolded her shoulders. She nuzzled her face against his chest and sighed, making his heart tighten. Gods, he loved this woman, and it killed him that she was struggling with this news. "Are you feeling well? I thought you were resting?"

"I was. I lay down about four hours ago. I'm not surprised you didn't notice… I could feel you seething through the door." Her teasing tone made him chuckle, and she glanced up at him with an impish smile. Unable to resist the impulse, he leaned down and captured her lips in a gentle kiss, smoothing his hands over her back. When he finally broke the kiss, it was just to murmur softly against her mouth. "I'm sorry if I kept you from sleeping. I was deep in thought."

"It's all right. I was in and out of sleep, doing some

thinking of my own." Her thoughtful tone made him draw back farther, looking at her inquisitively. She took a deep breath, nodded as if to confirm her decision to herself, and spoke. "I'm going to start drawing up plans tomorrow to begin the seeding, and once they're finalized, I want to begin immediately."

He froze, flooded with sudden terror. What if she harmed herself, forcing plant life to grow on Ironhold? Could she exert herself so much that she actually died? What if the energy that had changed her cells required reenergizing from Greenwell itself? Would she grow weak and sickly if she failed to get it? Swallowing the taste of fear that flooded his mouth, he nodded slowly. "I can tell you're certain, so I won't ask if you are. But I want you to promise me something."

"Only if I find it reasonable." She grinned up at him, and he smirked, relishing her squeal of surprise when he pinched her delightfully plush backside.

"Minx. If you start to feel weakened or otherwise negatively affected by your efforts, I want you to stop. That's the promise I ask of you." She was visibly confused by his question, although something warm flashed in her vivid green eyes. It made his breath catch. Could she possibly have feelings for him? No... they were friends, lovers, but the idea of her loving him in return was ludicrous.

Wasn't it? Suddenly, he wasn't so sure.

"Very well, Zavier. I promise."

There was a great deal of work to be done, terraforming a planet, even just to the minor degree she had planned for Ironhold. Soil composition, moisture levels, water sources, weather patterns, geography and topography... all had to be taken into consideration when deciding where to start, when, and which plants would be best for what region. As convenient as data slates were in terms of size and portability, Alexia realized that she worked better with something she could actually put her hands on. This was what found her small office practically papered with maps of all sizes, organized in a sort of ordered chaos that only she could comprehend. She was deeply focused on one against the wall beside her window, shading an area in muted orange as she muttered to herself, when she heard the door slide open.

Turning to see the source of the interruption, she grinned at the sight of Zavier. Setting down her pencil, she rounded the desk and eagerly went into her husband's arms, rising up on her toes so that she could greet him with a quick kiss. "This is a surprise. Did I work through lunch again?"

"Not at all. It's actually a little early. I was originally coming to see if I could seduce you before we eat, but now I'm curious enough to ask how things are going."

His hands cupped her posterior, and she rolled her eyes with a laugh. "I somehow doubt you're as uninterested in seducing me as you profess to be. As for how it's going, I'm nearly done. I estimate I'll have things properly laid out in two days, and I've had teams organizing the seeds by region and importance since I finished. I should be able to begin seeding efforts in the farthest reaches within three days."

"Hmm. Is that so?" He murmured the words thoughtfully, his keen gaze assessing her maps before dropping to her face. Something in his expression softened, making her stomach lurch pleasantly as he pulled her closer against him. "I worry about you, being out there all day without me."

"I'll be fine, Zavier. I'll have Kit to protect me, and Elea will be there to keep me well fed and hydrated. Not to mention, I saw you'd added some of your personal guard to mine just for these outings." Her tone was playfully chastising, enough so to have a tiny smile raising one corner of his lips. She smiled and pressed herself more fully against him, watching with growing excitement as his eyes darkened with desire. "Now, I do believe there was mention of seducing me. You should get on with that."

His lips crashed onto hers, and that was the last thing she said for quite a while.

Things were falling apart. Owen hated to admit that he was losing his grasp on his empire. Everything he'd worked for, the tyranny he'd done away with, the freedoms he'd given, were proving to be utterly pointless. Why? All because his brother had fallen in love, and one planet had cut itself off from the rest of the galaxy. There were other agricultural planets, of course, but Greenwell exported more than all of them combined. Those planets were struggling just to keep themselves afloat, let alone provide food for others.

And as though to laugh in this face of his struggle, Calla was pregnant again. Between his wife's temper and the state of the galaxy, the god-king was at his wit's end. That meant, when his holo-comm signaled with an incoming message from Kade, he groaned and dropped his face into his hands. What could possibly go wrong next? Sighing, he lowered his hands and swept the message forward, so he could meet his younger brother's holographic gaze. "This had better be good news, Kade, or I'm going to glass your planet."

"You can't glass a planet that's ninety-eight percent water, Owen, and you know it."

Normally, Kade was the jovial sort, a jarring contrast to Owen's vainglorious ego, and to Zavier's solemnity. To see him so serious now, sent a surge of dread through the god-king. If it worried Kade, he should *definitely* be panicking.

"Well, spit it out. What's going wrong now?"

"I've had to flee Oceanis. There was an uprising, and the populace stormed the palace. Ingrid and I got the children aboard the Aquarius, and we're on our way to Golden Cloud now."

Unable to believe his ears, Owen slumped back in his chair, staring aghast at his brother's image. The Azure Citadel, taken by the citizens? He couldn't imagine such a thing! But his brother wouldn't joke about a topic so serious. Rubbing at his mouth with one hand, he floundered for a response. "Why?"

"They're starving, Owen. Yvonne's embargo is slowly killing the galaxy. You know we can only harvest a certain amount of wildlife from Oceanis' oceans, or there will be a price to pay. When I couldn't bring in resources from outside, they rioted, it turned violent, and we were forced to run."

It was just what he'd expected, but it was happening far too quickly. Clearly, he'd underestimated just how swiftly things would make a turn for the worse without Greenwell's produce to feed the people of his empire. Inhaling sharply, he nodded. He had decisions to make. And soon. "I'll send ships and military personnel to retake your palace and restore order. Bring your family here, where you'll be safe. We'll come up with a solution together and make one last effort to get Yvonne to see sense. If that doesn't work…"

"Zavier will have to give up his wife." Kade's tone was just as somber as his face, and he knew why. Kade's marriage had been a love match from the start, which meant he had no doubt that the aquis king was thinking of how he would've felt in Zavier's position.

Owen sighed and nodded. "Let's pray it doesn't come to that. But I fear we'll have no other choice... and neither will he."

Chapter 13

It was extremely satisfying to watch the fruits of her labors coming to life, she mused. A field of tall grass was lightly rippling in front of her, with shoulder-high trees to her right and a small lake just past them. Much to her surprise, the exhaustion Zavier seemed so worried about was nonexistent. Instead, she felt wide awake, her body thrumming with energy, and the plants appeared to respond. The leaves on the trees grew more lush and shiny, almost as though in reaction to her high spirits. She smiled, turning away to start back toward the shuttle. Even though she wasn't tired, she could feel her stomach tightening in preparation to grumble and knew she needed to eat very soon.

When she saw Kit cupping Elea's cheek and kissing her softly, Alexia froze, her eyes widening in astonishment. Same sex partnerships were far from uncommon on Greenwell, but she'd had no indication that her loyal guardswoman and handmaiden were involved. She averted her gaze, not wanting to seem the voyeur, and leaned down to inspect the field of grass intently, if pointlessly. Once she saw Kit depart in her peripheral vision, she straightened and proceeded toward the shuttle once more. As she neared, she saw Elea's cheeks were flushed and her lips curved in a dreamy smile. Not so long ago, Alexia would've been puzzled by the expression, but now, she well understood the look of a woman in love. That wouldn't save Elea from being teased, though.

"How long have you and Kit been together?" She bit her lip to silence a laugh when Elea jumped and looked at her, the pink in her face darkening noticeably.

"Your Majesty! You ah… saw us, I take it?"

"Yes I did. I had no idea you were a couple." She patted Elea's shoulder and stepped past her into the shuttle, moving to dig out the small cryo-crate that held their lunch from among the crates full of seeds and bulbs. Elea joined her a moment later, helping to dig out the food and drink that had been provided for everyone.

"It's a… recent development. I thought Kit was involved with Benji, which, it turns out, is funny, because Benji and Maksim have, apparently, been a couple for many years."

Alexia considered that, then realized it made sense. The excitable scientist and the studious, mild-mannered steward were a good match for each other. Just like the stoic guardswoman and the gentle handmaiden. Smiling at that thought, she looked up at Elea. "You two make a very striking match. I hope you'll be happy together."

Elea blushed vividly beneath the compliment and well-wishes but said nothing and, instead, carried the cryo-crate outside to share with the others. Before long, everyone was gathered on a large swath of canvas that had been spread out to protect them from the rocky soil.

Sampling a fruit-filled pastry, Alexia scrolled through the data slate on her lap, halfway listening to the conversations around her, until Kit addressed her. "What's on the rest of the agenda for the day, Your Majesty?" The guardswoman peered upside-down at the data slate on her lap, turning her head to try to make sense of the image on the screen, which made Alexia chuckle.

Licking a bit of flaky crust from her lower lip, she tapped on the screen, enlarging the section of map on display. "Since this patch seems to have taken well, I want to move on to Haven and seed there next. Once the plots are sown, I'll instruct the residents on how to care for them, and then we can return to the Citadel. Let's finish our lunch first. Everyone deserves a break."

"Understood, Your Majesty." Kit nodded and returned to her meal, talking quietly with Elea. Alexia turned the data slate off and set it aside, looking up at the plot of plant life nearby.

Just that little spot of green seemed to change everything. How much longer would it be before all of Ironhold was so beautiful and verdant? Would her dream become real? Would she soon stand on plains of tall grasses, her body large with child, and Zavier at her side? Her hand fell to her belly, and she caressed the flat expanse with silent longing. She prayed it would be so.

The *Aquarius* and the *Apotheosis* dropped out of lightspeed just beyond sensor range of Greenwell, and Owen glanced at the captain. A deceptively young-looking man with sharp topaz colored eyes, Captain Erik nodded and began issuing commands in a steely voice.

"Weapons at the ready. All hands to battle stations. Shields at full strength. I want the full range of sensor sweeps, find out if there are any Greenwell ships out there, and try to discern their defenses. Comms, raise the *Aquarius*, and once the aquis king is on the holo, query the Verdant Palace."

There was a flurry of activity, and the lights on the bridge took on a faint red tinge as the ship readied itself for a potential assault. The holo-comm in the heart of the bridge flickered to life, displaying the image of Kade, with his coral crown on his brow. He nodded firmly, then glanced at Erik, who gestured to indicate the comm-line to Greenwell was open, although there had been no answer as of yet. Owen squared his shoulders and raised his chin, feeling the full weight of his opulent golden crown on his head and all the souls who trusted in that symbol.

"This is God-King Owen, of Golden Cloud. I have come in conjunction with Aquis King Kade of Oceanis to speak with the Verdant Empress Yvonne of Greenwell. The crimes the empress has committed against my empire are unforgivable, and we have come as a united front to demand redress for these affronts."

There was nothing but silence for several long moments, and Owen began to wonder if they were going to have to launch an attack of their own just to get a response. Then, much to his relief and surprise, the image of Yvonne appeared alongside that of Kade. The empress was cool and haughty, but there was a seething rage in her tone that couldn't be mistaken.

"You speak of crimes committed against your empire, Owen, but what about the crime committed against mine by your brother? Zavier stole my daughter, my heir, and lied about it. I told Calla this, but I'll say it to both of you, since you seem to be incapable of understanding. Greenwell's borders will remain closed to all trade until Alexia is returned to me. Leave now, or face the consequences."

Before either man could so much as open their mouths

to respond, the connection went dark, and the two brothers stared at each other. She was clearly dead set on maintaining her current course of action, which left him no choice. Pressing his lips together, he bit back a sigh and glanced at Erik. The captain grimaced, then nodded and settled into his chair all the more firmly.

"Weapons at maximum power. Forward shields at full. Proceed toward Greenwell at half-speed. Prepare to fire on my command." The *Apotheosis* was his flagship and, as such, was a massive starship with a full complement of advanced weaponry. He could feel the vessel humming, as energy reserves were diverted to the weapon systems and the forward shields and the engines propelled them forward quite swiftly. Greenwell grew larger on the viewscreen that spanned the front wall of the bridge, but it was only as they neared that he saw the precisely spaced collection of small satellites encircling the planet.

"Captain, there's an unfamiliar energy signature starting to envelop Greenwell. Orders?" a technician called out from one of the sensor stations, glancing in their direction. He could hear someone saying something similar across the comm from the bridge of the *Aquarius*, which had joined them as they advanced. The satellites visible on the viewscreen shifted noticeably, revolving so that the protrusions at the center of the concave dish mounted on them were facing toward the pair of formidable starships.

Owen was filled with a powerful sense of impending dread just as the protrusions in the dishes began to glow a virulent green. Then bedlam exploded on the bridge as that energy then lanced outward from all the nearby satellites, slamming into the shields at the front of both the *Apotheosis* and the *Aquarius*. The ship shook violently beneath the onslaught, and he gripped the railing in front of him tightly to keep from falling over while Erik snapped out orders. He watched as charged balls of plasma shot from the port cannons toward the nearest satellite, only to explode several hundred yards out, plasma rippling out across the surface of an invisible energy shield.

He realized with dismay that the whole planet was enveloped in a powerful shield. One that could easily deter their strongest weapons. Erik looked at him expectantly, and Owen knew there was only one order he could give. "Full retreat, and jump to lightspeed. Take us back to Golden Cloud immediately."

"There are really better things we could be doing with our time, you know."

Alexia glanced up at Zavier as he spoke, arching a brow and giving him her most imperious look. "Really? Better things than sharing a sensual picnic with your wife and queen? I think I'm offended by the insinuation." She saw his gaze sharpen on her, then flick down to the wicker basket in her arm. The wheels turning in his head were obvious, something that made a wide, wicked grin spread across her face.

"You didn't mention the word 'sensual' when you first dragged me out here. I reconsider my stance. There's nothing better I could possibly be doing at this moment."

This time, she didn't hold back her laughter, and was delighted to see him grinning in reaction. Zavier's smiles and laughs were becoming far more common these days, and it did her heart good to see him coming out of his dour shell. There was a man with a loving heart inside all that darkness. She just wished she knew whether or not that heart loved *her*. This little expedition into one of the rich fields outside the Ebon Citadel was just one of her more recent efforts to tease some indication of feelings out of the iron king.

Nearly three months after she'd begun her seeding efforts, Ironhold was almost completely covered in flora. Harvesting had already begun in the fields around Haven, with seeds from the various grains milled into flour for bread and other baked items. There were also small fruits and vegetables being gathered, although the larger fruit and vegetable bearing trees would take a little longer to mature. They were discussing reaching out to negotiate with other planets to import herds of animals for milk and meat, and once that was achieved, Ironhold would be completely self-sustaining. Her life was nearly ideal. All she wanted to make it complete, was to be fruitful herself.

Trying to ignore the guards that hovered a respectable distance away, she stopped beneath a few of the larger trees she'd seeded near the Citadel and handed the basket to Zavier so she could spread out their blanket. The folded-over grass made a nice, thick padding beneath the soft cloth, and after removing her shoes, she settled down on the ground with a contented sigh. Soon enough, they were lounging comfortably in the sun-speckled shade, feeding each other bites of Oceanic cuisine. She took advantage of that fact to swirl her tongue around his fingertip and watched with glee as the color of his eyes deepened to that lusty steel hue.

"If I didn't know any better, I'd think you were trying to seduce me, my queen."

She shivered, hearing the amorous rumble of his voice, and fluttered her lashes at him in a parody of innocence. "Me? I'm sure I would never do anything so underhanded, my king." She could tell he didn't believe her. Especially not when he captured her hand and drew it toward his mouth. Her breathing began to come faster as he pressed his lips to the inside of her palm, then dragged the tip of his tongue over the pulse point in her wrist. She watched, utterly enthralled, while he moved his mouth gradually up the inside of her arm, nipping playfully at the sensitive interior curve of her elbow, and finally broaching the slope of her shoulder. By that time, he'd slid entirely on top of her, his mouth latching onto the tender spot beneath her ear and making her moan.

"You drive me to madness, Alexia." His words were husky against her ear, and she could feel his hardness pressing insistently against her. Reaching down between them, she expertly flicked open the fastenings of his trousers and slid her hand inside the sheltering fabric. Immediately, her fingers met hard, hot flesh, and she didn't hesitate to curl her fingers around his length, something that made him groan against her throat and thrust help-lessly into her grasp.

"I can tell. Make love to me, Zavier." She turned her head, whispering the words in his ear as she stroked him slowly. Her eyes closed and her head tilted back when his mouth roved over her clavicle, laying heated kisses on her skin, until he reached the neckline of her gown. Pulling it down, he bared her breast to his eager attentions, sucking her nipple into his mouth. The pink peak pebbled in those warm confines, a powerful bolt of arousal shooting straight to her core as he teased it with his tongue and teeth.

Pushing his trousers down, she pulled her skirts up and parted her legs, allowing his hips to fall effortlessly into the cradle of her thighs. Propping himself up on one arm, his other hand groped downward and found her center, pausing at the feel of slick, bare flesh and no fabric to bar the way. He let her nipple slide out of his mouth and looked up at her with eyes that had gone pure black with need, his voice a hoarse growl against the full curve of her breast.

"You led me out here, with no undergarments on? How depraved of you, my dear."

She was unable to form words as his talented fingers slid gently between her folds and began to stroke her tender bud. Her hips rocked toward his touch, a pleading mewl was torn from her throat when he freed her other breast and began to lave the taut tip with his tongue. She was already burning with desire for him, so when he suddenly withdrew, she gasped in surprised indignation. Before she could think to ask what he was doing, she suddenly found herself pulled upward, and in a display of strength that left her breathless, he carried her over to one of the large saplings growing nearby. The smooth bark rubbed against her back as his weight pressed her into the young tree, her legs instinctively circling his waist while he fumbled between their bodies until his length sprang free.

He slid home in one powerful thrust that had her gasping against his mouth, her hands gripping fistfuls of his jacket while their tongues battled, feinting and plunging and twisting together in a mad battle for supremacy. He gave no quarter, meeting her motions eagerly as she began to writhe and buck against him, the angle stroking a spot deep inside that had her seeing stars. The knowledge that any of their guards could turn and see them, would know what was happening between their king and queen with just a glance, just made the entire moment all the more thrilling. Her body tightened with excitement, her hips moving to meet his with an energy borne of desperation, as she scrambled toward that moment of perfection with all she was worth. It exploded within her several moments later, her cries of ecstasy swallowed up by his eager mouth. At the same moment, she felt something else stir within her and seemingly rush outward, a fact she only became aware of as she sensed the trees near them moving. Her eyes snapped open just as Zavier groaned and pushed himself to the hilt within her one last time, tilting his head back and flooding her with the heat of his seed. Alexia raised her own head to see that the tree behind them was even now growing at a fast rate, its branches elongating while new leaves sprouted, and buds appeared before bursting into lush blossoms.

"Zavier, something is happening." She gasped the words and lowered her gaze, to see that the grasses between them and the Citadel had grown even higher, the blade tips weighed down by newly-formed seeds. It was an effect that spread outward from their location, stopping a dozen yards distant, where their guards were standing watch. He turned his head and noticed the trees, uttering a grunt of astonishment, then carefully set her on her feet. He fixed his clothing while she made herself decent again, just in time to see one of the guards hurrying their way.

"Your Majesties! The *Apotheosis* and the *Aquarius* have just entered the Ironhold system and are sending word that the god-king and the aquis king will be coming planet side shortly."

As much as he hated to do it, especially in light of what had happened during their coupling, Zavier was forced to leave Alexia behind while he returned to the Ebon Citadel. He didn't know what his brothers were doing here, but he wanted to intercept them and get them off his planet as soon as possible. A knot of dread formed in the pit of his stomach as he pondered what circumstances could be so dire that *both* of his annoying siblings felt obliged to make a personal appearance. The list of possibilities was short, and all of them had him frowning mightily.

By the time he arrived, he could see the glint of shuttles high in the atmosphere, so he made a direct path to the landing pad. There he waited, his expression thunderous, and watched them land. As soon as Owen and Kade emerged, looking weary and resigned, he stormed forward, snapping at the pair. "Say what you came here to say, then get off my planet. Both of you."

"I suggest you redirect your hostility to the proper target, Zav. Owen and I are here to try to *help*, you stubborn—" Kade cut off with a gesture from Owen, and that was enough to pull Zavier up short. Kade never bowed to anyone except his wife, unless he had no other choice, and certainly not their eldest brother. That was enough to make Zavier rein in his ire, just enough to direct a questioning look at Owen.

The god-king sighed, lifted his eyesore of a crown from his head, and raked his hand back through his hair. "This situation can no longer continue, Zavier. The citizens of Oceanis rioted and attacked the Azure Citadel, forcing Kade and his family to flee to Golden Cloud. From there, we approached Greenwell in the *Apotheosis* and the *Aquarius*, to demand that Yvonne open her borders and lift the embargo. She refused, insisted on the return of Alexia, and attacked us with a defense system like I've never seen before. She has a planet-wide energy shield, Zav. It deflected our plasma cannons like they were nothing.

"It's over. You have to send Alexia back to Greenwell, or the galaxy is going to starve."

Those words rang in his head like a death knell. To hear that his brothers had even attempted violence, and that Yvonne had repelled them so thoroughly, was beyond shocking. Just as he opened his mouth to respond, to once again deny that Alexia was going anywhere, he heard his queen's voice from behind him.

"How could you keep this from me?"

She knew she should wait. Zavier had seemed enraged when he ran off to confront his brothers, and she should give him time to work out whatever it was that had brought them there. But something in the back of her mind told her that she needed to be there, to hear what it was, because somehow, she just *knew* Zavier wasn't going to tell her himself. She was out of breath when she trotted onto the landing pad, just in time to hear Owen begin to speak. Pausing a short distance away, she listened with mounting horror while the god-king explained what had brought them there.

The galaxy was starving. It was easy to piece together what had happened, with that information. Yvonne knew she was here, knew she was married to Zavier, and wanted her back. Until Alexia was back on Greenwell, the galaxy's largest exporter of agricultural goods was on lockdown.

And Zavier had known all about it.

"How could you keep this from me?" Everything seemed to be moving slowly as Zavier heard her question and whipped around to face her, the gazes of three kings falling upon a lone woman who didn't feel like a queen at all in that moment. Her chest ached, and it felt like her very veins were afire with rage. They'd sworn to be equals. Partners. But he'd *lied* to her, had hidden this terrible truth.

Why?

"Alexia, I–"

Whatever he was going to say, she couldn't stand to hear it. Blinking back the salty sting of tears, she spun around and ran back toward the Citadel. Servants watched as their queen rushed past, wending her way through familiar hallways until she came to the queen's chambers. For the first time in her marriage, she went straight through her sitting room, into her bedroom, and locked the door behind herself.

The beauty of the room, with delicate furnishings of warm, golden wood, green fabrics, and a wealth of plants, was completely lost on her. She was deep in the throes of agony as she began to tear her dress off, sorrow making her gasp laboriously, struggling just to breathe through her tears. People were starving, and possibly dying, because of her. Oh, certainly, Zavier was the one who'd taken her from Greenwell and who had kept the information from her, but she was the cause.

With her dress abandoned on the floor in a crumpled heap, she entered her bathing room and stepped into the cleanser. The glass door slid shut and frosted over, and water began to fall like rain from the nozzle in the ceiling, drenching her while simultaneously filling the room with steam in moments. The answer to this problem was simple. If she returned to Greenwell, her mother would lift the embargo, trade would resume, people would no longer be starving, and peace would be restored to the galaxy.

But she would have to leave Zavier. The thought of never seeing him again, never tasting his lips or feeling his skin, never watching him smile or hearing him laugh, made bile rise in her throat. Could she live like that? Could she walk away from the man she had come to love with every inch of her being, her very soul?

Could she give up her happiness to save countless lives?

"Open the gods-damned door!"

"I'm sorry, Your Majesty. The queen has locked it from within, and the protocol preventing entry into the queen's chambers has been part of the programming since the Citadel was first built. We can't do anything."

The voice of the Ebon Citadel's lead security agent sounded remorseful over the speaker, which was all well and good, but that was definitely not what Zavier wanted to hear. Alexia had hidden herself away in the queen's chambers, which was frustrating enough, but to have locked herself in? That terrified him. Had he lost her? Would she leave him and run back to Greenwell? Slamming his fist into the door a final time, he then flattened his hand on the cold metal and leaned forward until his brow was pressed against it.

The awkward clearing of a throat drew his attention, and he turned his head to see Elea standing nearby. The handmaiden glanced meaningfully upward, and he followed her gaze, to see the speaker mounted in the wall above the door. It took him a moment to understand what she was trying to indicate, then after calling himself six different kinds of idiot, he spoke. "Patch the audio through to the queen's bedchamber and let me know when the connection is made."

There were several beats of silence before the security agent's voice was heard again. "Audio connected, Your Majesty."

Giving Elea a brief but infinitely grateful look, Zavier stepped back, raking his hands through his already disheveled black hair. It was so hard to wrap his mind around how, less than an hour ago, he'd been making love to his wife in a field. Now he was just trying to get her to speak to him. Thankfully, he heard Elea leave the room, which made it much easier for him to think of what to say.

"Alexia, please. I know you're in there. Just open the door... let me in. No, no, you don't have to let me in, just... come out and speak with me. Let me explain. Please."

Silence. Never in his life, had Zavier ever felt the weight of silence like he did in those moments. Had she heard him? Was she all right? Was she purposely ignoring him? He swallowed thickly, steeling himself to try again, when the door slid silently open.

She stood there, hair damp and wrapped in her robe, staring at him with hollow eyes. She looked so lost in that moment, it made him want to rush to her and hold her, but the wary exhaustion in her tone made him keep his distance as his heart sank. "All right, Zavier. Explain. Quickly."

Quickly. How was he supposed to 'quickly' explain what he'd been thinking over the past few months? Opening his mouth, he said the first thing that popped into his head, "You can't go back to Greenwell."

It was, apparently, the exact wrong thing to say. Her eyes flashed with anger, and her hand clenched into a fist where it gripped her robe.

Blessedly, she no longer seemed half-dead with weariness, but he could've done without the fury that threaded through her words. "I *can't?* Is that how it is? You're back to ordering me around, forbidding me to do things, like your *prisoner?*"

Oh. Yes. That was definitely the wrong thing to say. Floundering in the face of her ire, he struggled to correct his mistake. "You... I mean... I don't *want* you to go back. You can if you want to, of course, but I..." He trailed off, the words sticking in his throat. Why couldn't he just say it? Why couldn't he tell her he loved her more than anything? That he would give up his crown, his planet, everything, if it just meant he could have her at his side for the rest of his days?

She seemed to soften and took a half-step toward him, her face twisted into a mask of sadness. "You *what*, Zavier? Give me a reason to stay!"

A reason to stay. He could give her that, couldn't he? Was his love reason enough? Would she leave if he laid his heart in her hands? Unwilling to risk that she would retreat if he moved, he watched her helplessly across that unfathomably long distance between them and took the plunge. "I'm completely, unchangeably, in love with you, Alexia. If you leave me, I don't think I'll ever recover."

Of all the things he could've said, that was the last one she expected. It was also what she needed to hear most. She'd thought all her tears were dried up, but they welled anew, spilling over her lashes and running down her face. While she couldn't yet forgive him keeping the truth from her for so long, she now understood why he'd done it, and she was learning that when love was involved, forgiveness came easier. A sob tumbled from her lips as she stumbled, but blessedly, Zavier moved forward to catch her. As he drew her close, they sank to the floor, her face hidden against his chest.

"I love you, Zavier." She heard his breath hitch, felt his heart begin to race beneath her cheek, and his arms tightened around her. His lips pressed fervent kisses to her hair, her brow, moving steadily lower until they found her own. The embrace of lips was infinitely tender, making her heart sing with happiness. Gods, it felt so good to finally tell him, almost as good as it did to hear he felt the same. Her hands slid upward to cup his face, her thumbs stroking his cheeks, until they broke apart to gasp for air.

"Does this mean you'll stay?" She'd never heard him sound so uncertain, and when she opened her eyes to look up at him, his brow was creased with worry. The thought of returning to Greenwell hurt even more, now, knowing that he loved her in return. But all those people... She needed time to think, to try to come up with some sort of solution. But for the moment...

"Yes. I'll stay. But no more lying, Zavier, no more keeping things from me." His relief was palpable as he slumped against her, pressing his brow to hers and holding her so tightly, she wondered that her bones didn't creak beneath the strain.

"I swear it. I'll never lie to you, or keep anything from you, ever again."

She knew his word was as good as his bond, and some of the weight lifted off her shoulders. But there was still so much she needed to sort through, so many factors to consider. Wrapping her arms around his waist, she closed her eyes and exhaled slowly.

How was she going to fix this mess?

Chapter 14

Much to his relief, it took no coaxing to get Alexia into bed with him. Neither of them were particularly hungry, after the stress of the day, so they retired immediately, and he left strict instructions with Benji that they weren't to be bothered unless it was an extremely dire and imminent emergency. He supposed that a galaxy-wide famine constituted an emergency, and one of epic proportions at that, but passing on the message from Alexia that she would speak with his brothers in the morning seemed to be enough to keep them at bay. For now.

Clearly overwrought by the emotions of the day, Alexia immediately fell asleep, her back pressed to his chest and his arm over her waist. Deep in thought, Zavier simply lay there, watching her breathe. She loved him. He didn't understand how it was possible that someone so vivacious, so generous and gentle and kind-hearted and beautiful, could possibly love him in return. And yet, somehow, she did. It was the greatest gift he'd ever received, and he would be forever grateful.

But those wonderful qualities of hers that he so adored spelled trouble. Alexia couldn't stomach the notion of people starving, dying, because of her actions. This, he knew, as surely as he knew watching her return to her home world would break him. Would she leave him, for the good of the galaxy? Or would she choose him, choose love, over the lives of countless trillions? The thought made his arm tighten unconsciously, pulling her more firmly back against him, and he started when she huffed a soft laugh.

"Can't breathe, Zav." He loosened his hold, looking down at her as she wriggled and shifted until she was facing him. Her eyes slowly slid open, and she gazed up at him with a small, plainly sleepy smile.

"I'm sorry. I didn't mean to wake you." His hand began to stroke her back, rubbing light, soothing circles. He could sense the tension in her body and felt infinitely guilty for disturbing her rest. That guilt abated only slightly when she reached up to caress his cheek. Even after everything he'd done, not just today, but from the very start, he was amazed by the tenderness she showed him.

"I know. I wasn't very deeply asleep, anyway. I could feel you thinking. Tell me what's wrong." He frowned at her murmured words. She shouldn't be comforting him. He was the one who had ruined everything and upset her so badly. But maybe if he told her, she'd go back to sleep.

"Alexia, I know you said you would stay, but I want you to know that if you *do* decide to leave..." His words trailed off as she placed her fingertips lightly on his lips and shook her head a fraction.

"Don't. I love you, and in this room, that's all that matters. No talking about things that make us sad. Consider that a royal proclamation from the iron queen."

Her lips curved into a warm, loving smile that tugged at his heart.

Kissing her fingertips, he nodded his agreement, and when she lowered her hand, he dipped his head to gently kiss her brow, then murmured against her skin, "You're my queen, but the title of iron queen doesn't suit you. You're my queen of spring... my rose of winter."

The thought of eating made her feel ill, so she had no intention of doing so. But Benji had informed them that Owen and Kade were in the formal dining hall, waiting for them, with breakfast. She would make an appearance to inform them of her decision, then leave. She knew her nerves were the main reason she felt nauseous at the idea of food, but there was nothing to be done for it. Especially since her plan was still only half-formed. Would they accept it? More importantly, would Owen? She turned these thoughts over in her head as she walked arm-in-arm with Zavier, shaking them aside only when they entered the room.

Both kings stood at their appearance, bowing their heads slightly in respectful greeting to the royal pair. Owen may be the god-king, and Ironhold technically within his empire, but while on this planet, decorum dictated he was the lesser of royals. She only hoped he would remember that when she explained herself.

"Please, sit, both of you. I won't be here long." The brothers shared a look, then glanced back to the two of them but didn't take their seats. Not a good sign. Perhaps they didn't respect her as much as she initially believed?

"You won't be joining us for breakfast, Queen Alexia?"

Somehow, she doubted that was their only reason for

questioning her. But she shook her head a fraction and squared her shoulders. "No. I have much work to do. God-King Owen, I understand my mother's actions are harming your empire, and I'm deeply sorry for her rash behavior. But I won't be returning to Greenwell." He opened his mouth to speak, and she immediately raised her hand. Much to her surprise, he fell silent. Good. Maybe he was willing to listen after all. "I have a plan to correct this situation, but I need time to put everything in motion."

"I... see." Slowly, Owen sank back into his seat, propping his elbow on the arm of the chair and cupping his chin in the curve of his index finger. She could see him absently stroking his jaw with his thumb as he pondered this, then ventured carefully, "I'll be blunt, Your Majesty. I don't see how Yvonne can be persuaded to see sense without your return to Greenwell. I'll allow you two weeks to present your own solution, but if your plan doesn't meet with my satisfaction, I'll have no choice but to take you into custody and return you there myself."

Kade started at the statement and shot his brother an angry look. At her side, Zavier tensed and took a threatening step forward.

She stopped him by laying her hand on his forearm and took a deep breath before replying. "Of course. I understand. I hope it won't have to come to that."

"So do I." His words were solemn, and she believed him. Zavier relaxed marginally, but when she turned her back on the room and made to leave, he gently grasped her bicep, halting her progress. She looked up at him, meeting his gaze when he turned his head to face her.

"Do you really have a plan?"

The meeting had gone better than he anticipated, but hearing Owen state that he'd take Alexia by force had raised his hackles. Looking down at her now, he saw the bleak despair in her gaze and knew that no answer to his question was necessary. Schooling his features into a blank mask, he let go of her arm and let her leave the room without further incident. Feeling oddly numb, he crossed to the table where his brothers sat and eased into a chair midway between them both, unable to keep himself from slumping. He felt so... defeated. It wasn't a feeling he liked. At all.

"Zav, I know she means a great deal to you—"

"Don't." He snarled the word at Owen, who at least had the decency to look chastened by his poorly phrased attempt at consolation. Attempting to quell his temper, Zavier clenched his hand into a fist, then slowly uncurled his fingers, gradually working the tension out of his muscles. "If she goes back to Greenwell, I'm abdicating."

Under any other circumstances, the sight of Owen dropping his fork in shock would've been highly gratifying. As it was, he felt only the briefest flicker of amusement and a mild curiosity at the very intent look Kade aimed his way.

"Zavier, you can't. You have no heir. Who would rule Ironhold?"

"You can damn well name a regent until I produce one. I am *not* losing my wife," he snapped at his oldest brother, but his anger was turned to Kade when the bearded brunette chuckled. "What's so funny?"

"I never thought I'd see the day you were so madly in love, Zav. It suits you. I support this course of action." Winking at Zavier in a conspiratorial manner, he returned to shoveling food into his mouth, leaving the youngest of the three brothers quite bewildered by this response. Owen stared between the both of them, then threw his hands in the air, before pointing sternly at Zavier. "You had better hope she comes up with a good plan, because if you *do* abdicate, I'm going to make your life miserable until you produce an heir."

Hunched over a data slate in her office, Alexia cradled her head in her hands and rubbed circles on her temples with her fingertips. She had a massive headache, and the information she was able to access wasn't providing any help at all. Mostly, she felt like a fool. How could she have been so blissfully happy that she didn't realize what was going on in the galaxy? Word of the famine, the riots, the mounting death toll, was *everywhere*. And here, she had been so focused on making Ironhold self-sustaining, so stupidly in love with Zavier, desperate to have a child with him, that she just... missed it.

As her eyes began to sting with tears, she covered them with her hands and tried not to break down. More and more people were dying every day, because of her selfishness, because of her mother's inability to let her live her own life. How many of them were children? Babies? Men and women just trying to get by? They deserved as much of a chance at happiness as anyone else. Shouldn't she give that to them? Shouldn't she go back to Greenwell?

"I can't stay. But if I leave, it will break my heart... and worse, it will break his." She whispered the words to herself, then folded her arms atop her desk and laid her head on them. For the first time in her life, she felt utterly and completely hopeless.

As he often did in times of distress, Zavier was going to the garden. He wanted to be with Alexia, in truth, and part of him hoped he'd find his wife there. But when he stepped into the room with its domes of crystal, he stopped, his heart surging up into his throat.

Everything was dying.

"Get Warren and Maksim in here immediately." He barked his command at the guards outside the door and didn't even bother to turn and see if they'd obeyed. He could hear them running at top speed. Warren's quarters weren't far, so he arrived first, and when Zavier turned to face the aged gardener, the man's expression of horror told him everything he needed to know.

"Your Majesty, I swear, it wasn't like this yesterday! I-I don't... how could this have happened?"

"How could what have... Oh gods, the gardens are dying." Maksim stumbled in, a small crate full of equipment in his arms, and gaped at the sight. There was a carpet of shriveled leaves on the ground, the fruits and berries had all begun to rot, and the flowers had wilted to nothing.

"Warren, you know this garden better than anyone. See if something is amiss. Maksim, I want you and your team to run a full analysis on everything. See if something has contaminated the gardens." Not waiting for their responses, he moved out of the garden and addressed the two guards standing there, wide-eyed. "No matter what happens, do *not* let the queen or any of her staff in here. Understood?"

They snapped crisp salutes, closing the doors behind him, and stood at attention. He had to head this off as quickly as he could. If this was what he thought it was... Their hands truly were tied.

A week later, Zavier stood confronted with the uncomfortable truth: Everything Alexia had seeded was dying. It had taken longer to begin, outside the range of her influence, but there was no denying it when the reports started coming in from Haven. Rubbing his hand over his face as he looked at the holo-display, showing fields of dead grass and sickly trees, he knew he couldn't keep this from her. Not just because he'd promised he wouldn't, but because it meant all of her hard work was going to waste. She would want that even less than she would the famine to persist. She had been so determined to see Ironhold made green, and now, it was all falling apart.

Turning off the holo-display on the desk, he exited his study and proceeded through the halls until he reached Alexia's study. Hesitating outside the door, he considered how to broach the subject. He would need to handle it delicately. She was already fragile as it was. Barely eating, sleeping too much, constantly at work trying to untangle the mayhem they'd all caused. Finally, having gathered his courage as much as he was able, he stepped into the room. Alexia looked up from the data slate in front of her and gave him a wan smile.

"Excellent timing. I think I may have found a solution. It will take a while to enact, but… What's wrong?" He realized too late that he was frowning, and she'd seen it easily. Crossing to where she was sitting, he offered his hand, and after a few moments, she took it. Pulling her gently to her feet, he led her out of her office and through the few hallways that separated her space from the gardens. The guards moved aside at their approach and opened the doors for them.

Her gasp of dismay struck him like a blow, and he

winced. He'd wanted to prepare her for this, but the situation was too far gone now. He let go of her hand, watching as she entered the barren garden. The grass, dry and dead, crunched beneath her feet as she approached the nearest tree, which had begun to dry up. He saw the moment she figured out what had happened, as she froze and then turned slowly to face him, her eyes full of tears. "The fields…"

"Dying." He spoke the word gently and cursed beneath his breath as she began to cry. Closing the space between them, he tenderly cupped her face, his thumbs stroking the wetness from her cheeks. "We couldn't have known this would happen."

"This is my fault. The galaxy is starving, and my misery is killing everything here. All our work…" She laid her brow against his chest, and he wrapped his arms around her, pulling her tight against him. They remained like that for what felt like an eternity, but it wasn't nearly long enough, until finally she spoke, her words muffled against his sturdiness. "There's only one thing left to do."

"I know." He swallowed thickly, closing his eyes against the sight of his garden in its death throes. He was losing his birthright, his home, his crown, but he was keeping his wife. That would be enough. He would suffer Greenwell if it meant he got to remain by her side. When he felt her moving, he opened his eyes and looked down at her, surprised to see the spark of determination in her gaze.

"I'm going to send a message to Calla. I have one last card I can play, and I'm going to do it."

That astounded him. He'd thought certainly she would ask him to take her back to Greenwell. But if she had a possible alternative in mind… He leaned down and lightly pressed his lips to hers. "Whatever it is, I'll be by your side."

"You want to do what?"

Alexia sighed. Calla was looking at her through the holo-comm like she'd lost her mind. Which was, admittedly, a valid response. This was her most desperate bid yet, but she was trying to have it all. Didn't she deserve to be happy and still restore peace to the galaxy?

"I want to use the *Pyxis* as a neutral meeting ground to discuss terms with my mother, and I'd like you to serve as a mediating party. She wants me back, but I'll be damned if I give her what she wants without getting something in return."

Alexia looked at the god-king's wife as she pondered this and felt a brief surge of jealousy. Calla's belly was visibly round with child, and she was absently stroking the curve of skin as she considered the request. Why couldn't she be carrying Zavier's child, too? Shaking aside those thoughts as the older woman sighed, she waited for her response.

"If you can get Yvonne to agree, then I'll do it. Send me information with the time and location."

"Thank you, Calla. I'll be in touch." The holo-comm flickered off, and Alexia slumped briefly in her seat. Well, that much was done. Now she just needed to get her mother to agree. And that, she suspected, would be the true test. Taking a few moments to settle her nerves and gather her wits, she activated the holo-comm once more and straightened in her seat.

"What can I do for you, Your Majesty?"

"Connect me to the Verdant Palace on Greenwell, please." Lifting her crown from its cushion on top of her desk, she settled it carefully on top of her head and waited.

She hoped she looked queenly. After a moment, an unfamiliar face flickered into view on the holo-comm. She might not recognize the communications officer, but clearly, they recognized her, as the young woman's eyes widened.

"Princess!"

That address sent a flicker of fury through her. Was her mother even denying her marriage? That simply wouldn't do. Her anger giving her calm, she arched a brow and spoke in a cool tone, full of confidence. "No. I am Iron Queen Alexia, and I need to speak to the verdant empress immediately."

"Um, yes, of course, Your... Majesty. Just a moment." The display flickered slightly, and she gripped the arms of her chair. After a few heartbeats, the face of her mother appeared. She seemed to have aged a decade since Alexia saw her last, but to her surprise, the former princess felt no guilt, only a mild irritation.

"Alexia! Thank the gods, you've come to your senses. When are you coming home? And what is that on your head?"

Of course. Yvonne would never see her as anything other than a wayward child, incapable of making her own decisions. Pursing her lips, she refused to respond to anything her mother had said and, instead, proceeded with the carefully scripted address she'd planned out hours before.

"Empress, this embargo of yours must be lifted, for the good of the galaxy. I am requesting a meeting of equals in neutral territory. In two days' time, the *Pyxis*, personal vessel of Queen Calla of Quartz Spire, will be in the free space just outside the Greenwell system, and I will be aboard it. I wish to discuss terms. Can I count on your participation?" She felt a brief surge of vindictive satisfaction when she saw how floored her mother was by what she'd said.

It was short-lived, however, as Yvonne scoffed, "Stop this nonsense, Alexia. I don't know what that bastard has done to make you behave this way, but I–"

"That is *enough*." The sharp but quietly spoken words were enough to cut the empress off mid-diatribe, and she gaped in silence. Taking advantage of the moment, Alexia continued, her tone frigid with displeasure. "You will not speak of my king and husband in such a manner. You are an empress. Behave like one. Be on board the Pyxis in two days, or you will never see me again."

It was a bluff. A big one. But it seemed her change in attitude was making Yvonne reconsider her tactics, and the woman eyed her daughter thoughtfully for a moment, then slowly nodded. "Very well. In two days."

Without warning, the connection dropped, and Alexia covered her mouth with her hands. She'd done it. She'd gotten her mother to agree to talk if nothing else. Now, she just had to browbeat the stubborn woman into agreeing to her proposal. It was her last chance to save Ironhold, the galaxy, and her own sanity.

It had to work. It simply *had* to.

"You did *what?*"

Too exhausted to flinch, Alexia lolled her head to one side on the pillow and looked at Zavier. Normally, she would've been far more interested in his half-clothed state, and although she felt a minute stirring of arousal, she was too wrung out to try to seduce him. As it was, she sighed and gestured vaguely in his direction from her spot in their bed. "I got Calla and my mother both to agree to meet on board the *Pyxis* in free space, in two days. I want you, Owen, Kade, and Ingrid there, too. A show of solidarity and force."

"Alexia, this is madness. Do you really think Yvonne is going to agree to whatever you're asking of her just because we act tough?" She watched as he shed the last of his clothing and slid between the sheets, moving closer to her. Rolling onto her side, she immediately relaxed when he pressed up behind her. The heat and muscle of his body was decidedly soothing, as was his hand resting protectively on her flat stomach.

"No. I'm thinking she's desperate enough to get me back on Greenwell that she'll agree to whatever I say, to a point, to make it happen." Letting her hand drift down to where his was lying, she twined their fingers, then guided their joined hands upward so that she could kiss his palm. Feeling his nose nuzzle into her hair, she put their hands back on her abdomen and sighed, turning her head to rub her cheek against his. "I can't lose you, Zavier. But I can't let Ironhold die, or the galaxy starve, either. I have to find a middle ground. This is the only thing I can think of."

"What is this middle ground proposal of yours?" He dragged his nose along the curve of her cheek until he was half-poised above her, looking down at her. Much as she wanted to tell him, she knew that if she did, he'd find a way to keep her from going to the meeting. And that, she couldn't allow. So she shook her head and brushed her lips against his.

"No more talking. I just want to feel you tonight." She urged his hand down between her thighs and gasped as he began stroking her expertly, feeling his hardness stirring against the curve of her backside. Closing her eyes, she relished in the feel of his mouth on her neck, his teeth scraping across her pulse point while his fingers swirled and caressed, rousing her passion readily.

A short time later, he pulled his hand away from hers and cupped her thigh, lifting her leg upward and sliding his own between it. She could feel his length pressing against her opening, and arched her back, reaching down to grab him and guide him into where he belonged. He slid home easily, their bodies so accustomed to each other by this point that coming together was as easy for them as breathing. His breath on her shoulder, she reached behind herself and threaded her fingers into his hair, his hand moving to cup her breast while he drew back. When he pushed forward again, it was slow and achingly tender, his pelvis meeting with the curve of her posterior before he withdrew once more.

She whimpered with desire as his thumb circled her nipple, teasing it to hardness while his strong fingers moulded the plush heaviness of her breast, shifting her hips back to meet his next thrust. He was taking his time, drawing it out, no doubt imprinting every moment of this on his mind as though it would be the last time. Did he think he was going to lose her? Did he believe this *would* be the last time? The thought made her heart ache, and when she finally came undone, it was sobbing his name as she trembled in his arms.

He whispered her name when he spilled inside her, then bundled her close and kissed her cheek, holding her like she was the only thing in the universe that mattered. She couldn't lose him. She could only pray her mother would see that separating them would be like cutting a plant off from the sun. She would falter, fail, and die.

They boarded the shuttle together, Kit and Elea accompanying them. If she was to return to Greenwell, she wanted to have two people she knew she could trust unerringly with her. She knew that the guardswoman and her handmaiden would do everything they could to get her off the planet if it came to that. But as the shuttle ascended through the atmosphere, she saw it wasn't the *Nightfall* they were approaching. She'd seen visuals of the imposing dark-hulled starship when she was learning more about Iron-hold. The vessel they were approaching was smaller, with sleek curves, and was plated with a brilliantly iridescent silver metal that reflected the light. Her brow crinkled in puzzlement as she peered out the viewport at the ship, then turned to look at Zavier.

"That isn't the *Nightfall*." He had been watching her, she realized, and when she made the rather obvious comment, he smiled.

"No. It isn't." His enigmatic response just made her frown. Why was he being so mysterious?

"Well, what is she called, then?"

He didn't answer at first. Instead, he took her hand and brought it to his lips, pressing a gentle kiss to her fingers, before finally responding.

"That's for you to decide. She's for you, after all."

Her eyes rounded at that, and she looked out the viewport again. "But... how? You got me my own ship?"

"The Golden Cloud system is rich in resources. I commissioned one of Owen's engineers to design it and funded the construction. I was just waiting for the right time to tell you. Now, if things don't go the way you want..." He paused, clearing his throat, and a glance at him told her he was struggling with his emotions. He didn't like to display them in front of others, but she could see the sadness in his eyes. "If you have to go back to Greenwell, you'll at least have a way to come home."

She squeezed his hand. Of course, he'd be prepared. What was meant to simply be a gift of status for a queen, was now proving a thoughtful method of escape should she need it. Looking back out the viewport, she admired the elegant lines of the ship as it hovered in orbit, waiting for them. The perfect name came to her, bringing a smile to her lips.

"*Elysium.*"

"I'm… not familiar with that word. Does it mean something?"

She inhaled slowly, and as the shuttle had approached the docking clamps, she turned to face him. "It's a lily that grows on graves on Greenwell. Legend has it that it only appears when the departed's soul is happy in the beyond."

His eyes flashed as he comprehended what she wasn't saying. He pulled her closer, and she went gladly into his embrace, neither of them caring that Kit and Elea were witnessing their moment of tenderness. She might very well need that ship, and they both knew it. Once the shuttle had docked and the airlock pressurized, they exited into the ship. He gave her a brief tour, showing her the bridge and introducing her to the crew, before they made their way to her quarters.

Emotionally drained as they both were, they tumbled into the plush nano-gel bedding and remained entwined for the duration of their lightspeed flight to the edges of known space. The areas beyond the settled systems were a breeding ground for the dregs of society, where smugglers and thieves roamed freely. Which was why, when they dropped out of lightspeed and relocated to the bridge, she wasn't at all surprised to see not only the *Apotheosis,* the *Aquarius,* the *Pyxis,* and her mother's ship, the *Bountiful,* but also a range of battleships from both the Golden Cloud system and Greenwell. Just as they neared the collection of vessels, shuttles emerged from each one and started crossing empty space toward the *Pyxis*.

Hand-in-hand with Zavier, they boarded the shuttle and made the same journey. Calla was there to greet them when they disembarked, looking far from pleased, even as she embraced them both. As much as she was able, given her burgeoning belly, that was.

"Your mother is being an absolute terror, Alexia. I hope you have something spectacular planned, because she seems ready to move on to all-out war."

The words were far from comforting, and she felt anxiety knotting in her chest at the thought of seeing her mother in person again. On a holo-comm had been bad enough, but when physically confronted with Yvonne's domineering presence, would she crumble? Or would she do justice to the crown nestled in her hair? Gripping Zavier's arm tightly, they followed Calla into the largest lounge on the *Pyxis*, where a massive oval table dominated most of the floor space. Only four chairs sat along its edges, clearly meant to seat herself and Zavier, Yvonne across from them, and a place for Calla squarely midway, as was appropriate for an arbitrator.

Owen and Kade were standing near a trio of lushly padded chairs beyond the far end of the table, along with the Aquis Queen, Ingrid, clutching his arm. She'd not met the woman in person yet, something she wanted to remedy once all this was over, but she could veritably see the nerves in every taut line of muscle in the older woman's body. Now, was absolutely not the time to go introducing herself.

Especially not when Yvonne was standing behind the chair meant for her occupation, looking as detached and cold as ever. Something flashed across her face, an emotion

Alexia couldn't recognize, when her mother saw the two of them together, clearly not intending to part anytime soon.

Thankfully, Calla sensed the tension in the room and cleared her throat as she bustled to her seat. "Well, with all parties assembled, I think it's high time we got on with all this. Take your seats, everyone, if you would."

As they approached the table, Zavier stepped forward and pulled out a chair for her, then pushed it in before taking his own. She tried to ignore her thundering heartbeat as her mother sank gracefully into the chair across from them, resting her hands on its finely carved arms as though it was her throne in the Verdant Palace. Did she look as regal and commanding? Did Yvonne still see a child sitting across from her? Refusing to look away from her mother's piercing gaze, lest it be seen as a sign of weakness, she reached over and lightly touched Zavier's hand.

Her husband cleared his throat, then spoke in a firm voice. "How shall we proceed?"

"Since this meeting was Queen Alexia's idea—" Calla cut off as Yvonne scoffed at the title, which earned her a heated glare from the red-haired queen and Zavier both. Something that made Alexia smile slightly, just enough to make her mother purse her lips in irritation. "I think she should be the first to speak."

"Thank you, Queen Calla." Folding her hands on top of the table, she straightened and stared at her mother. "Empress Yvonne, your embargo is causing widespread suffering across the galaxy. I think we all know what your terms are to cease this foolishness. You wish for my return to Greenwell. I'm here to offer a compromise. I will return to Greenwell with you, *temporarily*. Just until the situation has been rectified. Once this is the case, I will return to Ironhold, with my king and husband."

Before Calla could do more than open her mouth,

Yvonne slammed her hands down on the table and stood so swiftly that her chair nearly toppled over backwards. Recognizing the look on her mother's face, Alexia braced herself for the yelling that was soon to come.

She wasn't disappointed, as Yvonne's voice echoed in the chamber. "Absolutely not! Alexia, you will come home this *instant*—"

"Empress Yvonne, there will be no raising of voices during these negotiations—" Calla attempted to interrupt and speak over her, and Alexia felt a surge of fury. How dare her mother speak to her this way? In front of her husband, her peers, her family by marriage?

Without raising her voice, she snapped at the golden-haired empress, her tone so frigid, she wondered the view-ports didn't frost over. "Sit. *Down.*"

Yvonne's mouth fell open, but she obeyed, dropping into her chair like an abandoned child's doll. Perhaps too stunned by her daughter's reaction, she said nothing else, for which Alexia was grateful. She gestured to Calla, who grimaced.

"Perhaps we should've laid some ground rules first. There will be no raising of voices, no physical displays, no threatening, and no insults. Are we clear on this?"

Alexia nodded, as did her mother, and she spotted Zavier doing the same in her peripheral vision. Calla inhaled deeply, then turned her focus on Yvonne, a bit more calmly, this time. "Empress Yvonne, you may *calmly* offer a rebuttal to Queen Alexia's suggestion."

Being given permission to do something, clearly irked the verdant empress, who shot Calla a withering glare. Visibly seething, she clasped her hands on the table, her grip so tight that the skin across her knuckles paled almost to translucency. "You are my daughter. Your place is with me. This so-called 'marriage' is a farce, and illegal. I'm willing to let the transgression of any physical violation go unpunished, so long as you return home to Greenwell immediately."

Alexia arched a brow. Well, that was an interesting take. Her mother thought her marriage was illegitimate, did she? Turning her head to look up at Zavier, she met her husband's gaze and was secretly delighted by the purely malicious smirk that raised one side of his lips.

Reaching into the interior pocket of his coat, he withdrew a data slate, which he slid toward Calla. "Queen Calla, would you please review the contents of this data slate?"

Calla took the slate and immediately began reading the items on the screen. Alexia knew exactly what she was seeing. The official record of her own birth, which very clearly stated the year she'd been born, and thus, her age. And directly after that, was the signed and sealed marriage contract. Her lips twitching with the threat of a smile, Calla then slid the data slate over to Yvonne, who took it with obvious displeasure. "Empress Yvonne, is that first item the official record of the birth of Princess Alexia of Greenwell, your daughter and heir?"

Yvonne looked at the document, glanced up at Alexia, and frowned as she replied, "Yes, it is."

"So the date on it is correct?" Calla leaned forward intently, and Alexia bit back a smile.

"Yes. Your point is?"

"So then, according to the date on that document, how old is your daughter?"

This was clearly not the line of questioning Yvonne had been expecting. She looked from Calla, to Zavier, then finally let her gaze settle on Alexia. "Twenty-three standard galactic years."

"Which, as per galactic law, makes her an adult, does it not?"

Alexia saw the moment her mother realized what had been done. Her eyes rounded in alarm and dropped back to the data slate, where she scrolled from her birth record to the marriage contract. Her mother's hand began to shake as she read the contents of the contract and saw that it was, in fact, completely legally binding. Despite being a self-proclaimed empress, the Greenwell system nonetheless fell under the domain of the god-king, and the contract was completely legally binding. Pushing the data slate away, she leaned back in her chair, appearing dazed. No one spoke for several long moments, then she suddenly sat up straighter, narrowing her eyes on Alexia.

"Fine. She's legally an adult, and the marriage contract is legal and binding. But I refuse to lift the embargo unless she returns to Greenwell, and *not* just until the galactic famine has eased. Permanently."

This was what she'd been afraid of. Her mother was stubborn, and at this point, Alexia was certain it was largely a matter of pride and needing to feel like she still had control over her daughter's life. That simply wouldn't do. But she knew that if she returned to Ironhold and let the famine persist, she would only continue to feel guilty and unhappy, and that would cause damage to the planet she'd invested so much time and energy in. That, she couldn't allow. There was only one move left she could make, and she knew that no one at this table was going to be happy about it. But being a ruler meant doing what was best for the people. "Very well, Mother. This is my final offer. You will lift the embargo, and I will return to Greenwell for a period of exactly half a standard galactic year. No more, no less. After which, I will return to Ironhold and remain there for the exact same amount of time. Then the cycle will repeat, until you pass the rule of Greenwell on to me, at which point, the agreement becomes null and void, and I will do as I see fit."

"No."

The flat, immediate answer was precisely what she'd anticipated. What she hadn't expected, was to feel Zavier's hand gripping her knee beneath the table. Although he appeared outwardly calm, she could practically feel the dread emanating from his body at the prospect of losing his wife. She reached her foot over and lightly touched his, attempting to reassure him, as she met her mother's furious gaze.

"I'll be blunt, Mother. I don't know what these defenses are that you've formed around Greenwell, but I know that as powerful as they may be, if you continue to pursue this all-or-nothing way of thinking, the galaxy won't tolerate it. People will learn that they're starving because of you, and what do you think will happen then? Their leaders will band together and formulate a way to overcome your defenses. They'll swarm across Greenwell like a plague, and you'll be lucky if you survive the assault. Greenwell will suffer, and so will the people. If you don't accept this offer, that is exactly what will happen. And I won't raise a finger to stop it."

She could see that her mother wasn't the only one completely stunned by this cold, grim assessment of the future of her home world. She knew it seemed out of character for her. But she suspected Zavier was the only one who knew it was a farce. She would be miserable, and she would hate herself for it, but she'd decided the time had finally come to take a stand. She couldn't let her mother rule her life any longer.

After several long minutes of silence, Yvonne seemed to deflate. Finally, she nodded. "Very well. I agree."

Chapter 15

Zavier was in shock. Not just because Yvonne had actually accepted the terms, but because of the offer itself. He watched, somewhat numb and detached, as the formal agreement was drawn up, signed by his wife and her mother, and witnessed by Calla. Gradually, people began to trickle out of the room, until he was left alone with his queen. He started when her hand fell on his shoulder, and pushed up from his seat, turning to face her.

Without preamble, he took her in his arms, crushing her to him fiercely. His face was buried in her hair, knocking her crown askew, but he couldn't care less. And judging by the way she was clutching the back of his coat, he suspected she didn't give a damn, either. His throat felt tight, realizing this would be the last time he held her, breathed in the scent of her hair, for half a year. It felt like an eternity.

"I'm so sorry, Zav. It was the only thing I could think to do." Her words were muffled, but he could hear the tears in her voice. Drawing back just enough to look down at her, when she raised her face and met his gaze, his heart twisted with agony. He hated it when she cried.

"I'm willing to give up my throne, to follow you to Greenwell. Let me abdicate." He sounded desperate, he knew, but he couldn't just let this happen. He couldn't bear the thought of being apart from her for so long. How could she think he would be content with such a thing? When she shook her head vigorously, he felt the sharp pain of betrayal spear him through the gut.

"No. You can't. I know Mother, and she'd separate us somehow. Exile you, imprison you… possibly even kill you. This way, we can still be together. I'll find a way to get her to pass on the rule of Greenwell to me, sooner, rather than later, so I can put an end to this stupid arrangement."

The pain in his chest eased, if only a fraction. So that was it. She was afraid her mother would find a way to keep them apart permanently. She feared for his life. And she was prepared, was already coming up with a way to take matters into her own hands. Pride and sorrow blended in his chest, too intense for him to fully process at the moment. Rather than speaking, he lowered his head and kissed her with everything he had. He could taste her tears, a salty flavor melding with the perpetual floral flavor of her mouth, and knew that it would have to be a memory to sustain him for many long months. When he broke the kiss, he buried his face against her neck. "I love you. Never forget that. You are everything to me."

"I love you, too. I'll always come back to you."

It was done. She'd said her goodbyes to her husband, who remained on board the *Pyxis*, awaiting the imminent arrival of the *Nightfall* to take him home to Ironhold, and boarded the *Elysium*. Keeping a safe distance from the *Bountiful*, the two ships traversed into the boundaries of the Greenwell system and made for her home world. In a way, she was glad to see it again, but it still represented a prison for her. Would she ever look fondly on the Paradise planet again?

Disembarking from her shuttle with Kit and Elea in tow, she entered the Verdant Palace and turned to face her guardswoman and her handmaiden.

"Elea, find a woman named Vienne and tell her to show you to the best guest quarters. I'll be residing there during my time here. Kit, come with me. I need to speak with the empress."

Elea curtsied and hurried off to do as she was bid, while Kit remained at her side. Making her way through the palace toward the royal family's wing, she bypassed her former suite of rooms and made her way to her mother's chambers. Kit remained outside, stationing herself at the door, while Alexia came face-to-face with her mother. Yvonne seemed visibly surprised by the intrusion, but she smiled as she approached her daughter, her arms extended with the clear intent to embrace her only child.

That was, until she found a blade pressed to her throat. Her eyes grew wide as she glanced down at the gleaming black metal, and she let her arms fall. "Alexia… what are you doing?"

"Shut up, Mother. I am so very tired of listening to you. So, for the first time in your miserable life, you're going to listen to me. This is Ironhold iron, and if I so much as nick your skin, you'll bleed out in moments. Do we have an understanding?"

Unable to form words, Yvonne simply nodded and stood there. Alexia raised her chin, glaring at her mother. When had she gotten so small? She'd always seemed bigger than life. Now, the daughter realized she was taller than her mother. She had outgrown her. In so many ways.

"You lied to me, all my life. You never told me who my father was, because you couldn't." Yvonne gasped, and Alexia snorted, a cruel smile appearing on her lips. "Yes, I know your little secret. I know how I came to be. Well, guess what, Mother? Those amazing abilities you terrified me into hiding? I've used them to make Ironhold a world of beauty, one that will come to rival Greenwell itself, in time, if I have my way. I'm going to dedicate my life to ruining your legacy, and I'm going to start by revealing how I was conceived, which clearly violates the galactic law against creating hybridized alien life. Unless, of course, you agree to abdicate within the next two years. In which case, I'll make certain all evidence of my origin is destroyed forever. Do you understand me, *Mother?*"

"Perfectly... Your Majesty." Hearing those words falling so weakly from her mother's lips, was a sweet reward. Lowering the knife and tucking it up her sleeve once more, she turned away and left her mother's rooms without a second glance.

"Your Majesty, the *Elysium* just entered the Ironhold system."

The words roused Zavier from a troubled sleep, and he sat bolt upright in bed. Was he dreaming? He knew Alexia was due to return today, but he hadn't known when. He'd at least expected he'd be out of bed when he got the alert, but this was far better. In a flurry of activity, he hauled on the first items of clothing he laid hands on and was still tucking in his shirt, even as he ran out the door.

Servants were rushing toward the main entrance,

spilling out into the courtyard between the Citadel and the landing pad, but they parted before their king. They knew how much he'd been aching for this day, yearning for the return of his beloved queen, and no one was foolish enough to stand in his way. Rushing onto the landing pad, he shielded his gaze against the glare of the rising sun and raised his eyes to the sky, watching as the shuttle descended and came to rest on the metal plateau. As soon as the door swung open, he was starting toward the shuttle, then, there she was. A mane of silver hair, moonlight pale skin...

The urge to run to her faltered when she fully emerged, and he stopped dead at the sight before him. It was absolutely his wife; she was as beautiful as ever, but there was a lot *more* to her than he remembered. He heard gasps and the hum of conversation behind him, then the cheers began. That was enough to spur him into motion again, and he strode briskly to Alexia, who was looking up at him with a positively manic grin.

"Alexia... you?"

Taking his hands, she guided them forward and placed them against the rounded swell of her belly. His eyes widened when he felt motion beneath his palms, a fluttering staccato beat of pressure, and then stillness. He'd been wondering if perhaps she was playing a very cruel joke, but, no. There could be no denying it.

His wife was with child.

"I wanted to surprise you. Telling you over holo-comm that I was carrying your heir seemed very cruel."

She could see him struggling with his feelings, with his words, and she reached up to cup his face. Urging him down, she tilted her head up and pressed her lips against his, tasting the flavor of his mouth for the first time in far too long. In that moment, everything faded away. There was nothing but them, their child, and their love, on the world they'd built together.

Finally, she was home. Where she belonged.

Blushing Books

Blushing Books is the oldest eBook publisher on the web. We've been running websites that publish steamy romance and erotica since 1999, and we have been selling eBooks since 2003. We have free and promotional offerings that change weekly, so please do visit us at http://www.blushingbooks.com/free.

Blushing Books Newsletter

Please join the Blushing Books newsletter
to receive updates & special promotional offers.
You can also join by using your mobile phone:
Just text BLUSHING to 22828.

Every month, one new sign up via text messaging will
receive a $25.00 Amazon gift card, so sign up today!